F

MW01136543

A University Mystery

Brenda Donelan

Best wishes!

Brenda Donelan

Fatal Footsteps

This book is dedicated to my dearly departed cat, Taffy. She was the inspiration for Pippa in the first four books in the University Mystery Series. Every day as I typed at my kitchen table she sat an arm's-length away in her cat bed atop the table. I'm guessing most people don't let their cats lounge on the table, but Taffy proved early on to be untrainable. Instead of teaching her not to get on the table, I trained myself to get over it. And that, in a nutshell describes my almost-sixteen years with the independent, lovable, temperamental, Taffy Kay Donelan.

ACKNOWLEDGEMENTS

My beta readers, as usual, are the true heroes when it comes to publishing my books. They read the manuscript when it's still rough and in need of some guidance. They see mistakes that I don't, firm up plot lines that I thought were finished, and contribute to an overall better end product. Thank you to Dayle Tibbs Angyal, Stacy Jundt, and Audra Bonhorst Hawkinson for reading my early work and providing valuable feedback.

Brian Schell, my editor, gets a major shout out for helping me through this process. Thank you for your diligence, Brian.

Thank you to Samantha Lund Hillmer, who designed my book cover and business cards and also helps me with technical snafus on my website. I'd also like to thank borchee for the cover photography, courtesy of iStock.

Once again, the majority of the first draft of Fatal Footsteps was written in November during National Novel Writing Month (Nanowrimo). For the past several years, this program has been invaluable to me in starting or completing a novel. I'm looking already looking forward to the next Nanowrimo.

A huge thank you to everyone, mainly family and friends, but also some people trapped in the airport with me, who've listened to me talk on and on about my current and future books. Some may think I can only talk knowledgeably about books, but that's not true. I also know a lot about cats.

Contents

How might my life have turned out differently? Would I have a successful career in business administration? A happy marriage to the man of my dreams and two adorable children? Or maybe the tables would have turned against me, and I'd be a down-and-out bar hag hanging out at the local watering hole. We'll never know because I died when I was just 19 years old.

Chapter 1

"You jackass," Marlee mumbled to herself as she sorted through the first of many boxes she had lugged up from the basement the previous day. She dug through the mishmash of papers, attempting to categorize them into some type of system. Marlee's hands and eyes dealt with the stacks of papers before her, but her mind was focused on that no-good, cheating, lying dirt bag, Hector Ramos.

Marlee met Detective Hector Ramos the previous year when he investigated the suspicious death of one of her college students on a class trip. The two began seeing each other off and on, and Hector eventually moved to Elmwood when he was hired on with the local police department. He was in the process of moving into Marlee's house when a woman who worked at the Elmwood jail showed up and announced she was pregnant with Hector's baby. That was the end of the "happily ever after" with Marlee, and she had cursed Hector's very existence since then.

Not one to hold grudges, Marlee tried to let Hector's betrayal be a thing of the past. Try as she might, she couldn't do it. She couldn't forgive, and she certainly wouldn't forget. The mere mention of his name still made her blood boil all these months later. She had only seen him around Elmwood twice since their break-up. The first time, she was driving by the police department and saw him exiting the front door of the old brick building. Her heart raced, and she fought the urge to swerve up on the sidewalk and run over him with her Honda CR-V.

The second sighting was in Food World, the local grocery store. As she rounded the corner to the produce section, Marlee saw Hector pushing a grocery cart with his baby daughter cuddled up in her car seat secured atop the cart. He inspected the broccoli by picking it up and turning it from side to side as the little pale-yellow bundle kicked her feet and made baby noises. Trish Riley, the baby's mother, walked alongside reaching into the cart to adjust the baby's blanket. Marlee turned her cart on two wheels, causing a loud screech which caught the attention of both Hector and Trish.

"Marlee, wait up," called out Hector as he fast-walked toward her. Marlee kept walking, pushing her cart as far away from the produce section as fast as she could manage. Of course, the cart had developed a sticky wheel which was now locked up while the other three wheels moved with ease. This slowed down Marlee's pace and added an extra clatter to the already noisy cart. Grabbing her purse, she abandoned her cart and the intended purchases within as she rushed for the door.

"Hey, wait!" Hector yelled, now that he had caught up to Marlee. "I know this isn't the time or the place, but I just wanted to..." His voice trailed off as he searched for the right words to say to one's ex-girlfriend when they see you with your new girlfriend and your baby.

"Piss off, Hector! I don't have anything to say to you. Go back to your little family and leave me alone!" The fire in her eyes was convincing, and Hector backed away, slack-jawed, as Marlee marched out of the store.

She stormed into the parking lot toward her car, unsatisfied with her interaction with Hector. Turning on her heel, she marched back into Food World and grabbed a navel orange from the sale display inside the door. Rage burned in her heart as she found Hector walking back toward his family. Marlee drew her right arm back and hurled the orange in Hector's general direction. Her aim, or lack thereof, resulted in the firm orange striking Hector in the back of the head. The dented orange fell to the floor, and Hector whirled around, his hand clutching his citrus-induced injury.

Satisfied with how things ended, Marlee walked toward the door. She reached in her purse and pulled out a dollar bill and handed it to a shocked teenage employee who was standing near the fruit display. "This is for the orange that that idiot just destroyed," Marlee said, nodding toward Hector, who was still rubbing the back of his head.

Since that time, Marlee had not seen nor heard from Hector, and she was happy to keep it that way. Their relationship, which had been built on lies and deceit, was over, and Hector had moved on with his new girlfriend and their baby.

"We'll just see how long before he cheats on her," Marlee grumbled out loud to herself as she continued rifling through boxes and tubs of papers. She adjusted her glasses, which were not working as well as they should because the print on everything seemed so small. She peered at a crumpled manila folder she had just extracted from a dusty cardboard box. Marlee opened the folder, and she spread out the contents on her cluttered dining room table.

"*What's this?*" Marlee thought as she sifted through the newspaper articles, hand-written notes, and a jumble of other memorabilia. Pippa, her hefty gray Persian cat, lifted her fluffy head from the round pet bed where she napped atop the dining room table. After a mighty yawn, she readjusted herself and continued napping.

Marlee clutched a newspaper article captioned: COLLEGE STUDENT FOUND DEAD. Her heart pounded as all the memories of Beth Van Dam's disappearance from their dormitory and eventual death came flooding back. All of a sudden, Marlee's memories transported her back to 1987 when she was an undergraduate student and had a front row seat at the death investigation of a friend. A friend, who as it turned out, she never really knew.

There's nothing quite like a college house party to get everyone stirred up. The drinking, the romance, and the backstabbing rival that of most soap operas.

Chapter 2

"Keep it down! I'm trying to sleep," grumbled Marlee from her lofted bunk bed as her roommate, Jasmine, charged in. Her blue backpack landed on the floor and her coat was flung toward a chair.

"It's nearly noon, and you missed your first two classes," Jasmine chided, still not reducing the noise. "And you missed The Young and the Restless!" Missing class was completely acceptable, but Marlee, Jasmine, and several of their friends and dorm-mates gathered in the first-floor dayroom to collectively watch soap operas when they didn't have classes or chose to skip them.

Marlee sat upright, her short stature preventing her from hitting her head on the ceiling. Flinging back the covers, she swung her legs over the side of the bed and faced her roommate. "For your information, Miss Nosy, I went to my classes, watched most of The Young and the Restless, and then just came to the room a few minutes ago to get a little shut eye before my Bio lab this afternoon." She stared at Jasmine, hoping this would be enough to quiet her down.

"Oh, I thought maybe you were out too late drinking at Nickel Night." One of the local bars held a special every Wednesday night in which patrons could buy a glass for five dollars and then each refill of beer only cost five cents. Anyone who could scrounge up five dollars and fifty cents had more than enough for a night of fun. Nickel Night was the downfall of many a college student and was the leading cause of poor attendance in Thursday morning classes.

"I went to Nickel Night, but left early and walked back with Angie and Beth. It was boring, and no one was out. We went to their room and ordered pizza. You were snoring when I came in," Marlee reported.

"You're lying. I don't snore. I've never snored, and

I never will," Jasmine said with a huff as she continued to pull books, art supplies, and papers from her backpack and fling them on her desk.

She enjoyed winding up her tall, wispy roommate. Marlee struggled to get down from her lofted bed, using the built-in desk and then the wooden chair as steps. She glanced at the Jon Bon Jovi poster attached to the cinder block wall with rubber cement. It would be a bitch to remove the poster intact and then cover up the rubber cement remains, but she would do her best, so she could get her dorm deposit back at the end of the semester.

"Did you have lunch yet?" Jasmine asked, redirecting the conversation from her supposed snoring.

"Nah, I'll just graze on what I have here in the room," Marlee said, grabbing a loaf of white bread, which had been on sale for 33 cents at the grocery store near their dorm. "How about you?"

"I'm avoiding somebody in the Commons, so I'll probably do the same. But I don't have any bread," Jasmine said with an exaggerated sigh, looking forlornly at Marlee's nearly full loaf.

"I'll trade you two pieces of bread for two cheese singles," Marlee suggested, remembering Jasmine's stash of plastic-wrapped cheese.

"Deal." Jasmine reached into the mini-fridge and pulled out two individually wrapped cheese slices from a twenty-four pack and tossed them to her roommate. Within five minutes, they were both enjoying toasted cheese sandwiches. Jasmine sat cross-legged on the floor while Marlee reclined in a lawn chair that doubled as her bed on nights when she was too tipsy to navigate into her lofted bed.

"So, who are you trying to avoid, Jazz?" Marlee chewed the last of her meal and considered making a second sandwich until she remembered that her Levis were getting uncomfortably snug around the middle.

"I think you can probably guess. He's a sophomore, has long blonde hair, and always wears

Zubas." Jasmine grabbed a Coke from the fridge and rolled her eyes as she spoke about Nick, the cutie from Texas who was overly blessed with the gift of gab and enthusiastic about animal-print athletic pants.

"Why do you keep avoiding him? Is he a creep?" Marlee reached behind the curtains on the window sill for a gallon-sized plastic container which originally held mustard. It had been thoroughly cleaned and now held sun tea. She balanced the full container against her stomach and glugged room-temperature tea into a stainless-steel glass, one of four her mother sent with her to college.

"Not really. I mean, he's nice, and he's cute, but he just won't stop talking to me." Jasmine sighed. She carried the weight of the world on her shoulders.

"He's probably one of those nervous talkers who just can't shut up when he's around someone he likes." Marlee giggled. "He thinks you're foxy, and you make him nervous." She ducked as a banana clip whizzed by her head.

"Very funny," said Jasmine as she searched for some other object to hurl at her roommate.

"Did you hear about the party at Stairway to Hell tonight?" In her morning classes, Marlee heard from a friend that mutual acquaintances were throwing a party at their off-campus house. That meant lots of beer, loud rock music, and plenty of hot guys.

"I wanna go! What's the plan?" Jasmine asked.

"No plan yet, but I'll see if we can catch a ride with Lisa or Angie. I heard they are having two kegs, and it's only three dollars for all you can drink. And there might even be garbage pail punch!" Marlee loved the concoction of apples, oranges, and other fruits soaked in Everclear and whatever other form of alcohol the makers had on hand at the time. Everything was mixed with Kool Aid, poured into a large container, often a garbage can, and people scooped up the beverage and fruit with plastic cups.

"I've never had garbage pail punch before. I can't wait to try it," said Jasmine, already planning what she would wear to the big event that night.

"Make sure you don't eat too much of the fruit because that's where the alcohol is concentrated," Marlee said knowingly, having learned this the hard way. "If you stick with the liquid, you should be okay, as long as you don't drink too much of it."

A loud knock on the open door frame interrupted their party discussion. "Did I hear something about a party?" asked Kristie, their next-door neighbor. Kristie had a heart of gold and the mouth of a sailor. She acted the same around everyone and didn't see a need to put on airs, which was the reason she was liked by everyone in their wing of the dorm.

Marlee and Jasmine filled Kristie in on the details, and she made plans to join them. "All we need is a ride there," Jasmine said. Kristie, like Marlee and Jasmine, didn't have a vehicle and was dependent upon friends for rides.

"I can ask Polly," Kristie said with an eye roll, referring to her roommate. "But if we ask her for a ride, she'll want to come to the party and hang out with us."

The three stood silent, weighing the pros and cons of inviting Polly. She could be overbearing and kind of bitchy, but she had a car and was usually willing to drive. Polly wasn't much of a drinker, so she could be counted on for a ride back from the party too, which wasn't the case with everyone who provided transportation to off-campus festivities. In the end, the trio decided it would be easier to put up with Polly for the night than to find someone else to drive them. And there was no way they were walking to the event, even though it was less than a mile away. It was one thing to walk home from a party, but it was uncool to show up afoot.

The outside of the two-story party house was in fair shape; at least it appeared that way in the dark, which was the only time anyone other than the renters were there. White paint was chipped and peeling in most places. Two windows on the upper level were cracked and had been sealed with duct tape. Unattended trees skirted the edge of the yard while unruly bushes and dead weeds clustered against the base of the house. Snow blanketed the unraked leaves on the ground. A widow's walk faced the west with one of the boards from the railing hanging loosely.   Bedrooms were both upstairs and in the unfinished basement. The guys renting the house had installed a bar in the basement consisting of stacked cement blocks and sheets of plywood.

The party had yet to gain momentum by the time Marlee, Jasmine, Kristie, and Polly arrived at 7:30 pm. Marlee always liked to get to a party early, have a few drinks, and get the lay of the land before everyone else arrived. The four women stood in a corner of the living room sipping foamy beer from red plastic cups and chatting among themselves. Stairway to Hell was in dismal shape and should have been renovated decades ago. Flowered print wallpaper peeled off the walls in spots, exposing harsh yellow paint. Brown carpeting covered every room and had been matted by years of foot traffic, party spills, and grime. Holes were burned into the carpet, the orange flowered couch, and the one lumpy, stained chair from unattended cigarettes. An additional couch was normally in the living room, but had been hauled out to the front porch to air out after someone puked on it the previous weekend. After a week or two of fresh air, the cushions would be flipped, the couch would be moved back into the house, and activities would resume as usual.

Tim, John, and two other guys rented the decrepit old house located in the center of town. Marlee knew Tim from her western div class, and he had introduced her to John at the bar a few weeks ago. Tim welcomed people at the door and collected three dollars per person to cover the cost of alcohol. John reportedly ran to the liquor store in quest of more booze. A few other guys milled around the house, but Marlee was unsure who were roommates and who were party guests.

By 9:00 pm, the party had picked up. A Van Halen cassette blared from the boom box, and the garbage pail punch was fully assembled and ready for consumption, thanks to John. Marlee reached in the trash can with her empty beer cup and scooped out a generous portion of the red drink. A slotted spoon, caked with rust, rested on the counter for anyone who wanted to dig deep for booze-soaked fruit.

Marlee and her friends, now well-buzzed, split up and mingled with others at the party. She gazed around the room, noticing several people from her dorm and her classes. The majority of the people there she didn't recognize. It was Marlee's first year on campus. She attended another in-state school her freshman year, but after finding an interest in psychology, she transferred to a school across the state that was well-known for that program. Marlee was just learning the ropes at her new university, but she had already made a bunch of friends, was frequently invited to parties, and wasn't flunking any classes, so she was off to a good start.

"Hey, Marlee! Isn't this party radical?" Beth Van Dam screeched as she danced her way through the growing crowd, holding her drink cup in the air. Her blonde, permed mullet rustled against the collar of her nylon jacket. They lived in the same dorm, and Beth was in Marlee's biology lab. Earlier that afternoon, they had discussed the party.

"Yeah. I didn't know you'd be here. I thought you had to work late." Marlee continued to sip from her red cup, beginning to feel the effects of mixed alcohol punch on top of keg beer.

"I left 7-11 early. Told my boss I was getting sick and needed to go home," Beth laughed as she chugged from her plastic cup. Beth sloshed some of her clear-colored drink onto the carpet as she navigated through the party, cigarette in hand. The matted carpet instantly absorbed the liquid, leaving only a small wet spot, which was dwarfed by a multitude of other stains of unknown origin.

Marlee spied Paul in the kitchen helping himself to more garbage pail punch. She'd had her eye on him since last semester and saw this as her chance to visit with him. He was alone, and Marlee had consumed enough drinks to think she was funny, charming, and beautiful. She walked into the kitchen, her flowered high-top tennis shoes sticking to the semi-dried spilled punch on the linoleum.

"Hey, aren't you in my criminology class?" Marlee asked, sidling up to Paul to refill her own cup.

"Yeah, I guess so," Paul said as he turned around to face Marlee. His blue eyes were fringed with long, dark lashes, and his shoulder-length blonde hair was parted on the side and hung straight. He wore acid-washed jeans with holes in both knees. They were pegged at the bottom, revealing his white, scuffed high-tops. Reaching into his jean jacket pocket, he pulled out a pack of Marlboro Lights and offered one to Marlee.

"No, thanks. Not a smoker," Marlee said as Paul procured one from the pack and lit it up. "Are you ready for the quiz? I think it's on Monday."

Paul took a long draw on his cigarette and exhaled the smoke through his nose. "Nah, I really don't worry much about quizzes. How about you?"

Wanting to appear as cool as Paul, Marlee downplayed her own dedication to the criminology class. "No way. I just pay attention in class, and then I don't have to study." In reality, Marlee loved criminology and read everything assigned. She also did extra research on topics that interested her. Math and science, however, were quite another story. If she didn't care about the classes then she didn't apply much effort.

They chatted about their shared class, the eccentric professor who taught it, and one student in the front row who always asked stupid questions. Paul looked away from Marlee and nodded at somebody across the room. "Look, I gotta go talk to this guy, but maybe we can get together sometime."

"Yeah, sure. That would be great," Marlee said as she put her hand on the counter in an effort to look casual. She hit the rust-encrusted slotted spoon which fell into the punch with a mighty splash. Paul was quick on his feet and jumped back before being covered in red punch. With an awkward laugh, he walked away.

Jasmine was in the middle of the room, surrounded by three guys competing for her attention. The skin-tight blue dress fit her like a glove, and her black heels had her towering over one of her male admirers. She laughed riotously and tossed her hair from side to side, enjoying being the focal point.

Kristie, clad in jeans, a blue t-shirt, and tennis shoes, was in a heated debate with two guys from their dorm about the necessity of fire alarms in the dorm rooms. Some students in their dorm disabled the fire alarms in their rooms because blinking red light disturbed their sleep. This was discovered during a routine safety check of dorm rooms and the offending students were forced to write reports about fire safety. Kristie was pro-safety, while the two guys were involved in disabling the alarms. When Marlee saw Kristie raise her hands above her head, she knew she needed to intervene before Kristie went ballistic.

Walking past Jasmine, Marlee observed Polly standing alone by the window. She had a pinched look on her face and wasn't enjoying herself. When she caught Marlee's eye, Polly pointed to her Swatch watch and mouthed "Let's go."

Marlee made it over to Kristie and pointed toward Polly. "The warden says we have to leave," Marlee said in Kristie's ear.

"Already? We just got here!"

"Polly's not having any fun, so she wants to make sure no one else does either," Marlee said with an edge of bitterness. This wasn't the first time Polly pulled the plug on a social situation if she wasn't getting any male attention.

"Fine," huffed Kristie as she walked over to Jasmine and relayed the bad news to her.

"The bitch says we have to leave," Kristie said to Jasmine, nodding her head in Polly's direction. Jasmine's mouth fell open as she obediently followed Kristie.

"Polly, why do we have to leave now?" Jasmine whined. "We just started having fun."

"It's almost midnight, and I have class tomorrow. I can't blow off my Friday classes like some of you do," Polly snapped as she headed for the door. "You don't have to go back to the dorm with me, but I'm not waiting around any longer." Since none of them had alternative transportation, they sullenly filed along behind Polly.

It was a quiet ride back to the dorm as Marlee, Kristie, and Jasmine all silently fumed about their early departure. As mad as they were, they didn't say anything for fear of jeopardizing future rides to parties, the bar, and the mall. One thing was obvious, they needed to find a new friend with a car. And fast!

I hate it when somebody tries to steal my man! That's an unforgiveable offense.

Chapter 3

The next morning the alarm rang way too early. Marlee hit the snooze twice then finally shut it off. When she awoke, it was past 11:00 am. Jasmine was still in her pajamas but out of bed. She looked horrible with tousled hair, bags under her eyes, and a glassy stare.

"I feel like death warmed over in a tin pan in the microwave," Jasmine mumbled as she sipped from a can of 7-Up.

"How many glasses of punch did you drink, Jazz?" Marlee sat upright and maneuvered down from her lofted bed. She felt sluggish, but had taken two aspirin and drank several glasses of water when they got home, so there was no headache.

"I wasn't counting. Actually, I thought maybe I was drinking non-alcoholic punch because it didn't even taste like alcohol."

"I'm not familiar with any parties that serve non-alcoholic punch," Marlee laughed. "Unless it's held in a church basement."

"I'll keep that in mind." Jasmine rubbed her temples with her forefingers in an attempt to alleviate her headache. "Maybe it's a good thing Polly made us leave early after all."

"Polly can be a real bitch sometimes. We need to find another friend with a car. I've had it with her." Marlee had put up with Polly's bullshit for a semester and a half and was done dealing with her.

"And they have to be willing to give us rides to parties and not insist we leave before everyone is ready," Jasmine added.

Marlee nodded, getting ready to rag on Polly some more when there was a sharp knock on their door. They both yelled "come in" at the same time, as they rarely locked their door except when they were both out of the room for an extended period of time.

Kristie stomped into the room, a scowl on her face. "I can't believe my roommate. After she made us leave early last night do you know what she said?" Not waiting for an answer, Kristie continued. "Polly said I owed her five dollars for gas money because she drove us to the party and also to the mall last week!"

"You're kidding!" Jasmine gasped.

"I can't believe she has the nerve. Is she going to charge us too?" Marlee asked, incredulous that Polly would ask for gas money. "We're doing her a favor by letting her hang out with us."

"Yeah, and the party was only a mile away. I know her car is old, but there's no way Polly used five dollars in gas. If she charges me for gas then I'm charging her for my jumbo bag of M&Ms that she ate while she was studying for her chemistry test." Kristie was livid and would've marched back to her room and confronted Polly right then had Marlee and Jasmine not stopped her.

The three groused on about Polly for a few minutes until there was another knock at the door. It was Polly, wearing a teal half-shirt that read "Life's a Beach" in fuchsia lettering. She was smiling and upbeat. "Hey, everybody. Hope you didn't have too much to drink last night. Have you heard the big news?"

"No," Marlee said sullenly, giving Polly the silent treatment by turning her back toward the unpopular neighbor.

"Sorry, I made us leave earlier than you might have liked," Polly asked sweetly, making everyone hate her even more.

When no one asked about her big news, Polly took the hint and left. But not before she made a final remark. "Well, if you all can't handle your alcohol then maybe you shouldn't party on weekdays." With that gem of advice, Polly sashayed her lumpy body out the door in her too-tight jeans and brightly colored half-shirt.

The door was no sooner closed than Marlee, Kristie, and Jasmine began bitching about Polly again.

After the novelty of that wore off, they shared stories of who they talked to at the party.

"Jazz, I saw you talking to a bunch of guys, and you looked like you were having a good time. Are you interested in any of them?" Kristie asked.

Jasmine perked up and recounted her flirtation with three guys from Dorner Hall, one of which she knew from her hometown. "Joey seems like a nice guy. I gave him my number. Let's see if he calls." She looked wistfully at the phone hanging on the wall, wishing for it to ring. "How about you, Kristie?"

"I got into an argument with some guys about disabling fire alarms in dorm rooms. They were the idiots that unhooked their alarm last semester. I'm going out with one of them on Saturday night."

"What? You have a date? What's his name?" Marlee asked, excited for her friend.

"I didn't catch their names. Guess I'll find out when he comes to pick me up on Saturday night," Kristie said, unfazed.

"Well, I finally got to talk to Paul. You know, the guy I've been lusting over since last semester?" Marlee reported.

"Yeah, what happened?" Jasmine asked.

"I talked to him, and then I nearly splashed him with punch. Then he had to go talk to someone else," Marlee recounted, realizing how pathetic it sounded. "Baby steps."

Jasmine and Kristie erupted into a fit of laughter. "By the time you graduate, you might actually have a date with him," Kristie said.

"You two are hysterical," Marlee grumbled, laughing in spite of herself.

"Ow, my head. Quit making me laugh," said Jasmine. "I drank way too much last night. But at least I didn't yak."

"You know who was really having fun when I saw her? Beth Van Dam," said Marlee, recalling her quick chat with her friend. "Let's call her room and see if she wants to come down here to rehash the night."

Marlee picked up the receiver and dialed Beth's room. After a quick conversation with Beth's roommate, Angie, she turned to Jasmine and Kristie. "Angie said she never came home last night. I wonder if she snagged some guy at the party."

"I saw her going upstairs a little after 9:00 with one of the guys who lives there. Maybe she stayed with him," Kristie suggested.

"It was after that when I saw Beth. Which guy did you see her with?" Marlee asked.

"I don't know his name, but he has black hair in a ponytail and has a mustache. He looked like a creep." Kristie shuddered recalling the man's appearance and demeanor.

"I don't know who that is. I don't even remember seeing anybody by that description last night," Marlee said and Jasmine agreed.

"They were talking and laughing as they walked upstairs, so I know he didn't force her to his room. Of course, I don't know what happened after they got upstairs." A frown crossed Kristie's face as she thought about her friend with the creepy guy and what may have transpired after they reached his room.

"I'll call Tim. He lives at Stairway to Hell and can tell us if Beth is still there," Marlee suggested. She placed the call and moments later hung up. Her face was white and her hands were shaking. "Tim said Beth was found in their yard this morning. She's dead."

When I hear them say, "She was my best friend. We hung out together all the time," I just think bullshit! Most of the people saying this never took the time to get to know me. They were too busy with their own little problems. They wouldn't know a real problem if it hit them over the head.

Chapter 4

"What?" Jasmine and Kristie chorused, their mouths agape.

"Are you serious? How can Beth be dead?" Kristie sputtered. "I mean, we just saw her."

"Tim said he took his dog outside to pee this morning. That's when he saw Beth face down on the ground. He said she was cold, and he called 911 right away. The cops are still there talking to everyone at the house," Marlee said, robotically repeating what Tim just told her.

The three students sat in silence, each remembering Beth and the fun she brought to their lives in the short time they'd known her. Although the bonds Marlee, Jasmine, and Kristie had formed with others in the dorm were brief, they were strong. The loss of Beth was profound and knocked the wind out of each of them.

Jasmine struggled to wrap her mind around the late-breaking events, and tears streamed down her face. "What happened? How did she die?"

"Don't know. I didn't even think to ask Tim," Marlee said. "I don't want to call him right back, but maybe we should go over there."

"Why would you want to go over there? Just to get the gossip on how she died?" Kristie was beyond disgusted to think her friend was only interested in salacious news.

"No. Not at all. I thought we could go for moral support for Tim and his roommates. Sure, I want to know how and why Beth died, but the police will want to talk to everyone who was at the party last night. They'll especially want to talk to you, Kristie, since you saw Beth go upstairs with a creepy-looking guy," Marlee said, a bit sheepish when she realized she wanted more answers.

"Well, I guess that makes sense. But I don't want to go over to Stairway to Hell if Beth is still there," Kristie said, calming down now.

"Me neither. I don't think I could take seeing her

just lying there in the snow," sniffed Jasmine, dabbing her eyes and nose with a tissue.

"I don't want to see Beth either, but I know from my criminology class that the sooner the police have all the information, the better chance they have of solving the crime. Let's walk over there and get our interviews out of the way. I'm sure Tim, John, and the other roommates would appreciate our support too," Marlee said, standing up and searching for her coat.

Jasmine shook her head. "I can't. I just can't do it."

"That's alright. I understand," said Marlee. "How about you?" she said looking at Kristie.

Kristie took a deep breath and let it out. "Yeah, I guess I'll go with you. Give me a second to get my coat." She walked from the room, closing the door behind her.

"Marlee, are you sure you want to go over there? You were better friends with Beth than either of us. Won't it be too much to bear?" Jasmine asked.

"It is too much to handle," Marlee admitted. "But I need to know what happened. It doesn't make any sense that a perfectly healthy nineteen-year-old woman died at a party."

Kristie opened the door to their room without knocking. She was bundled up in a heavy coat, stocking cap, and gloves. Marlee met her at the door, and they trudged through the snow over to Stairway to Hell. It was late February and warm spring days would be on their way. But today was not the day. A brisk, biting wind cut through the duo, forcing them to seek refuge behind buildings twice before they reached the party house.

Police cars surrounded Stairway to Hell and officers were stationed on all sides of the house to prevent unauthorized people from coming or going. Yellow crime scene tape surrounded the perimeter of the yard.

Marlee recognized one of the cops standing watch outside the house. He was in her criminology class and had mentioned during an in-class discussion that he was an officer seeking his degree. She didn't know his name, but that didn't matter.

"Um, excuse me," she began.

"You'll have to keep moving along, miss. This is a crime scene," the tall, pudgy officer said.

"I know. Beth was our friend, and we were at the party last night. We thought we would come back here and give our statements. I don't know your name, but you're in my criminology class. My name's Marlee McCabe. I sit in the second row," Marlee said at a rapid pace before he could interrupt and send her and Kristie on their way.

"Okay, I recognize you now," the officer said grabbing for his walkie talkie and speaking into it. After a few seconds, a voice responded and instructed the officer to escort Marlee and Kristie to the front door. "I'm Officer Stevens. Barry Stevens," he said before leaving them at the door.

A short, stout man dressed in a gray suit and sporting a crew cut met them at the door and introduced himself as Detective Barkley. "I understand you were both at the party last night and saw Beth Van Dam." He was curt and straight forward in his delivery.

Marlee nodded. "Yes, we both live in the same dorm as Beth. She came here from work last night. She told her boss she was sick so she could leave early. I talked to her around 9:00 pm. Kristie saw something too," she said nodding her head toward her friend.

"What did you see?" Detective Barkley asked looking at Kristie. She relayed her story of seeing Beth walking upstairs with the creepy guy around 9:15 pm.

The detective followed up with several questions and then gathered their names and contact information before dismissing them. Marlee and Kristie looked at each other, not satisfied with their interaction. It had been all take and no give on the detective's part.

"So how did Beth die?" Marlee blurted.

"I'm not at liberty to discuss the details right now. We won't know until the autopsy is completed," Detective Barkley said, flipping shut his notepad and placing it back inside his suit jacket pocket.

"Autopsy? You mean they're going to cut Beth open?" Kristie said, horrified at the thought of her friend being dissected.

"Yes. Autopsies are standard practice in death cases. Thank you both for your cooperation. I'll be in touch," said the detective as he walked back inside the house.

Officer Stevens appeared at their side and ushered them outside the crime scene tape. "Thank you for providing information on this case."

"Can you tell us what's going on? Beth was a friend of ours. She lived in our dorm. We just want to know what happened," Marlee pleaded.

"We all want to know," Officer Stevens said with a sigh. "Do you two need a ride home?"

"Sure!" Kristie and Marlee called out in unison, glad that they wouldn't have to walk home in the freezing wind. The officer utilized his walkie talkie again and a car drove up beside them.

"This officer will drive you home. Thanks, ladies. We'll be in touch. If you have any further information, please let us know," said Officer Stevens as he opened the back door of the police cruiser and helped them into the back seat.

Kristie started to talk on their chauffeured ride home in the police car, but Marlee shushed her. "Anything we say might be recorded," she whispered, paranoid that they could unwittingly be pulled into the case. Kristie nodded and not another word was uttered until they were dropped off in front of their dorm and they thanked the officer for the ride.

Marlee let herself into her dorm room, and Kristie followed. Jasmine sat at her built-in desk, simply staring straight ahead. After a recap of their interactions with the police, Jasmine had questions. "So, was Beth... Was she still there?"

"I don't know. I didn't see her. We talked to a cop

who's in my criminology class and then a detective. After that, we were given a ride home. We didn't even get to see Tim or John to see how they were doing." Marlee was disappointed that she and Kristie hadn't learned more during their time at Stairway to Hell, but was glad they went and provided what little information they had.

"I wish I knew what happened when Beth went upstairs with that guy," Kristie said. "He looked like a weirdo, but I never thought about trying to steer her away from him. I figured she was a big girl and knew how to get rid of guys she didn't want hanging around her."

"It's not your responsibility, Kristie. You said Beth was laughing and talking as she went upstairs, so there's no way you could have known something bad could happen. Besides, we don't even know if that guy was involved," Marlee said.

"Maybe he had nothing to do with her death," Jasmine said, anxious to alleviate any burden Kristie felt about Beth's untimely death.

"I know, but I still feel guilty. I may have been the last person to see her alive, other than the creepy guy," Kristie said. "I wonder who he is. I haven't seen him before on campus or at parties."

Marlee reached into her closet and pulled out the university yearbook from the previous year. Even though none of the three had attended then, Marlee purchased the annual to familiarize herself with more of the students in her classes and find out about campus life at this school. An added benefit was that if she saw a guy in class she could always go to the yearbook and search for his picture to determine his name, hometown, and grade level.

"Let's start looking through this." Marlee plopped the annual down on her desk and gestured for Kristie to take the chair since she was the only one of them who actually saw the guy.

After several pages' worth of big permed hair, goofy smiles, and serial killers in the making, the trio decided to take a break. It was after 1:00, and none of them had eaten breakfast or lunch. They walked over to the Student Union and took the annual with them to peruse as they ate.

By the time they finished their meals and decided to go back to the dorm, they had combed the entire 1986 yearbook, and Kristie found no one looking remotely like the guy she saw with Beth. "Maybe he didn't get his picture taken," Kristie said.

"Or maybe he's a freshman or a transfer and wasn't here last year," said Jasmine.

"It's possible that he's not even a student. John is from Britton, and Tim is from here in town. I say we wait until this evening, then give Tim another call to see what he has to say. And also to make sure he and his roommates are handling everything okay," Marlee suggested.

Jasmine and Marlee hung out in their dorm room the rest of the afternoon. One by one, many of the girls on their floor dropped in to talk about Beth and try to make sense of her death. Kristie was meeting three fellow students for a group project in her English class, but after that was over, she joined them. None of them had any new insights or ideas, but gathering together in times of chaos was important.

"Beth was a character. I'll never forget some of the things she said when we went out to some of the bars. She was fearless and would say anything to anybody," Marlee reminisced. "She was one of the funniest people I've ever known."

Jasmine nodded. "Me too. She always knew how to cheer me up when I was having a bad day."

"That girl could drink more than most men I know," Kristie said, giving Beth a huge compliment. "And she wasn't that big. I don't know how she could hold all that alcohol."

"She could party, that's for sure. But she also carried a full load of classes and was always working at 7-11," Marlee said.

"You know, I never really saw her around the dorm

36

or on campus much. When I saw her, it was always at a bar or a party," Jasmine observed. After thinking about it, Marlee and Kristie agreed that Beth did not have much of a presence on campus.

"I never saw her roommate, Angie, around much either," Marlee said. "Maybe they just have different schedules than us."

Polly gave a quick knock on the door and came in uninvited. "Did you guys hear the big news yet? About Beth Van Dam?" Always excited to be in the power position with gossip, Polly rattled on, assuming that Kristie, Jasmine, and Marlee knew nothing of their friend's death. "I heard she died from blood alcohol poisoning because she was a severe alcoholic!"

"We already heard that Beth died. Where did you get your information, Polly?" Marlee asked, trying to keep the disgust out of her voice. Polly acted as if this was a story line in one of the daytime soap operas they watched.

"Blake, one of the roommates at the house told me," Polly said.

"Who's Blake? What does he look like?" Kristie enquired.

"Long, dark hair, usually pulled back in a ponytail. A mustache. He's a fox. I've had my eye on him for a while," Polly said with a giggle.

"Seriously? You're hot for that guy?" Jasmine blurted, not even attempting to hide her disdain.

"Well, yeah. Who isn't? Just look at him," Polly said, oblivious that the others in the room found Blake vomitus.

"When did you talk to him?" Kristie asked.

Polly turned beet red. "Um, this morning. Why?"

"What time this morning?" Marlee asked, even though she was pretty sure she already knew the answer.

"Around 9:30."

"How did it come about that you were talking to Blake that early in the morning?" Marlee persevered.

"Well, I wasn't going to say anything, but I stayed

overnight with Blake. I slept in his bed, but nothing happened," Polly said quickly.

"Wait. So, you went back to Stairway to Hell after you dumped us off at the dorm?" Kristie asked, having difficulty believing her roommate would do such a thing.

"Yeah, well, after we got back, you fell asleep right away," Polly said to Kristie. "I could hear you snoring. I couldn't sleep, so I called Blake. We'd chatted a bit at the party, and I thought we hit it off. When we talked, he asked me to come back to the party, so I did."

"Really? That's funny, because you were in such a big rush to leave last night. You didn't seem like you were having much fun," Marlee observed. "Why did you call Blake last night?"

Polly released a deep sigh. "Like I said, I couldn't sleep and just thought he and I had a connection, so I called the house and talked to him for about fifteen minutes. He said the party was dying down and asked me to come back so we could talk one-on-one without people interrupting us. So, I got dressed and drove back over there. We hung out in his room and listened to music and talked. We made out a little, and then we both slept with all of our clothes on."

"What about the class you desperately needed to attend this morning?" Marlee asked pointedly. "That was the reason you made us leave so early last night, remember?"

All eyes were on Polly as she stammered her way through a half-assed excuse. "I remembered late last night that the class had been cancelled for today. Sorry."

"How did you find out about Beth?" Jasmine interrupted, changing the topic before the conversation turned nasty.

"We heard a commotion downstairs, and Blake went to see what was going on. He came back and told me that Tim found Beth dead outside. After the cops got there, they talked to everyone in the house, including me. I hung out at Stairway to Hell for a while and then came home."

"Why do you think Beth died from alcohol overdose?" Marlee asked.

"Blake and I and some of the others at the house were talking, and it was the only scenario that made sense. I really liked Beth and thought she was a nice person, but we all knew she had a major drinking problem, right? Did you ever see her at a party or at the bar when she wasn't sloshed?" Polly said.

"Just because Beth liked to party doesn't automatically mean that she drank herself to death," said Jasmine.

"I know, but it makes the most sense. It's not like somebody at the party killed her." Polly indignantly defended her theory.

"Did the police give you any clues as to what happened to Beth?" Marlee asked, anxious to uncover facts rather than Polly's assumptions.

"No, they just asked questions," Polly said. "I asked them what they thought happened, and they didn't have an answer."

"When did you last see Beth last night, Polly?" Katie asked, curious if Polly knew anything about Blake and Beth walking upstairs together.

"I guess it was when I was in the kitchen getting a glass of water after I went back to see Blake. Beth staggered in and sort of fell against the counter. She was really drunk and slurring her words. I tried talking to her, but she wasn't making any sense, so I walked away." Polly scratched her head as she recalled the events of the previous evening.

"Did you see Beth walking upstairs? Or did you see her upstairs when you were with Blake?" Marlee asked, unsure how to approach the topic of Blake and Beth going upstairs together that evening.

"No, I only saw her circulating around the main floor talking to people and then in the kitchen when she was trashed," Polly replied. "Why all the questions? Do you guys know what happened?"

The three all shook their heads. "We've been talking about it, trying to make sense of everything. We don't have any inside information. I called Tim this morning, and he told me about Beth," Marlee said, purposely leaving out the fact that she and Kristie had walked over to the house and been questioned by the police earlier in the day.

After more discussion of Beth's passing and what could have caused such a horrible ending, Polly left and went next door to her own room. After Polly was out of earshot, Marlee turned to the other two and said, "We need to get some inside information on this." Kristie and Jasmine nodded in agreement.

And I think I know how I can get it, Marlee thought.

The truth is usually hidden in plain sight, but no one wants to see it. No one really wants the whole truth.

Chapter 5

After three phone calls, Marlee found the information she was looking for. A friend of a classmate's roommate led her to the contact information for Officer Barry Stevens, Marlee's classmate from criminology. He was a full-time officer, unmarried, and lived with two other guys, both of whom worked in law enforcement.

That evening, Marlee called Officer Stevens, asking to meet with him right away. She didn't say it, but implied that she had new information to share about Beth's death. They agreed to meet right away at the university library.

It was nearing 7:00 pm, and since it was Friday night, the campus was buzzing with activities and students rushing to get off campus in pursuit of night life. She breathed deep as she entered the library. Marlee loved the smell of books and absorbed the scent of them every time she went to study.

Officer Stevens was sitting on a bench just inside the front doors. No longer clad in his uniform, he sported jeans, tennis shoes, a sweatshirt, and a heavy coat. No one would guess he was an officer of the law by the looks of him. "Thanks for meeting me," Marlee said.

Barry Stevens stood up and motioned her toward the back of the library where there were small enclosed study rooms. They were mainly used by graduate students who spent the majority of their lives in the library, but any room that was unoccupied and unlocked was fair game. Finding an open room, Marlee led them inside and closed the door behind them.

"So, what did you find out?" the police officer asked Marlee as they both sat down in the cramped room.

Knowing she couldn't tell him outright that she didn't have any new information, she decided to pass on the hearsay Polly told them earlier. It wasn't factual, only the uneducated guesses Polly and some of the roommates at Stairway to Hell had conjured.

Officer Stevens furrowed his brow. "A person from your dorm told you this? Was she interviewed?"

"Yes, Polly said the police talked to her and all the roommates there this morning after Beth's body was found. Personally, I have a hard time believing Beth drank herself to death. I think there has to be some other explanation," Marlee said, hoping to garner additional information from the young officer.

"You know I can't talk about it," the officer chastised. "When information is meant to be released to the public, an announcement will be made."

Marlee took a deep breath, mustering all of her inner strength. "Look, Beth was my friend, and I'd like to see justice for her. I'm in your criminology class, and I know you don't really know me, but I plan on going into something in the law enforcement field myself when I graduate. I was thinking maybe we could work out some sort of arrangement."

"Like what?" The officer looked at her with a mix of skepticism and curiosity as he raised his eyebrows.

"You tell me about new developments and theories on the case, and I'll report anything I find out on campus directly to you," Marlee said.

"You need to report any new information to us no matter what," Officer Stevens said, scowling at the student.

"I know. The detective gave me his card and asked that I contact him with anything else. I just thought that maybe you were looking to make detective and that if I pass new info on to you that it might help you in getting promoted sooner."

"How do I know you won't repeat everything I say to your friends? I could get fired for releasing unauthorized information."

"I'm not a blabbermouth, and I won't repeat any of it. The only thing I want is for whoever's responsible for Beth's death to be held accountable. That's all," Marlee insisted, looking him directly in the eye. "I promise."

Barry Stevens looked at the floor, pondering his next move. "If anything I tell you gets out, I'll know it was you who gossiped it around campus. I can make life tough for you, you know."

Marlee was indignant. "You don't have to threaten me. I already promised not to repeat anything. You won't have to break my knee caps."

For the first time that night, Officer Stevens cracked a smile. "You watch too much television. We don't break knee caps, just give you multiple parking tickets."

Marlee laughed, glad he wasn't aware that she didn't have a car. "So, we have a deal? We share information, and nobody needs to know where we got it?"

"Works for me. As soon as I have something, I'll let you know." The officer stood up and zipped his coat.

"But wait! I have a couple of questions. When will the autopsy be done? And were there any injuries to Beth's body?" Marlee asked.

"We should have the autopsy results on Monday. As far as injuries, the coroner couldn't determine much at the scene. I wasn't there the whole time, so I don't know much about it. Again, we'll know a lot more after the autopsy."

Officer Stevens left the room, while Marlee remained to think over their discussion. It was quiet and isolated in the study room and allowed her some quiet time to process what had happened in the past twenty-four hours. An announcement was made that the library would be closing in fifteen minutes.

Marlee took her time exiting the building. She didn't want to return to the dorm. She knew Jasmine and Kristie would wonder where she'd been. Since she made a deal with Officer Stevens, she would have to keep anything she learned to herself. What was she going to tell her friends? And how would they react when they inevitably found out she had been keeping secrets from them?

Boyfriend? Define boyfriend.

Chapter 6

The only topic of discussion in the dorm that weekend was the death of Beth Van Dam. A large piece of posterboard featuring Beth's photo was placed near the communal bathrooms. Below the photo, students wrote their memories of Beth and condolences. It was the only way they knew how to pay tribute to a deceased dorm mate.

In addition to Polly's claim that Beth died from alcohol poisoning, an assortment of other theories presented themselves. In a twenty-four-hour period, Marlee heard that Beth was killed by a professional assassin because she knew government secrets, she was strangled by an enraged ex-boyfriend, and a gang of teenage thugs had beaten her to death when she refused to hand over her money. Because Marlee had sworn secrecy to Officer Stevens, she was not able to refute any of the outlandish claims. All she could do was listen, ask questions, and write down everything she heard.

"What are you writing?" Jasmine asked after watching Marlee intermittently scratch in a blue notebook on Saturday.

"Um, I need to get a paper ready for my history class, and I'm just jotting down some notes. They don't make much sense, but at least it helps me keep my mind off of Beth." Marlee felt like a heel for lying to her roommate.

"Are you going for supper tonight?" Jasmine asked. She and Kristie already discussed going at 6:00. "You can join us, or I can bring something back for you."

"Thanks. If you could bring me a chicken sandwich and a large orange juice, that would be great. I'll pay you back on my meal card another day."

Jasmine and Kristie had no sooner left than Marlee hid her notebook, put on her coat, and left the room. She needed to hear first-hand what had happened at Stairway to Hell. The best way to do that was walk over there and talk to the guys who lived there. She didn't know what she hoped to find out, but doing something, anything, was better than sitting around the dorm room.

Tim let Marlee in after she had knocked for a solid minute. "Hey, sorry I didn't hear you at first. I was downstairs." Tim was clad in gray sweatpants and a black crew-neck sweatshirt.

"I just wanted to come over and see how you guys were doing. It has to be a hell of a shock to have someone die at your house," Marlee said, easing into the conversation.

"It's hard to believe. Things like that don't happen around here." Tim led Marlee downstairs. He had been sitting at the bar, a can of Bud Light resting on the bar top and the stereo tuned to the local rock station.

"Where are your roommates?" It seemed eerily vacant in the house.

"John went home for the weekend, and the other two went to the bar. I wasn't in the mood to go out," Tim said.

"But your roommates were?" Marlee asked, trying not to sound too judgy.

"They thought it would help them get their minds off it."

"So, what do you think happened to Beth?" Marlee asked.

"Don't know. She was buzzing around the house that night and was drunk, but not out of control. Beth was loud and drinking quite a bit. She was just being her usual self," Tim recalled with a hint of a smile.

"Did you see her leave the house? Was she with anyone?" Marlee persisted.

"No, I didn't see her leave. She spent her time talking to a few different people that I recall," Tim said.

Not sure how to play her hand, Marlee finally blurted out, "Someone saw Beth go upstairs with one of your roommates. I don't know his name, but he's the guy

48

with the black pony tail and the mustache."

"Blake?" Tim asked, surprise registering on his face. "I never heard anything about that."

"Had you heard anything about them seeing each other?" Marlee asked.

"No. Blake had some weird chick from your dorm stay over the night of the party," said Tim. "But he has different girls over here all the time."

"What kind of guy is he?" Marlee asked.

"Oh, no! Don't tell me you're interested in him too," Tim said with an eye roll.

"No, not at all. I heard he was kind of creepy. I was just wondering what you thought of him," Marlee said.

"He's a ladies' man, that's for sure. He pays his share of the rent and cleans up after himself. Sometimes he can be a jerk, but I get along with him. We've been friends since we were kids. I've had roommates that are a lot worse than Blake." Tim reported.

"I assume the police interviewed you," Marlee said and Tim nodded. "Did you hear what your roommates said when they were questioned?"

"No, the cops talked to us separately, but we all talked about it after the police left," Tim said, taking a swig from the beer can. "None of us knew what happened."

"I know how everybody likes to talk and try to make sense when something bad happens. What were some of the theories you guys had?" Marlee asked.

"Everybody knows Beth is a big partier. No offense, I know she's a friend of yours, but she drinks a lot and usually gets really drunk at parties and out at the bars. She doesn't seem to know her limit. A couple of the guys thought she might have drank so much that her body shut down," Tim said. "That she killed herself accidentally by drinking too much."

"Then how did she get outside?" Marlee asked.

Tim shrugged. "I thought maybe she was walking back to the dorm, stumbled in the yard, and froze to death."

"I hadn't thought of that," Marlee said, realizing Tim's assumption was entirely plausible. "Did you see her laying in the yard?"

"Yeah. After I found her I started yelling, and everyone came running. We called an ambulance and the police, but we could tell she was already dead." Tim finished the last of his beer and crushed the can with one hand.

"Can you show me where she was found?" Marlee asked.

Tim led her to a door off the side porch, which Marlee didn't even know existed. He flipped on the outdoor light, and they stepped outside. "She was right over there." Tim pointed toward an area that had been covered with a light layer of snow but now was marked with foot prints, tire marks, and other marks. "Beth was on her stomach with her arms spread out and she was facing toward the tree."

Marlee shivered, not just because of the cold, but because she envisioned Beth's last moments alive. "Why would she be out here? I mean, if she was walking home, she would go out the front door. This is in the opposite direction from our dorm."

"Maybe she got confused. She had a lot to drink."

"Do you guys use this door very much?" Marlee asked.

"Not really. I think I'm the only one who uses it. I let my dog out here because nobody cares if he craps over here where no one ever goes," Tim said.

Tim and Marlee walked back inside and talked for a half hour before she finally left. He had no other information to share, yet seemed relieved to have someone to talk to about the death.

Before she left, Marlee turned to Tim. "I don't think you should mention to Blake what I said about someone seeing him and Beth going upstairs together. I don't know if it's reliable information."

On the chilly walk home, Marlee had ample time

to think about her conversation with Tim and his description of how Beth's body was found lying in their yard. Tears inched down her red cheeks as she pictured her friend, helpless, in the snow. "If only I'd stuck around. I could've walked back with her," she thought. Had anyone else walked out the side door they might have discovered Beth before it was too late.

When Marlee walked in the door, she was instantly confronted by an irate Kristie and a teary-eyed Jasmine. "Where were you?" Kristie demanded.

"I went for a walk. I just needed to clear my head," Marlee said, not feeling entirely like a liar since part of the story was true.

"I was scared. I thought somebody kidnapped you or something," Jasmine said, always the first to jump to wild conclusions. "We asked everybody on the floor if they'd seen you, and no one had."

"Sorry, guess I should have left a note. I didn't think I'd be gone but for a little bit, but then I just kept walking and walking. With so much going on, I just needed some fresh air and exercise to help me think." Marlee knew if either of her friends asked if she went back to Stairway to Hell that she'd have to confess. It was way too easy for either of them to find out she'd been over to visit Tim.

Luckily, the conversation took another turn. "Guess what we found out at supper?" Jasmine asked, snapping back into her usual good mood.

Before Marlee could fathom a guess, Kristie blurted out, "Beth just got dumped by her boyfriend because she was pregnant!"

"What? Who told you this?" Marlee demanded. "I didn't know Beth was serious about anyone."

"Cami, a girl who worked with Beth at 7-11. She said Beth confided in her that night before she left to go to the party," Jasmine reported. "Cami lives in this dorm. On third floor."

"Who's the boyfriend that dumped her? Anybody we know?" Marlee asked.

"Nope. He doesn't go to college. He's an older guy and travels a lot. Cami didn't know exactly what he did, but she thought he might be in a band," Kristie said.

"Were Cami and Beth good friends? I've never seen them together. It seems kinda odd that Beth would confide something so personal with a coworker," Marlee observed.

"She just told me that Beth was really distraught that evening and went into the bathroom crying. Cami went in to see what was wrong, and Beth told her about the breakup and the pregnancy. She made Cami promise not to tell anyone, but she told the police everything when they questioned her," said Jasmine.

"I guess Cami doesn't have any qualms about repeating the story now, huh?" Marlee was disgusted that Cami was telling Beth's private information all over campus.

"Well, she has a big mouth. Beth must have been really upset to tell Cami anything at all," Kristie said. "She said Beth called their boss to tell him that she was sick and needed to leave work."

"We need to find out who the guy is that broke up with Beth. He might have a lot of information about her. I wonder if he's been questioned by the cops yet?" Marlee asked.

"I don't know. That's all Cami knew," Jasmine said.

"Who else heard this conversation?" asked Marlee.

"Polly sat with us, so she heard the whole thing," Kristie said.

"Well, if Polly knows, then everyone else will too," Marlee said. Jasmine and Kristie nodded in agreement. Cami was a gossip, but Polly put her to shame with her ongoing commentary about anyone who wasn't in the room.

"Thanks for bringing me a sandwich. I'm gonna

run down to the day room and warm it up in the microwave. I'll be right back." Marlee grabbed her chicken sandwich and headed down the hall. She passed the day room and went to the pay phone in the lobby where she placed a call to Officer Stevens.

On the third ring, a male voice answered and turned her over to Barry Stevens. "Hey, I just wanted to update you on some new information." Marlee relayed the details of her conversation with Tim from Stairway to Hell and also what Kristie and Jasmine told her about Beth being pregnant and getting dumped by a boyfriend.

Barry thanked her for her information and suggested they meet again in the library the next day. The library didn't open until noon on Sundays, so they agreed to meet in the same location at 2:00 pm. As Marlee was turning to leave the pay phone, she bumped right into the two people she really didn't want to see.

"Who are you talking to? And why didn't you make the call from our room?" asked Jasmine with an irate Kristie by her side.

*What happened? Who hasn't landed
face down in a yard after a party?
Except most people don't have any
help in hitting the ground.*

Chapter 7

Frack! Marlee wasn't sure what to do. She knew she had to keep her promise to Officer Stevens, but she also had an obligation to her friends. Taking a deep breath, she pulled Kristie and Jasmine closer so they wouldn't be overheard by people walking by them in the lobby. "I can't tell you what I'm doing because I've made a deal with somebody who has inside information. The only way I can find out what's going on is by not telling anyone else. So please don't ask me anything else, okay?"

"Inside information? About what? You think this wasn't an accident?" Jasmine furrowed her brow.

"I don't know, but I think it's something we have to consider."

"You're not in any trouble, are you?" asked Jasmine, already leaping to conclusions in her mind.

"No, not at all. I found someone who was willing to trade information with me about Beth's death, but I can't tell you who it is or what that person shares with me. Just know that I'm doing everything I can to find out what happened to her," Marlee said.

"So, you won't tell us anything you find out?" Kristie huffed, none too pleased with the arrangement. "How would you like it if we kept secrets?"

"Kristie, I'm trying to find out what happened to Beth. We all are. It just so happens that someone I know is in a position to trade information. What would you do if you were in my shoes?"

Jasmine and Kristie looked at each other, their expressions unreadable. Taking a deep breath, Jasmine said, "I understand. It's just frustrating knowing that you won't share your information with us, but we'll tell you everything we find out." Kristie nodded, unhappy with the arrangement, but deciding to keep her mouth shut rather than delve into her true feelings.

"Thanks for understanding, you guys. When

everything's out in the open, I'll tell you everything I know. Keeping secrets was not my idea, but the person I'm in contact with insisted on it," Marlee said.

The trio walked toward their wing of the dorm. Marlee stopped off at the day room to heat up her sandwich, taking plenty of time to give Kristie and Jasmine time to discuss their conversation. When she got back to the room, only Jasmine was there.

"Kristie's pissed at you," Jasmine said.

"I know. How about you?" Marlee asked, upset that her friends were unhappy with her.

"No, I'm not pissed. I just wish you could tell us what you know. We're trying to get a handle on this too. Secrets aren't helping anyone," Jasmine said, looking at the floor.

"If I tell you and Kristie, or anyone, and my contact finds out, the shit will hit the fan. Not only will I be cut out of the information loop, but I can probably expect all kinds of trouble for the next few years until I graduate and leave this town," Marlee said.

Jasmine took a deep breath and waited a full minute before she spoke. "Just promise me that you won't put yourself in any danger."

"You said something before about thinking I was kidnapped. Where is this danger thing coming from? Do you think someone killed Beth?" Marlee asked.

"Maybe. I mean, we can't rule it out, right?"

"It's a possibility. We won't know much until the autopsy results come in. That will tell us how Beth died. At this point, we don't know if it was accidental or intentional," Marlee said.

"What do you mean by intentional? You think Beth killed herself?" Jasmine was incredulous, hardly believing what she just heard.

"At this point, I don't know what I think. But if Beth was pregnant, and her boyfriend, who I would assume was the father, just dumped her, then maybe she drank herself to death. Maybe that was intentional, and

56

maybe it was accidental. Or maybe she was going to walk home, since she was too drunk to drive and fell down. She might have passed out and then frozen to death. Or, someone may have killed her, although I haven't heard anything yet that pulls me in that direction." Marlee said.

"You know, that could have been any one of us. We've all walked home drunk after a party. Any one of us could have fallen down and been injured or frozen to death." Jasmine's tears were back now.

"I know. Let's promise right now that we will never walk alone when we leave a party or the bar," Marlee said, emotion bubbling up.

"Pinky swear?" Jasmine asked as they linked fingers.

"You never said what you thought happened to Beth," Marlee said as she swiped away tears with the back of her hand. She realized nearly everyone had voiced an opinion so far except Jasmine.

"It's probably alcohol-related. I don't think there's any crime to be solved," Jasmine said, "but I still worry when you disappear."

"What would you do if you found out you were pregnant and then your boyfriend left you?" Marlee inquired.

"I have no fucking idea," Jasmine said. "You?"

"Me neither. Luckily, neither of us have this problem," Marlee said. "I can't imagine what Beth was going through. I didn't even know she was seeing some guy that was in a band. Did you?"

"No. I see Beth all the time, but it's always out at the bars or parties. She's never really with any guys. She just sort of floated around and talked to everyone, and then she was gone," said Jasmine.

"And then she was gone," echoed Marlee.

A little before 2:00 pm the next day, Marlee left for the library to meet Officer Stevens. The building was abuzz with students researching topics, writing papers, studying for exams, and talking to each other about happenings from the previous night. She weaved her way through the clusters of people to the enclosed rooms and found the police officer standing in one with the door ajar.

She dared not tell Barry that her friends busted her last night as she called him from the dorm lobby. Even though she hadn't revealed his name or any of the information he'd passed on to her, he would be skeptical and might end their agreement.

At his request, Marlee gave the long version of Beth's supposed pregnancy disclosure. "I don't know if it's true. For all I know, Cami made it up just to act important."

"You need to talk to Cami yourself, in private. Try to figure out if she's being truthful. Also, find out more about Beth's boyfriend that dumped her," Barry directed.

"Got it. I'll get as much detail as I can," Marlee assured.

"The other thing I need you to do is stay in close contact with the guys living at the house where the party took place. Act like you're just there to console them, but find out everything you can, especially about Blake." Barry flipped open a small notebook, glancing at it.

"Okay. I'll go back over tomorrow to chat. I'm friends with one of the guys that lives there, so I really would be there to give them moral support," Marlee said.

"Sure. Whatever," Barry said, flipping through the pages in his notebook.

"Anything new that you've heard about the death investigation?" Marlee inquired. She'd offered up her information and expected Barry to do the same.

"No, not yet. Tomorrow will be a big day because the autopsy will be completed. I go on duty early in the morning and should hear something during my shift. I'll let you know after criminology tomorrow."

"Did you see anything that looked odd at the crime scene? I mean, was there anything that looked out of place or didn't add up?" Marlee questioned.

Barry scrunched up his face and ran a hand across his crew cut. "No, not really. I've been with the police department for eight years, and I've seen a few other instances when someone was found frozen to death. This case didn't look much different."

"Is that what you think happened? She either fell down and couldn't get up or passed out and then froze to death?" Marlee asked.

"We know she was dead when she was found. We also know that by all accounts, she was drinking heavily last night. No blood or weapons were found at the scene. Of course, we won't know until tomorrow whether there were injuries or trauma to the body," Barry recited as if testifying in court.

"I have a feeling that there's more to Beth's passing away than just alcohol and cold weather. See you tomorrow afternoon in criminology," Marlee said as they departed the study room and went their separate ways.

When she arrived back at her dorm room, Jasmine was gone, but she'd left a note saying she was meeting with others from her class to begin work on a group project. Marlee did a fist pump in the air. She would have some time to herself, and with any luck, might be able to get together with Cami. Marlee pulled out the campus directory and located Cami's room and telephone numbers. She chose to go to the room first, on the chance Cami would be there alone.

Cami opened the door a crack and peeked out. Her eyes were blurry, and her short brown perm was matted on one side.

"Sorry for waking you up. I was wondering if I could talk to you alone," Marlee said. They were acquaintances only, so Marlee knew there was a strong chance Cami would blow her off.

"My roommate is taking a nap too." Cami motioned with her head toward the other side of the room. "We were taking a break from studying." They agreed she would come to Marlee's room in a few minutes.

Cami showed up five minutes later, her eyes clear and her hair de-matted. "So, what did you want to talk about?"

"Kristie and Jasmine said you told them about a conversation you had with Beth the night she went to the party. I wasn't there, and I just wanted to hear about it directly from you," Marlee said off-handedly.

Always ready for attention, Cami launched into her story. "Beth and I were working some overlapping hours on Thursday. I noticed when I got to work she seemed really upset. Then she ran to the bathroom, and I found her there crying. She told me her boyfriend had broken up with her when she told him she was pregnant. I told her she should go home, so she called our boss and told him she wasn't feeling well."

"Had Beth taken a pregnancy test or been to the doctor?"

"I don't know. She didn't say," Cami replied.

"Did she say she was for sure pregnant or that she just thought she might be?" Marlee asked.

Cami glanced around the room. "I don't remember her exact words, but Beth really seemed to believe she was pregnant."

"Did you know her boyfriend or anything about him?"

"I saw him a couple times when he stopped in at 7-11 to see Beth. He's sort of scruffy-looking. He's older and has long hair, but it's not cool long hair. It's stringy and kind of greasy-looking," Cami reported.

"Did he have a mustache?" Marlee asked, wondering if the mysterious boyfriend was the creepy roommate from Stairway to Hell.

"No, he didn't. If I saw him walking around town, I'd think he was homeless because he always wore this huge greenish-colored coat with a big hood on it. It had several cigarette burns and looked grimy," Cami said.

"What did Beth see in him? Did she talk about him to you?"

60

"No, she never even called him by his real name. Beth just referred to him as Spark. I don't know if he goes by that, or if that was a nickname only she used. I'd tease her about him after he'd leave 7-11, but she'd just smile and wouldn't say much," Cami said.

"Was he in a band or something?" Marlee asked, recalling her conversation with Jasmine and Kristie.

"I overheard them talking about him going out on the road. Then he made some music references, so I assumed he was in a band. I know he lived in the trailer park by the pool."

"How do you know where he lived?" Marlee asked.

"Beth's car wouldn't start one night back in December when she got off work. I was in here picking up my check, and she asked if I'd drop her off at Spark's place, and I did," Cami said.

"Could you find the place if we went over there?" Marlee asked.

"I'm not sure. Maybe." Cami was hesitant. Either she knew how to find the location and didn't want to show Marlee, or she couldn't remember the way.

"What say we give it a try," Marlee suggested. "We'll have to take your car because I don't have one."

Cami continued to hesitate. "I really need to study. We might be having a pop quiz in Chemistry tomorrow."

Marlee gave her a hard stare. "Is that why you were taking a nap when I knocked?"

Giving a huge sigh to demonstrate her inconvenience, Cami said, "Let's go. But I need to make it quick."

They hopped into Cami's bright orange Gremlin and turned the heat full blast. A Poison song blared from the cassette player. On the short drive over to the trailer park, Marlee continued to question Cami about her conversation with Beth and what she knew about her. The more Marlee asked, the more evasive Cami became.

"So, what's with the non-helpful answers?" Marlee finally asked. "I can tell you know more about this than you're saying. Just tell me what you know."

Cami pulled into the trailer park and pulled off to the side of the road. She stopped the car and put her head down on the steering wheel. "I don't know what to tell you."

"What do you mean? Just tell me the truth," Marlee pleaded.

"I know who Beth's ex-boyfriend is. I'm dating him now," Cami whispered said.

The story changes depending on one's motive. Everyone has a reason for telling the story the way they do.

Chapter 8

"What? You're dating him? Did Beth know?" Marlee asked. "Were you two seeing each other while he and Beth were going out?" One question poured out after the other, not leaving time for Cami to formulate an answer.

"That's why I didn't want to tell you the specifics," Cami said. "I knew you'd freak out."

"I'm not freaking out!" Marlee screeched.

"There was some overlap between the time Beth was dating him and I did," Cami reported. "She couldn't accept that it was over. One night we were at his trailer, and we heard noises outside. Beth was sitting in a tree outside the bedroom window drinking and singing. And it was the middle of January."

"What? Why would Beth do that?" Marlee asked.

"To spy on us. And I bet she was drunk when she climbed up the tree. She had a bottle of something and was singing love ballads."

"What's the guy's name? You obviously lied about that since you're dating him."

"Eddie Turner. But Beth called him Spark."

"He must not be quite as gross as you made him out to be," Marlee said, recalling Cami's earlier assertion that he looked like a homeless man.

"Well, no. I exaggerated quite a bit. He's a little scruffy, but I think he's hot."

"Why did Beth keep him secret? She never mentioned anything to me, Kristie, or Jasmine about Eddie. Why didn't we ever see them together?" Marlee queried.

"Eddie's the bass player in a rock band, so he's gone Friday through Sunday every week; sometimes longer if they have a long distance to travel. He spends so much time in bars for work that he doesn't like to go to them on his days off. Mostly, he just hangs out around home," Cami reported.

"How were you and Beth able to work together civilly if you stole her boyfriend?"

"I didn't steal him. Like I said, there might have been a bit of overlap, but I didn't do anything to break them up. Eddie pursued me, and he said he ended it with Beth," Cami recalled.

"Just be honest with me. Did Beth really tell you she was pregnant?" Marlee asked.

"Yes, she did. I swear it," Cami insisted.

"Why would she tell you of all people?"

"Maybe to get Eddie back?"

Marlee had to admit that made sense. Whether or not Beth was actually pregnant was immaterial at this point. Beth might have suggested it to Cami in order to cause trouble between her and Eddie. The plan may have been to get Eddie back for herself and kick Cami into the dust.

"Why didn't you just tell me this back at the dorm? Why all the secrecy? You had to know it was going to come out sooner or later," Marlee chastised.

"I don't know. Now that Beth's dead, I didn't want everyone to think I'm a bad person because of Eddie," she whimpered. Saving face was a strong motivator, a branch that many would cling to if they were in Cami's shoes.

"So, show me where he lives," Marlee urged.

"He won't be home. He doesn't get home until Sunday nights at the earliest." Cami looked at her Swatch watch, confirming it was only 4:00 pm.

They drove to the end of the trailer park, and Cami turned off the car. The flash from the television set was visible from the road. "Guess he got home earlier than usual," she said. Marlee couldn't tell if she was genuinely surprised or if she was acting. Or if Eddie had lied to her about the time he'd be home.

"I think it would be best if I talked to him alone," Marlee said, wanting to compare Eddie's version of events with Cami's story.

66

Cami opened her mouth to speak, but then thought better of it. She nodded and turned the car back on to re-activate the heater.

There were at least ten trailer parks in town, but this one was the most rundown and shady. Marlee approached the off-white trailer, jumping when the dog tied up next door lunged at her and snarled. She climbed up the rickety steps and knocked on the door. The sound of a sporting event was audible through the flimsy door.

The door flew open, nearly knocking Marlee off the step. An imposing figure stood before her, glaring and holding a glass filled with dark liquid. "What do you want?" he challenged.

"Are you Eddie?" Marlee asked, knowing from Cami's first description that he was. She originally portrayed him as scruffy and dirty, but later implied that he was just rough around the edges. The first description rang true. He was barefoot and wore dirty jeans with more holes than denim. His blue sweatshirt contained stains appearing to be spaghetti sauce or blood. An actual string of pasta was curled up on his shirt under his chin.

"Yeah, who wants to know?" Eddie asked, eyeing her quizzically as if she might be a strip-o-gram sent by one of his buddies. His breath smelled strongly of alcohol and cigarettes.

"I'm a friend of Beth Van Dam's. I just wanted to talk to you for a few minutes," Marlee said, inching her way up to the top step.

"The cops already talked to me. They tracked me down in Omaha where we were playing," Eddie said as he motioned Marlee into the dark trailer. He went over to the TV and turned it down. "You want a beer?"

"Sure," Marlee said, thinking that to refuse his offer might make him less inclined to talk.

Eddie grabbed a can of Old Milwaukee out of the refrigerator and handed it to her, his hand making contact with hers for longer than necessary. He drank from his glass of dark liquid and sat in a saggy, stained recliner. He gestured for her to sit on the couch. Marlee hesitated, unable to distinguish fabric patterns from stains. She was wearing her best jeans and didn't want to ruin them by sitting in a puddle of God-knew-what. In the interest of building rapport, she sat gingerly on the very edge of the stained couch.

"So, how long had you and Beth been dating?" Marlee asked, hoping to put together a time frame of Beth's past.

"Dating?" Eddie burst out laughing. "We weren't dating. We were just... you know," he said as he waggled his eyebrows in a suggestive manner. "Is that what she told you? That we were dating?" He continued to laugh as if he just heard the world's funniest joke.

Marlee tried to brush off Eddie's cloddish behavior toward her dead friend. "What about Cami Fischer? Are you two dating?"

Eddie grabbed his stomach as he lurched to one side, still laughing. "Where are you getting this?" he gasped between guffaws. "Dating!"

"So, who are you dating?" Marlee asked, irritation creeping into her voice.

"I'm in a band, baby. I don't date anyone. I'm just out to have some fun. Why? Were you looking for some action?" Eddie asked, making what he probably thought was a seductive stare.

"Eww, gross!" The words were out of Marlee's mouth before she knew it. He was repulsive, but she didn't need him to know that.

"Oh, that's nice. You college bitches act all uppity. Like you're too good for the likes of me," Eddie snarled and took another drink. He grabbed for his cigarettes and ignited a Marlboro Light with his Bic lighter.

Marlee needed to do some backpedaling and fast or else Eddie would clam up without answering any more of her questions. "No, that's not what I meant, Eddie. I just meant it would be gross to go out with a guy that my friend was interested in." Marlee held her breath, hoping that

Eddie was dim enough or drunk enough to fall for her justification.

"Oh. I thought you were saying you were too good for me," Eddie said, blowing smoke out of the side of his mouth.

"Not at all," Marlee said, attempting an alluring look at the scruffy rocker.

Eddie raised his eyebrows and licked his lips. Before he could say something disgusting, Marlee interjected, "I just want to know more about your time with Beth. When did you meet?"

"My band had a gig here in December, I think it was. Beth was there, and she came up to talk to me when we were on break. After the show, she came back here with me. My band is Zenith. Have you heard of us?" Eddie asked, still leering at Marlee.

She had her eye on the door and knew she could outrun Eddie if he tried to put the moves on her. He was much taller than Marlee, but she felt confident that she could knock him off balance and get away since he was moderately intoxicated. "Oh, sure. I've seen you guys before. That's why I thought you looked familiar," Marlee said, lying. She hadn't heard of his band, and she was certain that if she'd seen a dirtbag like Eddie that she would have remembered him.

Continuing to puff on his cig, Eddie carried on with his story. "We came back here, she spent the night, and left the next morning. She stopped over here a couple more times, and I told her I didn't want a girlfriend."

"So, you only slept together that once?" Marlee knew it was a personal question, but Eddie didn't seem like a guy who would hold back if it dealt with bragging about sexual conquests.

"Oh, no. Lots of times. Once after I kicked her out, I came home one night and found that she broke in and crawled into my bed. The craziest thing was that she had dug a dirty Metallica t-shirt out of my laundry hamper and was wearing it," Eddie said.

"Did Beth tell you she was pregnant?" Marlee asked.

"What? No!" Eddie shouted. "I always wear protection." He picked up an oversized box of condoms from a TV tray next to his chair and waived it in Marlee's direction. "I'm in a band. I have to be careful. I have chicks chasing me around and trying to trap me. If Beth was knocked up, it wasn't because of me."

Looking around the old trailer with the stained furniture and at the disheveled musician, Marlee couldn't imagine why anyone would sleep with him, let alone try to trap him. "Was Beth seeing anyone else?"

"No idea what she was doing," Eddie said.

"How about Cami? How did you meet her?" Marlee asked.

"I'd see her when I stopped in to 7-11. She gave me her number. I called her, and she came over. End of story."

"What did Beth think of you and Cami being together? Did she get jealous?" Marlee asked.

"Don't know. Like I said, baby, I'm a rocker, and I don't have any use for a girlfriend. Now, unless you're going to take your clothes off, I think it's time for you to go," Eddie said, getting to his feet more quickly than Marlee would have predicted.

She jumped to her feet and edged toward the door. "Yeah, thanks for your time, Eddie." She opened the door and was nearing the car when the door opened.

"See you around," Eddie said, giving Marlee a lecherous look.

Marlee jogged to Cami's car and swung open the passenger side door. "What a pig! What do you see in him?"

Cami jumped. She'd been so into *Night Songs* by Cinderella that she hadn't noticed Marlee approach the vehicle. "Whoa!" she shouted in surprise. "What happened?"

She took a deep breath, wondering how much of Eddie's creepy behavior she should share with Cami.

70

Erring on the side of caution, Marlee said, "I'd be careful around him if I were you."

"Why? What do you mean?" she asked.

"Um, well, I think he has a lot of girlfriends. He seemed to think you two were just casually seeing each other rather than in a serious relationship," Marlee said gently. She and Cami were not friends. In fact, Marlee didn't have much time for her, but she didn't want to see Cami or any woman involved with this loser.

"Hmmm... looks like somebody's jealous," snapped Cami as she put the car into gear and drove away.

"Yeah, that's it," Marlee said, all of a sudden not really caring if Cami was being used by Eddie.

They rode home in silence, and Cami fast-walked ahead of Marlee into the dorm, slamming the entry door behind her as Marlee approached. She went to her room to find Jasmine back from her group project.

"How's the group project going?" Marlee asked, not really caring, but trying to think of something to discuss other than Beth.

"You'll never guess who's in my group now!" Jasmine shouted, not waiting for Marlee to guess. "It's Nick, the guy who's always talking to me! I'm so pissed!"

For the first time that day, Marlee laughed. It felt good to find something funny, even if it was at her roommate's expense. "Jazz, I bet you two will end up together before the end of the semester."

"Sick! I don't think so," Jasmine said, making a face. "He's totally not my type."

"You sure spend a lot of time talking about a guy that's not your type," Marlee observed. "Maybe you like him more than you think."

"Instead of interfering in my love life, maybe you should focus on your own," snapped Jasmine, not ready to accept Marlee's assertion. "By the way, how's it going with Paul?" she asked, knowing full well that Marlee's one and only contact with him had been at the party at Stairway to Hell.

"I have class with him tomorrow afternoon. I'll probably talk to him then."

"Yeah, right," Jasmine mumbled under her breath.

"You think I won't?" Marlee challenged.

"That's exactly what I think. You're too chicken to do anything," Jasmine said.

Getting agitated, Marlee temporarily forgot her anxiety about approaching Paul. "I think you might be very surprised at what I have to report tomorrow after class." She had no idea what she was talking about, but in the next twenty hours she should be able to think of something.

"Riiiiiight," said Jasmine in a dismissive tone. "Let's go to supper. I'm hungry."

Marlee's hunger overrode her agitation with her roommate. Jasmine could attract men right and left, to Marlee's chagrin. She didn't harbor jealousy toward her roommate, but wondered how she could go about gaining male interest at the drop of a hat. Maybe Marlee was a little jealous.

They went upstairs to the dorm cafeteria, and after selecting their meal, they sat at a small table, eating in silence. Marlee selected a hamburger, onion rings, and a large orange juice. Jasmine ate a grilled ham and cheese with fries and a Coke. The silence didn't last long, as Cami and her posse strode by and stopped near their table.

"That's her," Cami shrieked, pointing at Marlee. "She's the one who tried to steal my boyfriend!"

Friends can be the biggest backstabbers of them all. At least that's my experience.

Chapter 9

"Are you mental?" Marlee yelled, standing up to confront Cami who stood before them with her hands on her hips.

"I just called Eddie, and he told me everything! He said you hit on him and told him that I was seeing other guys," Cami hissed, her face getting redder with each sentence.

"Are you kidding me? Eddie is one of the grossest guys I've ever met. He's old, dirty, and not a nice guy. I wouldn't go out with him if you paid me five hundred dollars," Marlee said.

"You lie! I've had to deal with girls like you my whole life. You act all nice then try to take what's mine," Cami said, her voice cracking with emotion.

"I swear that I didn't hit on Eddie. He said if I wasn't going to take my clothes off, then I should leave," Marlee reported, shuddering at the memory.

"Yeah, right," Cami bellowed as she reached over and slapped Marlee hard across the face. "Stay away from Eddie, or you'll be sorry!"

The cafeteria, normally loud and bustling with activity, was completely quiet. Marlee blushed and put her hand to her sore cheek. She was in pain, but more than anything, she was embarrassed. Everyone in the cafeteria heard the accusations by Cami and saw her slap Marlee.

Jasmine stood up and grabbed their dining trays. "Come on. Let's go." Marlee walked self-consciously out of the dining room while her roommate dumped the remainder of their unfinished meals and caught up to her. Marlee had never been more thankful in her life. The accusations and the slap had both paralyzed her into inaction. Jasmine took the reins and led Marlee back to their room.

"Is this one of those things you can't tell me about?" Jasmine asked, once they were in the privacy of their room.

Marlee hesitated. Officer Stevens asked her to talk to Cami, but going over to Eddie's trailer had been her own idea. She decided to confide in Jasmine with at least some of the information. "After you and Kristie told me what Cami said about Beth being pregnant, I went to talk to her. She finally admitted that she was seeing Eddie, Beth's former boyfriend. I had her take me over to his trailer, and I talked to him alone for a bit. He's so gross. Anyway, he admitted sleeping with both Beth and Cami, but denied he was the father of Beth's baby. Eddie was concerned about women trying to trap him with a child, so he showed me his big stash of condoms."

"Ick!" Jasmine made a face. "Cami was seeing the same guy Beth was dating?"

"He's so gross, Jazz. I have no idea what Beth or Cami saw in him. He told me he isn't dating anyone, he's just having a good time. What I said earlier about him telling me to take off my clothes is true."

"Why did Cami say you were trying to lure him away from her?"

"He probably told her that to cover his tracks. Eddie's just interested in sex and wants to make sure Cami keeps coming over. I bet he thought I told her about him hitting on me," Marlee said.

"Why didn't you tell her what he said and did?" Jasmine asked.

"Because I was trying to spare her feelings. I'm no fan of Cami's, but he said some really cruel things that would crush her. I didn't want to tell her. I just wanted to warn her that he was a major pig," Marlee declared. "Now I don't really care about her feelings. Next time I see Cami, I'm going to tell her everything Eddie said." Marlee checked her face in the mirror. Her left cheek was red from the slap and tender to the touch.

"At least she didn't punch you in the eye. Or break your nose." Jasmine tried to lighten the mood. She was normally the one who saw the worst in every situation, but now she stepped up and helped bolster her roommate's spirits.

After catching up on her reading for Monday's classes, Marlee took her notebook and went to bed. She turned on the small reading light she had next to the wall on her lofted bed. Before going to sleep, she recorded everything that happened that day pertinent to Beth's case; the conversation with Officer Stevens, her talk with Cami, meeting Eddie at his trailer, and Cami's confrontation in the cafeteria. Her head swam with information, none of which seemed to fit together. Why would Beth be involved with Eddie, a guy that anyone could see was a total loser? Beth drank too much, even by college standards, but she was cute, fun, and smart. She wouldn't have any problem finding a decent guy. Why Beth spent time with Eddie was nearly as mysterious as her death. The more Marlee found out about Beth, the less she understood her friend.

Classes the next day went as normally as could be expected, given the death of a student. Rumors continued to circulate, and Marlee heard claims that Beth was a drug dealer, that she had ties to a Satanic cult, and that she died as a result of a hit-and-run accident. Although she didn't believe any of the stories, she listened carefully as the students in her classes discussed Beth. Marlee wondered how many of them actually knew her.

Death has a tendency to make people think they had a closer relationship to the deceased than actually existed. A mere acquaintance becomes a dear friend once death makes a visit. In psych class last semester, they discussed how people want to feel important and will place themselves at the center of a disaster even if they have no involvement in it. Another thing Marlee learned was that information is power. It doesn't even have to be correct, it's just important that the teller have an audience. That's why gossip is so powerful. The person spreading the information, whether it's true, false, or both, identifies as the dispenser of knowledge. In uncertain times, people want information, and that's what gossips provide.

Anxious to continue eavesdropping on conversations about Beth, Marlee ate lunch by herself in the Student Union rather than going back to her dorm room. After that, she went to the library to listen in on more conversations and see if she knew anyone she could visit with about the tragedy.

At long last, it was time for criminology class, and she would be meeting with Officer Stevens to share their findings. She was anxious to hear of the autopsy results. Making her way to her usual seat in the second row, Marlee glanced around looking for Officer Stevens. He wasn't there, but one of the guys he usually sat with was present. Toward the back of classroom sat Paul. Marlee smiled at him and he gave her a nod.

Dr. Eisner walked in and began chatting with students in the first row. He was a portly man, always sporting a nondescript suit and tie. He was eccentric, as most university professors tend to be. His main idiosyncrasy was rearranging his office five times each semester, including the floor-to-ceiling bookcases.

As Professor Eisner paced back and forth, glancing at his watch every thirty seconds, he continued talking about a recent episode of *Cheers* and his thoughts about it. Marlee was fascinated by all topics this man chose to espouse upon. She was a sponge and soaked up everything he had to say. It always pleased her that Dr. Eisner knew her name. She assumed she was a nobody in the large classrooms and when she needed to meet with her professors she always introduced herself and mentioned the class of theirs she was taking. After the second time she did this, Dr. Eisner said, "Yes, Marlee. I know who you are."

When it was time for class to begin, the professor activated the projector and darkened the room. He flipped a flimsy, plastic overhead on the projector and began talking about mala *in se* and *mala prohibita* crimes.

"*Mala in se* crimes are those acts we believe are evil; like murder. On the other hand, *mala prohibita* crimes are acts that are criminalized just because we think they should be. An example is driving under the influence. It's not an evil act, but as a society we prohibit drinking and driving because of the possibility of car accidents and deaths." Dr. Eisner engaged the class in a discussion, challenging them to justify why a crime was *mala in se* or *mala prohibita*. Marlee was so engaged, she forgot to look behind her to see if Barry Stevens had slipped in during the discussion.

Class ended way too soon for Marlee's liking. She knew she would take every class she could with Dr. Eisner because he was so intelligent and interesting. As she gathered up her belongings, she remembered Barry Stevens and glanced around looking for him. He exited the classroom without even glancing in her direction.

"Barry, wait!" Marlee called out as she ran after the police officer. He didn't turn around and kept walking down the hallway toward the exit. She caught up to him and grabbed the arm of his coat.

"Let go," he hissed as he jerked his arm free. "I can't be seen with you." He continued to walk and talk out of the side of his mouth as if that would fool people into thinking he wasn't actually talking to her.

"What's the deal? I want to find out about the autopsy results" Marlee said, nearly jogging to keep up with Barry.

"I can't tell you anything. We had a meeting before my shift, and the captain said anyone leaking information about the case will get suspended. I'm hoping for promotion as soon as I get my degree, so I can't talk to you. There is another officer taking this class, and I don't want him to see me talking to you." Barry continued walking and talking in low tones.

Marlee had to do some quick thinking, or she would lose her source of information. "Barry, you're not married are you?"

"What?" He looked at her like she was a crazy woman.

"Are you married? Do you have a girlfriend?" Marlee asked.

"No. Why? What does that have to do anything?" Barry asked, irritated.

Marlee dropped her coat and book bag in the hallway. When she saw the other officer from criminology approaching, she grabbed Barry, pushed him against the wall, and kissed him. To her surprise, Barry responded with enthusiasm. A few students made rude comments as they walked by, and somebody whistled.

When they broke free, Barry looked at Marlee with a dopey expression, instantly falling for her. "I didn't know you thought…"

Marlee interrupted him before things could get out of hand. "Now everyone will assume we're going out. So, you can tell me what's going on in the case." She picked her things up from the floor and grabbed Barry's hand as they continued to walk.

Barry Stevens was a dim bulb, and she felt bad for giving him the wrong idea. Marlee was no more interested in the police officer than she was the Easter Bunny. He wore a befuddled expression, unsure if he and Marlee had a connection. His lips tried to form words, but no sound came out of his mouth. After a few tries, he gave up.

They walked, hand in hand, out to the parking lot. When they got to his car, Marlee let herself in the unlocked passenger door. When he was settled inside, she clarified what was happening. "Thanks for playing along. I know the guy you sit with works at the PD, so I made sure he saw us kissing. Now all you have to do is tell him we're going out, and he will probably spread the word all over the department. Then you won't have to worry about someone thinking you're telling me secrets about the case."

Beginning to clue in to the ruse, Barry put both hands on the steering wheel, deep in thought. The more he thought, the redder his face became. "So, I'm supposed to make it known that we're going out, but we really aren't?"

"Right," Marlee said, still feeling guilty. "I hope you didn't get the wrong idea..."

"Oh, no, no, not at all!" Barry spoke a little too loudly and a little too nonchalantly to be believable, still blushing. "This should work perfectly. I assume you'll tell your friends about us."

Marlee hadn't thought about that. She planned to carry on as usual and let Barry tell his friends and co-workers of their pretend-dating status. She didn't want to be weighed down with a boyfriend, not even a pretend one.

"I guess if it comes up, I'll tell them," Marlee said. She didn't want to ruin her chances with Paul. Barry looked hurt, but didn't comment.

"So, what were the results of the autopsy?" Marlee asked, finally getting back to the real reason they were meeting; the investigation into the death of Beth Van Dam.

"The coroner didn't find any injuries other than broken fingers. He thought she broke them when she fell to the frozen ground. There was nothing to indicate she had been shot, stabbed, strangled, or otherwise killed by another person. Beth's blood alcohol level was 0.42, which is nearly dead. He ruled her death accidental. Based on the autopsy and the crime scene, it looks like Beth drank way too much and then tried to walk back to the dorm but fell down and passed out. Then she froze to death before anyone found her," Barry reported. "With that amount of alcohol in her system, she was on the verge of passing out. When Beth hit the ground, she either knocked herself out or passed out right away. Either way, she wouldn't have felt any pain when she died."

"There weren't any drugs in her system? Just alcohol?" Marlee asked.

"No drugs, but the amount of alcohol was at a lethal level. The heart can stop and so can respiration when someone has that much to drink. She could have just as easily died inside the party from the amount she drank."

"Was Beth pregnant?" Marlee asked, wondering if Cami's claims were true.

"Yes, she was. About six weeks along," Barry said. "Here's what makes me mad. Why was Beth drinking if she knew she was pregnant? Everybody knows it's bad for the baby if the mother drinks."

Marlee was at a loss for words as she thought about Beth's pregnancy and her gross ex-boyfriend who might be the father of the child. "I talked with Beth's ex-boyfriend, Eddie, and he said they slept together several times but that he always wore protection. He laughed when I asked him if they were exclusive. Apparently, Eddie isn't exclusive with anyone. When I asked him if Beth was seeing other guys, he said he didn't know. And I don't think he really cared." Marlee detailed the rest of her conversations with Eddie and Cami, including Cami's assertion that she tried to steal Eddie away.

"She slapped you? Really?" Barry asked. "Were there witnesses? Do you want to file a report?"

Marlee laughed. "No, she's just insecure, and I'm sure Eddie filled her head with all kinds of lies to cover the fact that he hit on me. Cami is no friend of mine, but I don't want to press charges against her... unless she hits me again. Then I want her thrown in jail."

Barry showed a slight smile. "If she does it again, you let me know. Nobody hits my pretend girlfriend and gets away with it." They both laughed, which reassured Marlee that Barry understood the nature of their non-relationship. At least she wouldn't have to deal with a love-sick cop.

They chatted amiably about the case and the coroner's ruling of accidental death. "I don't know why, but I feel like we're missing something," Marlee said. "I think there's more to the story."

"There always is," Barry said. "We never know all the details about the victim and what happened before their death. Beth had a boyfriend in a band. She was pregnant. There was a lot you and her other friends didn't know about her. Maybe Beth drank so much because she knew she was pregnant, and her boyfriend had dumped her. It could have been her way of committing suicide."

Marlee's blood began to boil. "I seriously doubt that. I don't know why she was drinking if she was pregnant, and I don't know why she didn't tell me or some of her other friends from the dorm. The only person she told, as far as I know, was Cami, and I think Beth only told her in a moment of weakness. Either that or to make Cami jealous since she's seeing Eddie now."

"Do you think Beth planned to have an abortion? If so, I guess it wouldn't matter if she was drinking. And if Eddie was the father and didn't want anything to do with her, Beth might have been ready to end the pregnancy," Barry said.

"I really wish I knew what was going on in Beth's life and in her head. It's sad that she had such a secret life that none of us knew anything about," Marlee said. "I don't know what I could have done to help her, but I would have listened and not judged her."

"Speaking of a secret life, there's more that we found out about Beth during our investigation," Barry said.

Marlee raised her eyebrows, unsure if she was ready for additional shocking information about her friend. In the span of a few minutes Marlee learned that Beth was pregnant, her blood alcohol level was at a deadly level, and that her death was ruled accidental. "What is it?"

"Beth was working as a prostitute."

Why do truck stops get such a bad rap? I've eaten some of my best meals at truck stops.

Chapter 10

"A prostitute? No way!" Never in a million years would Marlee have guessed this was the new information Barry was going to reveal. "You're kidding, right?"

The officer shook his head from side to side. "No, I'm not. It was brought up during our meeting this morning. Not that it makes much difference now since the case is closed."

"It does too make a difference. A big difference! And what do you mean the case is closed?" Marlee's head swirled as she took in the news. At least she was sitting down so there was no worry about falling down. In addition to being a little slow on the uptake, Barry was showing himself to be an insensitive clod too.

"I meant it didn't change anything with the case that Beth was a hooker." Barry continued to dig himself in deeper every time he spoke.

"She's not a hooker! Quit saying that!" Marlee shrieked. "Who said she was, anyway?"

"The manager of one of the motels over by the truck stop. He told detectives that Beth visited guys there regularly. The motel is known for prostitution, so we put the squeeze on the manager and he told us everything we wanted to know to keep himself out of trouble," Barry reported.

"How did the investigation lead to the motel in the first place? It seems like a reach to just conveniently stumble upon a motel where the manager reveals this to the police," Marlee said, skeptical that this information shook out the way Barry was reporting it.

Barry stammered, caught without a quick answer. "Detective Barkley didn't say what led him to the motel. I suppose it came out during an interview that Beth was a prostitute, so he went to the place the hookers hang out."

Marlee rolled her eyes with such force that they nearly stuck in the back of her head. "What did you mean the case was closed? Nobody's going to keep looking into Beth's death because of the autopsy findings?"

"There's nothing else to look for. There was no sign of foul play, and Beth's blood alcohol level was at a deadly level. What's left to investigate?" Barry was in serious need of sensitivity training.

"You're an ass!" Marlee yelled, jumping out of the parked car and stomping off toward her dorm. At this point, she didn't care what he thought since she most likely wouldn't be dealing with him in the future now that Beth's case was closed.

Barry opened his car door and watched Marlee storm off, but didn't say anything. He just shook his head, unsure what had provoked her, and got back in the car. "She must have her period," he mumbled to himself. He was twenty-nine years old, and he didn't know if he'd ever understand women.

In spite of the cold temperature and biting wind, Marlee had worked herself into a sweat by the time she arrived home. She stomped into her room, flung off her coat, and heaved herself into the lawn chair recliner.

Jasmine sat at her desk, poring over a text book. An opened can of Coke rested on the desktop along with a crumpled Hershey bar wrapper. "What's wrong with you?"

Knowing that keeping secrets didn't matter much anymore, Marlee bared her soul. She told Jasmine about Officer Stevens and their deal to share information, her conversations with Cami and Eddie, and the findings of Beth's autopsy. "They've closed the case. The police don't even care that Beth died. Since the coroner didn't find any injuries or bruises that someone else inflicted, he ruled it an accidental death!"

"You think it's something else?" Jasmine asked, not nearly as upset as Marlee would have liked.

"Well, I don't know. It just seems very quick for the coroner to make such a big decision. And too quick for the police to consider the case closed," Marlee said.

"Do you think someone killed Beth?" Jasmine asked, still level-headed.

"I don't know. Maybe. Probably not," Marlee babbled. "It's just too soon to come to this conclusion about Beth's whole life and her death." Her head spun. She couldn't articulate why she was angry. It wasn't as if she really thought Beth was intentionally killed. Marlee couldn't think of a clear motive for that, and she didn't have any suspects.

"You're just processing too much information that came to you at one time. It's overload, and you don't know how to handle it." Jasmine was the picture of calm, cool, and collected.

"Why are you being so calm?" Marlee asked. "You're usually the one falling apart, and I'm the sane one. I didn't get the memo that we were trading places today."

Jasmine laughed, and Marlee eventually joined in. She grabbed the Tickled Pink wine from the mini-fridge and poured half the bottle into an aluminum glass, sipping as she talked. "I just don't understand. Four days ago, Beth was alive and well. Now she's dead, and the police aren't investigating anymore, and the whole thing just keeps getting worse."

"Worse? How?" Jasmine asked.

"Beth was about six weeks pregnant. Also, Detective Barkley was told by a motel manager that Beth was a hooker." Marlee shook her head, her face wrinkled into a disgusted expression as she continued to drink wine.

"A hooker? I don't believe that!" Jasmine said in disbelief. "Do you?"

"I don't either. I think it might be some misinformation that a motel manager gave to detectives to keep himself out of hot water. Apparently, he runs a motel that allows prostitution. It's over by the truck stop on the edge of town. I'm sure the manager would say anything to keep the police away," Marlee said.

"That's bullshit! Why would Beth be a hooker? She

87

was working at 7-11, so she had money," Jasmine said, chugging her remaining Coke.

"That's exactly what I thought. Why would she be prostituting if she already had a job? Or, let's say she was a hooker, then why would she keep working at 7-11? None of it makes sense. I think the manager gave the police false information about Beth. Maybe it was intentional and maybe it was accidental, but either way, he lied." Marlee was feeling better already in the few minutes she had been discussing the case with Jasmine. Barry bought into the official story set forth by the police department. At least Jasmine joined with Marlee in seeing the potential holes in the official theory.

Jasmine rummaged through the mini-fridge and grabbed a can of Bud Light. "I'm so mad, I'm going to drink one of your crappy beers." She took a sip and made a face. "Well, I might not drink the whole thing."

"I'm going to the motels out by the truck stop tonight and talk to the managers to see which one said Beth was a prostitute, and then I'm going to ask him some questions of my own," Marlee said, finishing the remainder of her cheap, sugary wine.

"That's almost two miles away, and it's supposed to get below zero again tonight," Jasmine said, carefully taking another sip of the unsavory beer. "I can't go with you because I have to study for tomorrow's test. Maybe Polly can give you a ride."

"Ha! Polly would probably charge me for gas money and then insist on butting in when I was questioning the motel managers. I'd rather walk. Besides, this extra walking the past few days seems to be doing me some good. These jeans aren't as tight as the last time I wore them!" Marlee happily demonstrated that she could pull her waist band a few millimeters away from her skin. Just last week she'd been walking like the Tin Man because her jeans were so snug.

About halfway there, Marlee started to rethink her

plan of walking to the motels on the edge of town. It was dark, and the temperature had dropped from cold to bone-chilling. Before leaving on the trek, she ate a hearty supper at the cafeteria and put on an extra sweatshirt under her winter coat. The coat kept her warm, as did her heavy gloves. It was her feet and ears that suffered from the cold. Nobody wore a stocking cap or ear muffs unless they were a complete nerd, and Marlee wasn't about to go against convention. As for her feet, she forgot she was wearing white, thin-soled lace-up shoes without socks. Her toes began to crunch with every step, a sure sign of a poor choice in footwear, so she walked faster.

When she reached the truck stop, she went inside, mostly to warm up, but also to see if she could get some information. Rickety booths lined the walls, while tables and chairs filled in the center part of the building. Several men sat alone and in groups, smoking, drinking coffee, eating enormous meals, and telling stories. A counter with six silver stools attached to the floor was nearly empty, except for one grizzled old man in his mid-forties. He was bundled up in a parka, knee-high-laced snow boots, and an insulated hat with ear flaps. He barely even turned to look at her when she approached the counter and sat at the other end.

"What can I get for you?" asked a woman in her fifties, sporting a name tag that identified her as Helen. She wore dark pants and a light weight beige sweater with a pink apron over the top.

As Marlee settled onto the stool, she realized walking there had been the easy part. She hadn't put any thought into how she would elicit information about motels that catered to prostitutes. "I'll have coffee," she said upon realizing Helen was still waiting for her order.

She grimaced as she took a sip from the boiling coffee. Marlee was convinced that coffee was the ultimate bait and switch. It smelled delightful but tasted awful. How anyone could drink such a vile substance on a regular basis was beyond her. She reached for the sugar packets and emptied three into the coffee. It was marginally better, but still not good.

Helen swung back around and asked if there was anything else she needed. Marlee looked around and lowered her voice. "I'm looking for someone," she whispered, trying not to draw the attention of the truckers and other diners.

Helen eyed her up and down. "Who you looking for?"

"I don't know for sure. I heard he runs one of the motels that caters to prostitutes and ..."

"Oh, no! Wait just a minute! We don't deal with any of you girls and that kind of thing around here. Drink your coffee and hit the road!" Helen snapped, drawing the attention of the man sitting at the counter.

"No, that's not what I mean," Marlee stumbled over her words trying to speak as fast as she could, knowing she was on limited time before Helen bounced her out of the truck stop. "My friend died on Thursday night. Maybe you read about it in the paper? She went to college, but somebody told the cops she was a hooker. I don't believe it, but I need to find the manager of a motel around here. He's the one who told the police Beth was a prostitute."

"Yeah, I heard about her. Found outside a party house, wasn't she?" asked the man at the end of the counter.

"Yes. Her name is, I mean was, Beth Van Dam. She lived in the same dorm that I do. I'm just trying to find out why someone would spread lies about her," Marlee said.

"It doesn't make much difference now, does it?" growled Helen, unmoved by Marlee's account of her friend's death.

Taking a deep breath so as not to punch Helen in the nose, Marlee said, "No, it doesn't, but I bet if you died, you'd like someone to clear up any lies that had been told about you."

That did the trick. Helen, after thinking for a

90

second and putting herself in Beth's shoes, decided to show mercy on Marlee and her quest in clearing her friend's name. "Robbie at the Moon Glow Motel is who you want to talk to. It's the first motel east of here. All kinds of shady business going on over there. Not that I know any particulars. It's just what I hear people saying."

Marlee glanced at Helen and then the guy at the end of the counter. He nodded, as if in agreement with what the waitress said. She couldn't drink anymore of the horrid coffee, so she left money on the counter and thanked Helen for her help.

"Hey! Don't tell Robbie where you got your information, you hear?" Helen said.

She nodded in acknowledgement and walked back into the frigid night. As she peered to the east, she could see the flashing sign for the Moon Glow Motel. It was a few minutes away, which was nothing compared to the distance she'd already walked that night.

The Moon Glow Motel gave Marlee a creepy feeling as she approached it. It was a small, two-level motel, with doors opening to the outside. A small balcony with a wooden railing was on the top level. Strings of unlit Christmas lights, which had not been taken down, were wrapped around the balcony in a haphazard fashion. A young lady, in her early teens, paced back and forth on the balcony as she smoked a cigarette and drank from a dark bottle. Marlee mustered her courage and entered the motel.

The creepy feeling did not dissipate once Marlee was inside. The small lobby was consumed by two well-worn chairs, a shelf displaying pamphlets on area attractions, and a rickety table with an empty coffee pot. The front desk was only two feet wide and so high that Marlee could barely see over it. A bell and papers fastened to a clip board were on top of the desk, but no clerk was around. Marlee rang the bell and waited, looking down at the yellow carpet.

A man, about Marlee's age, appeared and asked,

"What can I do for you?"

She decided to go another route rather than the direct one. "I got a call from a guy here."

"Was his name Warren?" asked the desk clerk.

"Might have been," Marlee said.

"Okay, you can go up to room 202," the clerk said, pointing upward. "You know the way, right?"

Marlee just stared at the guy as she decided what to do. She didn't want to go to some strange man's room, especially if he was expecting a prostitute. On the other hand, she wanted to find out as much about Beth and the Moon Glow Motel as possible. "Why do you think I'm here?" she asked, giving the guy a hard stare.

His face changed expression as he realized he was not dealing with the prostitute that Warren in room 202 had requested. "Oh, excuse me. I think I have you confused with someone else. The man in room 202 was expecting one of his friends to arrive shortly, and I thought it was you."

Marlee burst into laughter. "Nice try. I'm guessing Warren asked you to get him some company for the night, and you thought I was a hooker."

"Who are you?" the man demanded. "Are you a cop?"

"No, I'm not, but I'll tell them everything if you don't tell me what I want to know," Marlee said.

"Depends on what you want to know," the man threw back at her, not easily intimidated.

"First, I want to know where Robbie the manager is," Marlee said.

"I'm Robbie, and I'm the manager," the guy said. "Why?"

"You're my age. How did you get to be a manager?" Marlee asked, curious as to how someone barely twenty years old could be in charge of a business.

"My uncle owns this place. Is that all you wanted to know?" Robbie snapped, disdain dripping from his voice.

"No, I wanted to know about a college girl named Beth Van Dam. I heard you told the police she was a hooker," Marlee said. "Is that true?"

"Yeah, it's true. She was in here from time to time, and I don't think she was selling Tupperware," Robbie said as if it were no big deal.

"How do you know for sure it was Beth?" Marlee asked, concentrating on what she hoped was chewing gum matted into the yellow carpet.

"Because the cops showed me a picture of her. I'd seen her around, but she never went by Beth. She called herself Dixie," Robbie reported.

"How did the cops know to come here when they were investigating Beth's death?" Marlee inquired.

"Guess somebody told them. I don't know who. Jeez, why don't you just leave me alone? I got the cops off my back, and I don't need any questions from you. Get outta here!" Robbie pointed at the door and when Marlee didn't move, he started around the counter to physically remove her from the premises.

"Okay, okay. I'm leaving." Marlee threw her hands in the air and backed out of the motel. There was no way she was turning her back on Robbie. No way in hell. If he was a pimp, then there probably wasn't much that he wouldn't do, including hurting Marlee. When the door slammed, she took off running. She only made it a block because she wasn't athletic. The run slowed to a fast walk, and after a few minutes it turned into a slow walk. Her toes were beginning to crunch again from the cold, yet she knew she needed to get back to the dorm as soon as possible. Marlee was scared, pumped up on adrenaline, and nearly frozen. As she got to the halfway point between the motel and the dorm, she became aware of a car driving very slowly behind her. Then it pulled up alongside of her.

"Get in!" commanded the person in the car. "Get in right now!"

How many cops does will it take to solve this thing? Jeez!

Chapter 11

The street light above was burned out, so she couldn't see who was in the car. She recognized the voice, which prompted her to move in for a closer look. Marlee had no intention of getting into a car based on someone's directive, but she was curious and wanted to determine the identity of the driver. Taking a tentative step toward the car, she leaned down to look in the front passenger window just as the door flew open. Sitting there was a man she'd never seen before in her life. He was bald and had a baby face, so it was hard to determine if he was prematurely bald or had a youthful face for his age. His eyes were squinty, and he had a blank expression.

The driver leaned forward and yelled again, "Marlee, get in the damn car!" It was Barry Stevens and he was in a pissy mood.

"Are you following me, Barry?" she snapped, irritated that she would now have to come up with a good story to cover for her investigation at the Moon Glow Motel.

"Somebody should be following you so you stay out of trouble! Just get in. We'll give you a ride home," Barry said, his voice evening out into a calmer tone.

"My mom told me not to get into cars with strange guys." She continued to stall, deciding if a warm ride home was worth the interrogation she would have to undergo. Comfort won out, and Marlee slipped into the backseat. She figured she could drum up enough bullshit on the ride back to the dorm that she wouldn't have to divulge why she was walking along the highway at night.

"This is Doug," Barry said, jerking his thumb toward the passenger. "He's a police officer too."

"Hi, Doug. Whose car is this?" Barry was driving a junky car that looked like it was ready to give up the ghost.

"This is a work car. We're going on a stake out," Barry replied, sitting up a little straighter and puffing out his chest.

"Where are you going? Who are you staking out? Can I go?" Marlee was so taken with the idea of surveillance, she forgot she was trying to get away from Barry to avoid his questions.

"No, you can't go. We're watching some people we think have been passing funny money around town. Besides, don't you think you've done enough sleuthing for one night?" Barry asked, making eye contact with her through the rear view mirror.

"I thought the police used white vans when they did stake outs. Or is that just the FBI?" Marlee hoped to stall Barry for another five minutes and then they would be in front of her dorm.

"Give it up. I already know that you went to the truck stop to find out about the motel manager that said Beth was a prostitute. Your roommate ratted you out," Barry smirked.

"Did you beat it out of her? Or threaten her?" Marlee accused, sure that Jazz wouldn't have volunteered Marlee's intentions without some sort of intimidation.

"No, I just let her know that there are a lot of criminal types that hang out at that motel, and you might be in danger. She told me everything, including that you blabbed about the stuff you were to keep secret," Barry said, staring her down via the rear view mirror.

"So what? The case is closed, and the PD isn't going to do anything else. What difference does it make that I told Jazz about our conversations? She was Beth's friend too," Marlee insisted, knowing she was on weak ground.

"It's all about you, isn't it? Little Miss College Girl," Barry said, bitterness creeping into his voice. "Nothing has changed for me. If the chief or one of the captains hears I passed on information to you, I might have a long time to wait before I get promoted. You probably torpedoed my career."

"I told Jazz not to mention anything to anyone," Marlee said, realizing Barry had a point.

"A lot of good that will do. I told you not to mention it to anyone, and you couldn't keep a secret," Barry accused.

"I can keep a secret really well. I have a bunch of them right now that I'll never tell anybody. After you said the case was closed, I was mad at you so I made the conscious decision to tell Jazz about our information swap. She won't tell anyone. I guarantee it." Marlee sounded more confident than she felt. For all she knew, Jazz was retelling the information to anyone in the dorm who would listen.

"She better keep her mouth shut," Barry said, but then realized that sounded like a threat. "Not that I'll do anything, but I just really want to make detective, and you two could wreck it for me if word gets out. Now tell us what you found out at the truck stop."

Marlee gave a full report of her evening, including how Robbie assumed she was a hooker and directed her to room 202. "When I asked him about Beth, he said she went by Dixie and that she'd been out there a few times before. He said he didn't know how the cops knew to talk to him about her. Then he got really snotty with me and told me to leave."

"So, if the cops know about Robbie and the prostitution at the motel, why doesn't he get arrested? Why doesn't the motel get shut down?" Marlee asked, disgusted that the police were aware of the criminal activity but chose to ignore it.

"His uncle is a big wig in this town. Nobody messes with him or his businesses," Barry said. "All we can do is put pressure on Robbie from time to time when we need information. Beyond that, there's not much we can do."

"But there was a young girl in her early teens there tonight. Working, I'm sure. Doesn't that bother anyone?" Marlee snapped.

"Of course it bothers us. There's nothing most of us on the force would like better than to arrest Robbie and his uncle and the guys who are paying for sex, but the word came down from our bosses to leave them alone," Barry reported with a degree of sincerity that Marlee believed to be true.

Feeling better about Barry and his stance on the prostitution at the motel, Marlee decided he wasn't such a dipshit after all. "I'll talk to Jazz right away. We'll keep everything about the case between the two of us," she assured him as she exited the car in front of her dorm. "By the way, you two need better disguises for the stake out. You totally look like cops."

Jasmine was a nervous wreck when Marlee entered the dorm room. She was pacing, chewing her fingernails, and had opened another can of Marlee's Bud Light. "Oh my God! Did they find you? Did you get hurt?"

"I'm fine, and yes, they found me. I assured Barry that you and I wouldn't say a thing about the case to anyone else. His career depends on it. You haven't told anyone else, have you?"

Jasmine shook her head. "No, I didn't talk to anyone except your cop friend. He said he was worried for your life."

"Barry exaggerated so you would tell him where I was and what I was doing. I don't think I was in any danger. Well, not really, although the guy at the motel thought I was a hooker and tried to send me to some guy's room," Marlee said, thinking Jasmine would get a kick out of the story.

"He what?" Jasmine's voice reached a high note Marlee hadn't heard before. Any higher and it would have been a pitch only audible to dogs.

"Relax. I came into the motel, and the clerk assumed I was there to meet a specific guy. I told him I wasn't and asked about Beth. He claims she worked there a few times and went by the name of Dixie. I asked some questions, he got mad, and then I left. End of story," Marlee said, leaving out what a creep Robbie was and how she was afraid to turn her back on him as she left.

"So what now?" Jasmine enquired.

"The coroner ruled Beth's death an accident, presumably from intoxication. The case is closed, and the police aren't going to do anything else about it. Barry said the motel clerk and his uncle are big shots in town, and the police were told to leave them alone. Apparently they're untouchable. The worst the police can do is pressure them for information, but that's it," Marlee repeated her conversation with Barry.

"That's it? Nothing else can be done?" Jasmine was incredulous.

"What do you think should be done?" Marlee asked.

Jasmine thought awhile, chewing her nails again. "I think we should talk to the guys at Stairway to Hell to see what they know."

"I already talked to Tim, but I never talked to any of the other guys. Whatever they have to say doesn't change the fact that Beth's intoxication level was almost at the lethal limit, but you know what? I don't think we'll find out anything that will reopen the investigation, but we might piece together more details about Beth and who she was. We've learned quite a bit already, and I for one want to know more. Who knows what other secrets are lurking out there." Marlee said.

"Let's go to Stairway to Hell tomorrow to talk to the guys," Jasmine said, calming herself and sitting down.

"It's only 9:00 pm. Let's go now," Marlee suggested, jumping up from the lawn chair and grabbing her coat. "But first, I'm putting on some socks and warmer shoes."

The temperature was hovering just above zero, but the wind chill made it feel more like twenty below. The roommates cut through as many buildings on campus as possible on their trek to talk to Tim and his roommates at Stairway to Hell. The Administration Building, which was open until midnight, provided a temporary respite for the nearly frozen coeds. They lingered until they could feel their limbs again and then fast-walked the remainder of the way to the party house.

Marlee's stubby legs were no match for Jasmine's long limbs. She had to jog just to keep up with her roommate's fast walk. "Dammit, Jazz. Slow down! We're not running a marathon, you know." Taking the icy cold air into her lungs was hard enough without adding panting onto it.

"Sorry, I'm just really, really cold," Jasmine said. Marlee knew she outweighed her slim roommate by at least forty pounds and that those extra pounds of blubber provided a good deal of warmth. If Marlee was freezing, she could only imagine the level of cold her skinny roommate was feeling.

They reached Stairway to Hell in record time, even with the warm-up stops on campus. When they arrived, Tim was just coming inside with his dog.

"Hey, what are you guys doing? It's a little cold for an evening stroll, isn't it?" he called out in a cheerful manner.

"We're here to visit you and your roommates. Can we come in?" Marlee asked, shivering.

Tim took his time maneuvering his dog up the steps to the deck and through the side door. Jasmine turned a light shade of blue by the time they finally made their way into the toasty house. "I think I'm going to die. There's no way I can walk back to the dorm!" Jasmine's chill, along with her flair for the dramatic, had kicked in.

"Don't worry, I'll give you a ride back to your dorm. Why did you decide to come for a visit on one of the coldest nights of the year?" Tim took his dog off the leash and put a pan of hot water on the stove. He opened a cupboard and withdrew packets of Swiss Miss hot chocolate and a bottle of peppermint schnapps.

Once settled in the living room with their hot libations, Marlee and Jasmine took turns telling what little they could reveal. Since Officer Stevens had reiterated his need for secrecy to protect his career, Marlee tip-toed around most of the facts and kept her questions

100

general. "Tim, did you know Beth very well, other than from bars and parties?"

"We were in English together last year. That's how we met. Why?" Tim picked up the bottle of schnapps from a TV tray and poured more into his hot chocolate.

"We've heard some rumors about Beth and don't know what to think. Jazz and I thought we knew her fairly well, but now we're wondering. I heard Beth earned money on the side through prostitution out at the motel by the truck stop." Marlee didn't add any qualifiers or additional information. She wanted to judge Tim's reaction when he heard her revelation.

Tim looked at the television, which was turned off, then the wall, then the floor. He would not make eye contact with either of his guests, which Marlee interpreted to mean that he knew something.

"Yeah, I wasn't going to say anything, but I've heard about it too," Tim finally said, glancing up at Marlee then Jasmine. "I mean, there wasn't any reason to tarnish her reputation. She was dead, and nothing was going to change, so why even mention it to the police?"

"How did you find out?" Marlee asked, again keeping the questions brief.

"A friend told me. I don't want to say who, but it was a guy I believe was telling the truth," Tim said, making direct eye contact.

"Was it fairly well-known that Beth was a hooker?" Jasmine asked, hugging her mug of hot chocolate to absorb its warmth.

"All of us guys here at the house knew," Tim said bluntly.

"There's no good way to ask this. Tim, were you or your roommates clients of Beth's?" Marlee asked, unsure if she had crossed a line.

"No! I don't have to pay for sex." Tim was indignant, but didn't seem offended.

"What about your roommates?" Jasmine asked.

"I can't answer for any of them," Tim said,

bouncing his foot against the edge of the coffee table.

"Is that because you know one or more of them paid Beth for sex?" Marlee asked.

Tim's look said it all, but he wasn't prepared to accuse his friends. "I don't know. All I can say for sure is that I didn't. We don't keep tabs on each other, so I can't say what my roommates do and don't do. You'll have to ask them yourself."

"Are they around tonight?" Marlee asked.

"John went to the library, and Blake went to see some girl at her apartment. Adam is in the basement. You can go talk to him if you want," Tim said as he got up from the couch and walked up the stairs to the top floor, not bothering to introduce them to Adam.

Jasmine gave Marlee a fretful look. "I hope Tim's still going to give us a ride home later." Marlee nodded in agreement as they opened the door to the basement and descended the stairs.

Adam sat at the makeshift bar, holding a can of beer and looking off into the distance as he listened to *Round and Round* by Ratt blaring from a boom box. He turned as he saw them come down the stairs and looked at them with curiosity. Adam was clad in a gray university sweatshirt and tight-fitting black jeans. His short, blonde hair offset his hazel eyes and sculpted cheekbones.

Marlee introduced them and mentioned that they had been at the house party on Thursday night. "We're friends of Tim's and were just upstairs talking to him about Beth. She was a friend of ours, and we lived in the same dorm."

"It's a sad situation. I've seen Beth around, and she always seemed to be the life of the party, you know what I mean?"

"Yeah, she was really bubbly and outgoing," Jasmine said with a trembling voice as she sat down on a barstool beside Adam. "I miss her so much already."

"So we're just asking around about Beth. You know, trying to piece together her life," Marlee said with an air of nonchalance. "Anything you can tell us about her, even negative stuff, will be helpful."

"Like I said earlier, I've seen her around. That's all I can tell you." Adam turned his swivel bar stool so that his face angled away from Marlee and Jasmine.

Marlee was cold, tired, and tired of all the bullshit. "Cut the crap, Adam. You knew she was a prostitute, didn't you?" She moved around so that she was face to face with him.

Adam's eyes darted around the room as he planned what to say. "Yeah, but I didn't want to say anything bad about the dead."

"I'm not buying it. There's some reason you and a lot of other guys don't want to talk about it, and I think I know very well what it is." Marlee made her accusation clear enough for even the most obtuse to grasp it.

"Hey, are you saying I paid to have sex with Beth? Because I didn't!" Adam jumped up off his barstool and glared at Marlee and Jasmine.

"Then why isn't anyone talking about it? Seems to me the reason no one is saying anything is because they were involved," Marlee continued with her accusations. She wasn't convinced that Adam was complicit, but she had struck a nerve and wanted to see his reaction.

"Who do you think you are, coming in here and making accusations like this? I don't even know either one of you. Get out of here, both of you!" Adam stood firm with his hands crossed in front of him. He was defensive, but Marlee couldn't determine if it was because he had something to hide or because Marlee made a mess of the interview.

"Fine, we'll leave. But one more thing. Did you know Beth was pregnant when she died?" Marlee asked, as she inched her way back from Adam.

"Beth was pregnant?" Tim gasped from the top of the stairs as he started walking down to the basement. That was when he missed a step, fell down the remaining stairs, and hit his head on the bare concrete floor, knocking him unconscious.

Burn, baby, burn!

Chapter 12

After Tim regained consciousness, the situation became calmer. Adam was no longer swearing, Jasmine wasn't freaking out, and Marlee had resumed breathing. The three dragged Tim to the purple bean bag chair in the corner and hovered over him until he began moaning and moving his limbs.

"What happened? Did you beat me up?" Tim asked Adam as one eye looked directly at him while the other eye roamed the room.

"You fell down the stairs and landed on your noggin," Adam said. "Nobody beat you up."

"Do you want to go to the hospital?" Jasmine asked. "You took a nasty tumble down the stairs."

"And you were out for a few minutes," Marlee added.

Tim rubbed his head in different spots as if the pain was moving all over rather than concentrated in one area. "No, I don't need a doctor. Maybe just some aspirin for my headache."

Adam jogged upstairs to retrieve the pain reliever Tim requested. He continued to recline haphazardly in the bean bag chair but then began to get antsy. Struggling to get up from the swishy chair, he slipped and fell backward into its plushness.

"You might have a concussion. I think you should go to the hospital to get checked." Marlee didn't know much about medicine or first aid, but she recalled an episode of Magnum P.I. in which someone suffered a concussion from a fall.

Adam galloped down the stairs, unafraid he could stumble and suffer a fall just like his roommate. "I called my mom. She's a receptionist at a doctor's office. She said someone will have to stay with you all night and wake you up every few hours to make sure you're still alive. Mom said you shouldn't have any aspirin."

"Can you do it, since you live here and all?" Marlee asked.

"Yeah. And I think it might be time for you two to take off now," Adam said, irritation returning to his voice.

"But Tim was going to give us a ride home because it's so cold," whined Jasmine, not relishing the bitter cold return walk to the dorm.

"Well, he can't drive now, and I'm not leaving him alone," Adam growled as he helped Tim to his feet.

"That's fine. We'll be alright," Marlee lied, knowing without looking that Jasmine was furious about the promised ride falling through. "I'll stop back tomorrow to see how he's doing. Do you need any help getting him upstairs?"

As Adam waved them off with a glare, Marlee and Jasmine found their coats upstairs and headed back out into the cold night. By the time they arrived back at the dorm their faces, hands, and feet were partially numb.

"I hate your stupid ideas," Jasmine grumbled as she put a second pair of pajamas on over the first pair. "I'm never going to get warm."

The hair dryer buzzed as Marlee waived it in front of her feet. "Do you want me to turn the hair dryer on you?"

As they did their best to get warm, a thought occurred to Marlee. "When Tim fell down the stairs he had just heard me tell Adam that Beth was pregnant. I wonder if hearing that was what made him fall?"

"Why would he be so shocked by that? He knew Beth was a prostitute, and he's the one who found her dead outside. Why would learning that she was pregnant be such a jolt to him, given the other things that have happened in the past few days?" Jasmine asked, her head becoming clearer now that she was warming up.

Marlee shrugged. "I don't know, but after I told Adam that Beth was pregnant, I heard Tim repeat it back, and he sounded upset. Then he fell down the stairs. It seems like an odd sequence of events."

"I guess, but unless Tim was the father, why would he care so much?" Jasmine asked. "I mean, I'm sure he cared because he knew Beth, but he told us himself that he'd never been a customer of hers."

"He said he wasn't a paying customer, but maybe they had been seeing each other. Or maybe they had a fling," Marlee suggested.

"But if Beth was a hooker, then she's been with a lot of guys, and any of them could be the father, regardless of whether or not she and Tim had sex," Jasmine said.

"That's a good point. I'm going back over there tomorrow to check on him and see how he's feeling," Marlee said. "Don't worry. You don't have to go."

"Now you've got me curious about Tim, and I want to go too. I just hope it'll be warmer tomorrow!" Jasmine said as she continued to pile on layers of clothing before going to bed.

Marlee shut out the light and climbed into her lofted twin bed. Jasmine was already settled into hers with an extra blanket pulled up to her chin. It was nearing midnight, and they'd both been busy that day. Plus, fresh air and exercise made them tired. It was nearly four a.m. when their phone rang.

"Dammit, who calls this early?" Marlee growled as she got out of bed as fast as possible without slipping from the lofted bed. "If this is a prank call, I'm gonna be pissed!"

"Hello!" Marlee yelled into the receiver, wanting to make sure the caller knew they had disrupted her sleep. "Oh, no. Is everyone okay?"

After hanging up, Marlee said to Jasmine. "There's been a fire at Stairway to Hell!"

"A fire? Who was on the phone?" asked a drowsy Jasmine.

"It was Barry from the police department, and he said the whole place is ablaze. The fire department won't be able to save it."

"Did everyone get out?" Jasmine asked, worry in her voice as she woke up.

"They don't know for sure. Tim's roommates all made it outside, but no one could find Tim or his dog."

A dog is a man's best friend. But why would a man with a head injury take his dog for a walk on one of the coldest nights of the year... while his house burned down? Does that make any damn sense?

Chapter 13

"Oh my God!" Jasmine shrieked. "Tim must still be in the house, passed out from his concussion. Adam was supposed to be watching him!"

"Barry said he would swing by and pick me up because he knows Tim's a friend. He and another cop were on a stake out. That's why they knew about the fire. Do you want to go over there too?" Marlee asked as she pulled on sweat pants and a sweat shirt over her pajamas.

Jasmine threw back her covers and maneuvered out of bed in seconds. "Just give me a minute," she said as she scrambled for sweats and warm footwear. The two stood inside the lobby door as Barry and Doug drove up. Marlee and Jasmine hopped in the back as Marlee began with the rapid-fire questions.

"Did the firefighters go in to look for Tim? He was knocked out earlier tonight and didn't want to go to the hospital. He may have passed out or gone into a coma from the head injury," Marlee said, hoping there was still time to locate and revive her friend.

"Two went in, but the fire was so intense that they had to leave. Tim still hasn't been located, but his roommates were hopeful that he's alright since his dog is missing too," Barry reported.

"Where would Tim and his dog go in the middle of the night? Is his car gone?" Marlee asked.

Barry shrugged. "I'll see if I can get some answers from one of the firemen I know. You two can't go with us, but I'll let you know what we find out." The two officers left their unmarked police car and walked three blocks to the smoldering house.

"We can't go with them, but we can still walk up there. It's a free country," Marlee pointed out as she opened the back door.

Jasmine, more worried than her roommate about getting into trouble, hesitated before following Marlee.

"Nobody will tell us anything. We don't know any firemen."

"No, but we might overhear something. And maybe talk with the roommates," Marlee said, not even noticing the cold even though she had already walked several miles in it during the past twenty-four hours.

Adam was standing across the street from the fire along with his roommates, EMTs, and multiple bystanders. Firefighters were in front of Stairway to Hell, most standing and waiting for the fire to burn out without spreading to surrounding homes. Adam stood alone, while John talked to a police officer, and Blake's arm was being tended to by medical personnel.

"Are you okay?" Marlee asked as she and Jasmine approached Adam. "Where's Tim?"

"I don't know where he is. I checked on him at 1:00 and again at 3:00. He was alright both times. I woke him up and everything. He said he still had a headache and was really sleepy. The next thing I knew, Blake was yelling at me to get up because the house was on fire. I ran to Tim's room, and he wasn't there. The other guys said he wasn't in their rooms, and I didn't see him on the main floor when we ran out." Adam was visibly shaken and seemed to forget that he had thrown Marlee and Jasmine out of the house just hours before.

"Where would Tim be? Is his car gone?" Jasmine asked, marching in place and swinging her arms to keep warm.

"His car is parked right over there." Adam motioned to the driveway along the side of the house. "Tim's dog is gone, and he loves that dog, so I think they went somewhere together."

"Where would they go on a freezing cold night like this? And why wouldn't he take his car?" Marlee asked. Adam's assertions just didn't ring true.

"Maybe somebody picked him up," the roommate offered.

"Did he seem confused when you checked on

114

him?" Marlee asked.

"No, why?"

"Because Tim could have woken up and forgot who he was or where he was. Who knows what was going on in his mind?" Marlee said.

"Where does Tim's dog usually sleep?" Jasmine asked.

"Inside the house during the winter. During the warmer months, he stays in a kennel outside at night. Rufus usually sleeps in Tim's room on the bed," Adam said.

"If Tim and Rufus were in the house when the fire started, I bet the dog would've barked, don't you?" Marlee asked, recalling what little knowledge she had about dogs.

"Definitely. Rufus was very protective of Tim and would have woken him and the whole house up with his barking if there was a fire," Adam relied.

"Were all of the other roommates home when the fire was discovered?" Marlee asked.

"John and I were here. And Tim, of course. Blake was the one who discovered the fire. He came home from his girlfriend's place and saw the blaze, so he ran in to wake us up and call the fire department," Adam reported.

"Any idea what caused the fire? Or what part of the house it started in?" Jasmine asked.

"No, we don't know anything yet."

"Did you look in the basement for Tim?" Marlee asked.

"No! The living room was full of smoke and flames were leaping up all over the walls. If I went downstairs, I might not have made it out alive," Adam said defensively, apparently feeling guilty for not taking extra measures to look for his roommate.

"We're not accusing you," Jasmine said quickly, not wanting him to feel any worse than he already did.

Marlee elbowed Jasmine and gestured for her to look across the street. Barry and Doug finished their conversations and were walking back toward the car. The girls took off running through back yards so they could make it to the car before Barry and Doug.

Huffing and puffing from the exertion of running through snow, Marlee and Jasmine hopped in the backseat of the unmarked patrol car just as the cops rounded the corner. Marlee worked to control her breathing by taking slow, deliberate deep breaths.

"What was happening?" Marlee asked innocently as Barry and Doug got in.

"Don't bullshit us. We saw you across the street," Barry growled as he turned in his seat to face Marlee. "I told you to stay away from the house!"

"No, you said we couldn't go with you. We didn't go with you. We walked over there by ourselves and didn't interact with you at all. No one knows you drove us over," Marlee corrected, even though she was on shaky ground with this argument. It seemed much more logical before they went.

"If I'd known you were going to do this, I never would have told you about the fire, and I sure as hell wouldn't have brought you over here," Barry said, disgust in his voice.

"We wanted to see for ourselves what happened, and we didn't think it would hurt anything if we just hung around like some of the other bystanders," Marlee said, doing her best to act contrite. She even stuck her lower lip out a bit in an attempt at a pout.

Barry turned back around and started the car. He was giving them the silent treatment and would not be forthcoming with anything he and Doug learned through official channels.

Marlee gave Jasmine the elbow. She was a pro at using her feminine wiles to get men to talk. With a toss of her hair, Jasmine said, "Barry, we're sorry. It was my idea to walk over to Stairway to Hell, and it was a bad one. I take full responsibility. But we just wanted to find out about our friend Tim. Can you please tell us what you know about him?"

116

Not even taking a beat, Barry said, "Tim still hasn't been located. His roommates all indicated that they didn't see him in his room or anywhere upstairs or on the main floor as they fled the house. Nobody had time to look in the basement, but there would be no reason for him to go there." Barry might be a good cop, but he didn't even realize that he'd fallen for Jasmine's charms.

"Did anybody check with the hospital?" Marlee asked, giving a recount of Tim's possible concussion.

"Nobody with Tim's name or fitting his description went to the emergency room in the past twelve hours," Barry said, irritation still in his voice when he addressed Marlee's questions.

"What did you find out from the other cops and firemen at the scene?" Marlee continued, hoping for more information and also that she could wear Barry down.

"Nothing other than the fire is contained. There's no longer a worry that it will spread to the houses next door, so the neighbors will be allowed to return home soon," Barry said.

"When will the fire fighters go in to see if anyone is still inside?" Marlee asked.

"Soon. Akers, my buddy from the fire department, said he would let me know after they've looked around, and the fire investigator will be coming later this morning to make a determination as to the cause of the fire."

"Did they have any theories about what started the fire?" Jasmine asked.

"It's an old, college party house, so there are several plausible theories. It may have been from an electrical problem in the house, somebody smoking and falling asleep, or something that was not fully extinguished was thrown in the trash, where it started a fire. Since the blaze began in the early morning hours, it probably wasn't a cooking fire," Barry reported.

"So, because the house is old and decrepit, and since college students live there, it won't be given as much attention as a fire in a family home or an apartment?"

Marlee asked, forgetting she was trying to get back on Barry's good side.

"No, not at all. It will get the same level of careful investigation as any other fire. I was just pointing out that it was an older house with possible maintenance issues, and since it's a party house, a lot of people are coming and going and not necessarily being careful," Barry said, quick to clarify his position. "I was just trying to give some explanation for what may have caused the fire."

"Okay. Sorry, Barry. I'm just really worried about Tim. Where do you guys think he is? He didn't take his car, so he's either on foot or someone picked him up," Marlee said.

"Or, worst case scenario, he's still in the house," Barry said.

"What's the likelihood he's still in the house? Honestly," Jasmine asked, wanting but not wanting to know the answer.

"I'd say it's more than likely that he's in the house somewhere. His roommates said he wasn't in his room, and they didn't see him as they left, so that's good, but the smoke was thick, and they didn't have much time to look around. He could have been in a number of different areas since the house is so big. And nobody made it to the basement, so Tim could be down there," Barry said.

"Adam told us that Tim's dog followed him everywhere and even slept on his bed at night. So they must be together now. Somewhere," Marlee said, hating to think of their burned bodies in the basement or elsewhere in the house.

"Why didn't Rufus bark and wake everyone up when he smelled the smoke and saw the flames?" Jasmine asked.

"Maybe he barked, but Tim didn't hear because of his head bump," Barry suggested.

"But if Rufus barked, the other roommates would have heard. He's a fairly big dog, so I'm assuming he has a mighty bark," Marlee concluded.

"Not if Rufus and Tim were in the basement, especially if the door was shut," Jasmine countered.

"Good point. We know Adam was probably really tired since he was getting up every two hours to check on Tim. Blake was at his girlfriend's place most of the night and is the one who discovered the fire when he returned home. John was there, but I don't know anything about his situation," Marlee said.

"Where will the guys from Stairway to Hell stay now that their house is gone?" Jasmine asked.

"One of them told Akers that they would all be staying with a relative outside of town," Barry said. Marlee felt relieved knowing they had a home, even if it was only temporary.

The cops dropped the girls back at the dorm, where they were able to get a couple hours of sleep before going to class. Marlee was so tired she didn't even bother showering or changing her clothes. She wore her sweats over pajamas to her morning classes, and when she realized she hadn't brushed her teeth that morning, she found a stick of gum in her book bag.

Classes dragged, as they always did when she was tired or had more important things to do. She was tempted to skip her 1:00 class, but knew a test was coming up, and she needed to learn as much as possible from lecture since the textbook made no sense to her. Philosophy was not her best subject. She found the material interesting, but her mind just didn't seem to bend the way necessary for understanding it.

Later that afternoon, Marlee dragged herself back to the dorm, crawled into bed, and slept for hours until Jasmine woke her. "Don't you have a night class tonight?"

"Oh, shit! I do, and I almost missed it," she said as she rushed from the dorm, still clad in her sweats and pajama combo with her hair sticking out on one side. The only stop she made was at the vending machine for a candy bar and a can of pop. She made it to class only five minutes late, which was fine because the professor was blathering on about his weekend. Boring!

Professor Warren was a trim man with a gray beard and mustache. He reminded her of Sean Connery in looks only. His demeanor was much more like a dictator or a prison warden. Professor Warren used the Socratic Method in his teaching, so he frequently called on students to answer questions. Marlee hated it, but had to admit that it kept her awake and made her read the assigned chapters before class. Usually. Tonight's class was an exception, and she prayed the professor would not call on her. Luck was on her side, as he chose to grill the football players sitting in the back row. Unfortunately, the only seats open in the classroom when she got there were in the front row. Now Professor Warren stood toe-to-toe with her as he lectured about criminal law. Marlee was sitting at her desk, and her only two choices for viewing were to look down at her notes or up at the front of the professor's pants. The choice was clear. She stared at her notes until her eyes were bleary, and she began to slip into a continuation of her nap.

When her head hit the desk, Professor Warren jumped backward with the speed of a jack rabbit. Marlee did a quick save by acting as if she dropped her pen and was just picking it up from the floor when she hit the desk. For the rest of the class, Marlee stared at Professor Warren's zippered brown slacks with the front pleats.

"Barry from the police department called you while you were in class," Jasmine announced as Marlee trudged through the door, too tired to close it behind her.

"What did he want?"

"He wants your body," Jasmine joked as she finished cooking ramen noodles in the hot pot.

"Shut up. What did he really want?" Marlee grumbled, not in the mood for jokes.

"He didn't say. He and Doug are on stake out again tonight, so he said he'd either call back or stop by. Say, does Doug ever talk?" Jasmine asked as she dished up two bowls of ramen.

"Not so far. Why?" Marlee asked, realizing she had yet to hear Doug's voice.

"I think he's hot!" Jasmine confessed. "He's so sexy. I'd like to see him in his uniform. Or out of it."

"Get control of yourself, Jazz. We're in the middle of a death investigation and a fire investigation. We don't have time for your love life," Marlee chastised. "Besides he's old and bald. I bet he's at least thirty!"

"I think we have time for all those things. Plus, it wouldn't hurt you to concentrate on your love life too. I know Barry likes you," Jasmine said.

"Barry's okay, but I don't have any attraction to him. He's just a nice guy. And sometimes he's not even all that nice," Marlee said. She hadn't told Jasmine about kissing Barry on campus the other day because it would just propel her into thinking Marlee and Barry were meant to be.

"Maybe you should give him a chance. Wouldn't it be fun if you were dating Barry, and I was seeing Doug? We could go on double dates," Jasmine said with a giggle as she blushed.

"Their idea of a double date would probably be a stakeout, and I bet they'd expect us to bring the snacks. No thanks. Although I would like to go on a stakeout," Marlee said. "Just not as a date with Barry." She slurped up the last of her ramen noodles, hungry for something else.

A rustling caused Marlee and Jasmine to look up from their makeshift table as they sat on the floor. Standing in the open doorway were Barry and Doug.

*There's nothing that could separate me
from my dog. Nothing!*

Chapter 14

"Oh, shit!" Marlee exclaimed, eyes as wide as saucers as her mind raced to think of an explanation for the conversation Barry and Doug just overheard. Jasmine was even more shocked than Marlee and looked as if she might pass out.

"You think I'm hot?" Doug asked Jasmine, a smile crossing his face. Not only was this the first time Doug had spoken, but it was also the first time he showed emotion of any kind. Up until tonight, Marlee had wondered if he was a robot.

Jasmine blushed a deep shade of red, which of course, was adorable on her. "Um, I might have said something like that." She looked at Doug, blushed even more, and then looked away with the hint of a smile.

"How about we go for a little walk around the dorm, and you tell me more about how you think I'm hot," Doug suggested, holding out his arm.

"Okay," Jasmine said suggestively as she took hold of the rugged cop's arm and left the room. "So tell me about yourself, Doug." Low tones of talking along with bursts of Jasmine's giggles were audible and then faded away.

"Barry, I'm sorry. I didn't mean for..." Marlee was without words, which was rare. She wanted to tell him that he wasn't supposed to overhear her conversation with Jasmine, but that would hardly make him feel better. She also wanted to make it clear why she wasn't attracted to him, but that would surely make Barry feel worse. She let the sentence hang in mid-air until Barry broke the silence.

"Marlee, you really don't have to worry about it. Seriously. I didn't have any attraction to you either, but when you planted a kiss on me, I started to think about you in a different way. Since then I've realized that I was just flattered with the attention. You're clearly not girlfriend material. No hard feelings?" Barry asked, sincerely not upset with Marlee's lack of interest in him and not realizing what a land mine he had just stepped in.

"What do you mean you're not attracted to me? Are you gay?" Marlee was incredulous. Not that she was a man-magnet, but she assumed a guy like Barry would be thrilled to go out with her. He was the male version of a Plain Jane and not all that bright. On a scale of 1 to 10, he was barely a 5, while she considered herself a solid 7.

"No, I'm not gay! Just because a guy isn't into you doesn't mean he's gay. Jeez, you have some ego!" Now Barry had adopted an attitude and was showing it.

She needed to walk a tightrope to get herself out of this mess. "No, of course you're not gay. I was just joking. At least we're in agreement that we're not meant to be a couple. That takes a lot of pressure off, and now we can focus on finding Tim."

Barry took a deep breath, no doubt trying to figure out what Marlee meant. He must have come to the conclusion that all was good, because he launched into cop mode. "That's what we came over here to talk to you about: Tim."

"What is it? Did you find him?" Marlee asked.

"No, but we found his dog," Barry said, lowering his tone to a level that Marlee knew suggested bad news.

"Where? Is Rufus okay?" Marlee asked, tears already welling in her eyes.

"The dog was found on the outskirts of town, not too far from the truck stop. He had a broken neck and was left in a ditch," Barry said.

"Somebody killed Tim's dog?" Marlee could not believe her ears. "Why would anyone break a dog's neck?"

"We don't have any other information yet. The dog was dead when a farmer called it in," Barry reported.

"Any sign of Tim? Do you think someone killed him too?" Marlee was beside herself with worry as she thought about Tim and his dog dragged out to the edge of town and killed.

"No, we didn't find any sign of Tim. Firefighters

didn't find any bodies in Stairway to Hell when they searched today. There was nothing to suggest Tim was anywhere near the dog. In fact, we suspect Rufus ran away when the fire started. As soon as someone opened the door, he probably bolted and ran. Then somebody found Rufus and killed him," Barry said, emotion creeped into his voice, suggesting he had a soft spot for dogs.

"What kind of pond scum would hurt a dog?" Marlee asked. "That's just disgusting. I think they should be arrested."

"Agreed, but the killing of a dog isn't going to take precedence over anything else, especially when we have a missing person and an unexplained house fire," Barry said.

Jasmine's giggles reappeared, and soon she and Doug were arm-in-arm back at the room. Since she was in such a good mood, Marlee figured Doug hadn't dropped any of the bad news on her. "I showed Doug all around the dorm," Jasmine said with a little laugh.

"Including the laundry room?" Marlee snarked, knowing that's where people went to make out when they couldn't stay in their dorm room. Plus, the RAs never went down there, so it was a good hiding spot when those in the female wing of the dorm had male friends over for a visit.

Choosing to ignore Marlee's remark, Jasmine pulled Doug into the room and pushed him down on her chair and snuggled up into his lap. Marlee was appalled. Jasmine barely knew this guy, who, although he seemed harmless enough, was still virtually a stranger to them.

Realizing that Jasmine really didn't care to hear anything about Tim while Doug was in the room, Marlee kept mum until the cops left. They were gone exactly thirty seconds when Marlee said, "Rufus was found dead on the edge of town. The cops still don't know where Tim is yet. But maybe you don't care anymore now that you have a boyfriend."

"Jealous?" Jasmine spat back, not appreciating Marlee's bitterness.

Marlee was contrite, realizing that her roommate was capable of having more than one area of interest at one time. "Sorry, Jazz, but you seem more interested in your love life than finding out about Tim."

"Of course I care about Tim. And I can't believe Rufus was found dead. Who did it?" Jasmine, who had already forgiven Marlee's brashness, sat on the edge of the chair.

"The cops think Rufus ran out of the house as soon as someone opened the door after the fire started. They don't have a theory on who broke his neck or why," Marlee said, knowing in her heart that there was a special place in hell for people who hurt cats and dogs.

"Well, the good thing is we know Tim didn't burn in the fire. Do the cops have any clue as to where he might be?" Jasmine asked.

"Nope. No ideas at all." Marlee was perplexed. Tim was a hometown boy and had lived here all his life. No doubt, he had friends and relatives who might have taken him in if he showed up on their doorsteps. "I wonder if he's staying with a relative or a high school classmate."

"But they would know Tim's house burnt down and that the police were looking for him, wouldn't they?" Jasmine queried.

"The fire has been on the news, but I don't recall hearing anything about Tim's disappearance," Marlee said. "Maybe the cops are keeping that secret."

"Why? Because they think Tim set the fire?" Jasmine asked, confused as to where the conversation was headed. "They don't suspect him, do they?"

"No! I mean, I don't think so. Barry never said anything at all about Tim being a suspect." Now that she thought about it, it seemed odd that Tim's name had never come up as a potential arsonist.

"I don't think Tim started his own house on fire and killed his own dog. That's too ridiculous to even consider. I mean, what would be his motive for doing either of those things?" Jasmine asked.

126

"Tim didn't have a motive. I can't believe he would set his own home on fire and leave his roommates to die. The only way it's possible that he set the fire is by accident. And then he left the house, maybe because he was still delirious from his fall down the stairs. There's no way in hell I believe he killed his own dog. You saw him with Rufus. He loved that dog. Even Adam said so. Besides, even if he did kill his dog, why would Tim take Rufus to the outskirts of town and kill him there?" Marlee asked.

Shaking her head back and forth and shrugging at the same time, Jasmine picked up her shower caddy and went to the restroom shared by that wing of the first floor. When she came back, freshly washed and with minty-fresh breath, she had a smile on her face.

"Out with it! I can tell you're dying to tell me all about Doug," Marlee said with a grin, no longer irritated or jealous of her roommate.

"First of all, he said to tell you that he's only twenty-eight, and he shaves his head on purpose. He's so nice. We walked around and talked. He asked me all kinds of questions about myself. Most guys just want to talk about themselves, so that was really cool. And we like the same kind of music. I think I might be in love!" Jasmine gushed as she continued on with Doug's many attributes.

"Don't start the wedding planning yet. You just met a few hours ago, and you've only had one conversation," Marlee warned, afraid her roommate was going to fall head over heels with the cop.

"I won't, but if we get married, do you want to be my maid of honor?" Jasmine asked with a straight face. After seeing Marlee's shocked expression, she broke out into a fit of laughter. "Puh-leez!"

"Whew, I was afraid you were going to pick out your wedding dress tomorrow," Marlee said with relief.

"Hey, I don't fall for every guy that shows me a little bit of attention," Jasmine said with a huff.

"If you say so," Marlee said with a wink and a grin, which prompted Jasmine to burst into a fit of laughter.

I don't have many friends. The people I allow into my life tend to stick around for a long time. Unless they betray me.

Chapter 15

Vomiting was not an option. Marlee sat behind the hard wooden desk in the second row of her western civilizations class and tried not to fall on the floor. She wasn't feeling up to par when she left the dorm that morning, but chalked it up to lack of sleep, poor nutrition, and spending too much time out in the cold. It was midway through the boring history lecture when she realized she might have a stomach bug.

The journey back to the dorm took forever, even though it was usually a ten-minute walk. She barely made it through class without getting sick, but was not so lucky on her walk home. Water gushed from the sides of her mouth, a sure sign she was going to puke. As she passed the administration building, she stuck her head in the leafless brown bushes and barfed until she saw stars.

"Whoa! Looks like you partied too hard last night," said Paul, the guy she had been crushing on for weeks. He looked sexy as ever with his pegged acid-wash jeans and a lined jean jacket.

She stood upright and wiped her mouth, trying to pull off an air of nonchalance. "Yeah, it was a huge party last night." Marlee attempted a smile as she walked away. She would rather be known as someone who drank too much at a party than a person who was about to shit her pants from the bug she had contracted.

Once she got back to the dorm, Marlee was surprised to find Jasmine in a similar state. "What the hell happened? Who gave us the flu?" Jasmine asked.

"I don't know, but when I find out, I'm going to punch them," Marlee said, after her third trip to the bathroom. "I'm not even going to attempt getting into bed again in case I have to rush back to the bathroom. I'll just lay here in my beach chair."

"What about me? I can't go back up to my bed either, and I don't want to lay on the bare floor," Jasmine whined, looking forlorn and even more helpless than Marlee felt.

"Take your blankets from your bed and make a cushion out of them on the floor. It won't be so bad," Marlee said, trying to get in a comfortable position.

The remainder of the day and through the night was spent drinking 7-Up, making frequent trips to the bathroom, and avoiding everyone in the dorm. By the next morning, both roommates were feeling somewhat better. Neither had vomited in the past few hours, and the body aches had subsided.

"I don't think I should go to class," Jasmine said in a faint whisper, as she lay on her pile of blankets on the floor. "I'm just too weak."

"Me too," Marlee agreed. "I wouldn't want to give the flu to someone else, so it's probably best not to go to classes today."

The roommates spent the day in their pajamas, eating food they asked Kristie from next door to retrieve for them from the cafeteria and talking about Tim's disappearance. "Even if Tim was out of his head from the fall, he would've come to his senses by now, wouldn't he?" Jasmine asked as she chowed down on a thick slice of banana bread slathered with margarine.

"Either that or whomever he's staying with would have taken him to the emergency room," Marlee added. She slurped chicken noodle soup straight from the plastic take-out container, not bothering with a spoon.

"Unless...," Jasmine let the thought hang in the air without continuing her thought.

"Let's not even think about Tim being dead. I think he's alive and well and at a friend or relative's house trying to recover from his head injury. The police keep checking the hospital, so we know he's not there," Marlee said.

"But are they checking any other hospitals other than the one here in town?" Jasmine asked.

"Why would Tim be in a hospital out of town? That doesn't make any sense," Marlee chastised.

130

"None of this makes any sense," Jasmine snapped.

"You know, you might be right," Marlee said as she thought more about the situation. "If Tim was walking and was out of his head, someone might have picked him up and driven him to a hospital in another town."

"Or maybe Tim was kidnapped," Jasmine said.

Marlee broke out into a laugh. "Why would Tim be kidnapped? He wasn't well-off, so I doubt there would be any money to pay ransom. He was just a regular broke college student. And who would want to kidnap him?" She shook her head as she continued to laugh at the prospect.

"I thought we were just throwing out ideas. I didn't know I was going to be judged by the high court," Jasmine huffed.

"You're right. No judgment. We should just list all possible ideas, no matter how outlandish," Marlee said in an attempt to placate her roommate. "I know some of my ideas are out there too. Let's go through every possible scenario we can think of."

"Ruling out shape-shifting and UFOs, right?" Jasmine joked.

"Yes, only thinking of realistic scenarios," Marlee said, relieved that Jasmine was in a good mood again.

"If he was kidnapped or killed, God forbid, who would have done it?" Jasmine asked. "Unless it was some deranged person who kidnaps and kills for fun, like a psycho or a serial killer or somebody like that."

"You know what I'm starting to think?" Marlee asked, but not waiting for Jasmine to reply. "I think Tim is alive and well. I think he's hiding out somewhere and doesn't want the cops or anyone else to know where he's hiding."

"Are you serious," Jasmine asked, peering at Marlee over her pile of blankets. "Why would he be hiding?"

"I don't know, but it's seems the only likely conclusion right now. Tim wasn't killed in the fire. He's not in the hospital. No one knows where he is. I assume the cops have talked to his family and friends here in town and elsewhere to see if any of them have heard from him," Marlee ticked off the reasons for her theory.

"If Tim's hiding, that means he must know something he doesn't want everyone else to know about. Or he did something and doesn't want to get caught," Jasmine said. "You know him better than I do. I just met him the night of the party."

"I don't know him very well. Most of our conversations were in class or at parties. Tim's nice, but doesn't offer up much information about himself. I always thought he was a bit shy around girls." Marlee said. "Now, I'm not so sure. Maybe he was hiding something all along."

"Did you hear anything about him doing anything illegal, like selling drugs?" Jasmine inquired.

"No, I never really heard anybody talk about him other than to mention a party at Stairway to Hell. We were put in a group together in western civ class. After that, we would chat before class or when we would bump into each other around campus," Marlee reported.

"Other than his roommates, who are his friends? Who does he sit with in class?" Jasmine asked.

"I never see him sitting with anyone in particular in western civ, and I don't know any of his other friends," Marlee replied. "I guess he's a bit of a loner, now that I think of it. Anytime I saw him, he was by himself, even downtown at the bars. We need to talk to his roommates."

"And maybe his family here in town," Jasmine suggested.

"Good idea. If anybody can tell us more about Tim, it's family." Marlee pulled the local telephone book out of her desk drawer and began to search for DeWitts. After finding four, she jotted down all of their names, phone numbers, and addresses. Tomorrow, she would track down Tim's family members to see what they revealed about him. Then, she would track down Tim's three roommates, wherever they were now staying, and talk to them. She was certain there were answers to be

132

uncovered, and it would just take some elbow grease to get it done.

Marlee felt she had no choice but to skip classes again the next day. This week was shot to hell due to her amateur sleuthing and the stomach flu. No sense in getting too involved in classes this far into the week. Jasmine, on the other hand, had a group presentation due and could not miss her class.

Right after a quick shower and breakfast, Marlee got down to work. She referred to the list of Tim's potential family members and their contact information. The first call she placed was to Betty DeWitt, which she thought sounded like a kindly grandmother. After identifying herself and her reason for the call, Marlee was on the receiving end of a string of harsh words and profanity.

"You and all the other reporters can go to hell!" Betty shouted before hanging up.

Even though Betty didn't answer any of her questions about Tim, Marlee knew Betty must be a relative. No one would get that worked up over a phone call unless they had some direct connection.

Call number two was to Edgar DeWitt. Marlee made no assumptions about this man before she placed the call.

"Hallooooo?" yelled the man.

Marlee went through her spiel again, this time emphasizing that she was just a college student and not a reporter.

"Sure, come on by. I'll tell you whatever you want to know about Tom," Edgar said, sounding excited to have company.

"No, it's Tim that I want to talk about. Tim DeWitt. Are you related to him?" Marlee asked.

"Sure, we fought in the war together. I'd never forget him, but I haven't seen him in over thirty years," Edgar said.

"Oh shoot. You know what, Edgar? I'm not going

to be able to make it over today after all. I'll call if I can come another day. Thanks." Marlee ended the conversation quickly when she realized Edgar was a lonely old man with a faulty memory.

Call number three was placed to Bernie and Nicole DeWitt, who Marlee suspected might be Tim's parents. She let the phone ring twelve times before hanging up. Probably both at work, she thought.

The fourth call was to Pam DeWitt, who lived within the county but outside of town. Pam answered on the first ring, out of breath.

"I guess I could talk to you. My brother and I aren't very close anymore, but I want to find him, and I hope he's alright," she said with some degree of hesitation. Pam gave directions to her farm a few miles outside of town.

"I'll be there in an hour," Marlee promised, although she had no idea how she would get there. The temperature was even colder than the previous day. The total distance was around five miles, which was too far to walk in frigid temperatures.

She placed another call, hoping that Barry was at home. A roommate answered and said Barry was sleeping because he'd been working the night shift.

"It's an emergency," Marlee said, even though this technically was not a dire situation.

"Whaaaaa?" said a groggy voice amid the clatter of dishes.

"Barry, it's me. I need you to give me a ride to see Tim's sister. She lives on a farm outside of town. Hurry up! We need to be there in an hour," Marlee said.

"I've had two hours of sleep. I'm not taking you anywhere," Barry growled.

"Really? I thought you were serious about making detective. I guess it was all just talk," Marlee said, twisting the knife.

A tremendous sigh was followed by, "I'll be there, but you're taking me out for lunch afterward."

"It's a deal," Marlee said. Not only was she without

a car, she was without money. No matter, she would worry about that later. Right now, she needed to concentrate on talking to Tim's sister.

Barry was in a sour mood and barely talked during their drive to Pam's farm. He balanced an enormous plastic glass between them on the front seat. In it, he'd poured four cans of Mountain Dew. Marlee felt confident that he would perk up once caffeinated.

Pam DeWitt was short with the sturdy build of a farm gal. Her dishwater-blonde hair was pulled back in a ponytail, and she wore jeans, work boots, and a heavy winter coat. She looked to be in her late twenties, which would make her around six years older than Tim.

"Come inside. It's cold out here," Pam said as they exited the car. "I just finished with chores, and I'm ready to warm up."

The farm house was quaint and kitschy with mismatched chairs at the kitchen table, a collection of Hummel figurines scattered throughout the front room, and a rusty tin coffee pot on the gas stove. "This used to be my grandparents' place. I took over when grandma died, and they moved grandpa to a senior home," Pam said as she moved a stack of bills and letters from the table.

"Is your grandpa Edgar DeWitt, by any chance?" Marlee asked. When Pam nodded, Marlee gave an overview of their conversation.

"Yes, his memory is slipping. He's in good physical condition, but he gets confused easily and is very forgetful. Grandma took care of him, but when she passed away we had to make sure he was being watched. Before we put him in the home, Dad found him walking down the road looking for Speedy. That was his dog when he was a kid."

Over cups of hot cocoa, Pam told them about Tim, a brother with whom she had become estranged in the past few years. "I always loved the farm and spent a lot of time here as a kid. Living out here and raising animals and crops was all I ever wanted to do. He wanted to take over the farm, but he was too young. Tim was still in high school when everything happened with our grandparents. The only ones interested in the farm were me and Tim. I never had any intention of going to college, and I wanted to take over, so it only made sense for me to move out here and continue what Grandma and Grandpa started fifty years ago."

"Tim held it against you?" Barry asked.

"He's never gotten over it, even though I told him after he finished college he could take over the farm if he wanted. Tim's always been a bit suspicious, and he probably thought I was lying to him," Pam continued.

"Did Tim stay in touch with your parents and your grandpa?" Marlee asked.

"Not really. He'd be there for Thanksgiving, Christmas, and Easter. Those were always big celebrations in our family, but he wouldn't stick around. It was like he couldn't stand to be around any of us for very long," Pam said with a hint of sadness in her voice. "And now we don't know where he's gone. The police have been by every day, and they don't know any more than we do."

Barry had not identified himself as a cop. He wasn't wearing his uniform, so there was no reason to think that he was with the police force. "What are the cops asking when they come here?"

"It's always the same questions. They want to know if Tim's been here, if I've heard from him, and if I have any new information on where he might be. I think they believe I'm hiding him, but I don't know why," Pam said.

"What do you think happened to Tim? Where is he?" Marlee asked.

"I wish I knew. A detective came by earlier this morning and told me Tim hit his head the night before the fire. That was the first I'd heard about it. Now I don't know if he's wandering around delirious, if he's been kidnapped, or something worse." Pam was working herself into an emotional state, and she wiped her eyes with the sleeve of her ratty sweatshirt.

136

"Is there anyone Tim might turn to or anywhere Tim would go in a time of crisis?" Barry asked.

Pam shook her head. "I don't know of anyone. Since we've been out of touch for so long, your best bet is talking to his college friends."

"Was he close with anyone in high school?" Marlee asked. "Maybe someone who still lives here in town?"

"He used to hang out with a neighbor kid we called Elvis when I still lived at home. Tim would have been around ten years old then. Of course, I have no idea if they remained friends throughout high school or after. Elvis's dad and mom still live here in town, just across the street from my parents." Pam took a napkin and jotted down their names and address.

"Will your parents be willing to talk to us if we stop by?" Marlee asked, admitting that she had attempted telephone contact with them that morning.

"Probably, if you can catch them. They both work during the day and have all kinds of activities going on at night. Dad goes to the Elks Club twice a week, plus he's on a bowling team, and he coaches kid's basketball. Mom sells Mary Kaye and Tupperware, so she's gone most nights for parties."

"Maybe I can catch them on the phone and set up a time to meet," Marlee said, more to herself than anyone else.

After they left, Barry suggested they swing by the neighborhood where Tim's parents lived. The DeWitt house was cool blue in color with white shutters. The two-story home was well-maintained and in a middle class area of town. Noticing a car in the driveway, they decided to stop.

A nervous woman in a brown polyester skirt and blazer answered the door. Her hair was mussed and her make up smeared. She only opened the door a crack, deciding if she would allow them into the house. After Marlee made a brief introduction and casually mentioned that Barry was with the police department, Nicole DeWitt invited them inside.

Her voice, which was quiet and timid at first, had now become loud and boisterous. "Please follow me into the kitchen," she yelled, walking through the house with heavy footsteps. "I can only talk for a few minutes because I have to get back to work."

"Where do you work?" Barry asked.

"Downtown at the First Bank of the Dakotas."

"And your husband? Where does he work?" Marlee inquired.

Nicole blanched at the question before regaining her composure. "He works at Thompson Manufacturing, but he's out of town today. He has a conference in Fargo and won't be home until tonight."

"Do you know where Tim is?" Barry asked.

"No, I don't. I wish he would contact us and let us know he's okay."

"What do you and Tim's father think happened to him?" Marlee asked.

"We've discussed it over and over, and we can't come to any reasonable conclusion. We're just so thankful he wasn't found in the house he rented. At least we think there's a strong chance he's still alive."

"Where do you think he might be?" Marlee asked.

"We don't see much of him, even though he lives here in town. Tim likes to keep his business private, so we really don't know his college friends," Nicole said.

"What about Elvis, who used to live across the street? Are they still friends?" Barry inquired.

"Sure, but nobody calls him that anymore. His name is Blake. He's one of Tim's roommates.

Here come the lies... one after another.

Chapter 16

"Looks like Mrs. DeWitt was entertaining a guest while her husband was out of town," Barry said as they got back into his car.

"What? How do you know that?" Marlee asked.

"I caught a glimpse of movement reflected in a mirror in the bedroom when we walked by. I guess she was having some afternoon delight."

"She did seem nervous when we were there. And she was a bit disheveled," Marlee observed recalling Nicole's mussed hair and make-up.

"Okay, you owe me some lunch. Where should we go?" Barry asked as he started the car.

"Before lunch, I think we should go across the street to Blake's parents' house to see what they know," Marlee said.

"Okay, but just so you know; I'm starving!" Barry said as they got out of the car and walked over to a white two-story house that looked much like the DeWitt home. It was obvious that someone was home because the curtain moved as they neared the house.

Thomas Rikers confirmed that Blake was his son and that he and the other roommates were staying at Blake's cousin's place north of town. He gave them directions to the rural home. "Sorry I can't invite you in. I'm battling some type of a stomach bug." His sunken eyes and pallor led credibility to his self-diagnosis.

A half-hour later, Barry and Marlee were seated at the end of a long table in the Student Union. Since she didn't want to waste what little cash she had on dining out, Marlee used her student meal card to buy them both the lunch special, which was spaghetti and meatballs.

"It's good, huh?" Marlee was slumped over her plate shoveling in pasta.

"It's alright," Barry said, as he poked through the entrée with a plastic fork.

"What's the matter? Is this not up to your standards?"

"I was really hungry earlier and now I don't feel that great. I need to go home," Barry said. Marlee finished her meal and took her Styrofoam cup of Diet Pepsi with her. He left everything behind, virtually untouched. Barry had to stop to throw up in the parking lot. He hadn't eaten much food, but several cans of Mountain Dew emptied from his stomach.

"It's a stomach bug that's going around. Jasmine and I already had it. It will only last a day or two, that's the good news. The bad news is that you'll probably throw up about ten more times, and you'll ache all over."

Barry handed Marlee the keys to his car as he crawled in the passenger seat and rested his feverish face against the cool glass window. On their way back to the dorm, Marlee got a great idea.

"How about if I drive you home to your place since you're sick," Marlee suggested.

"Then how will you get home?" Barry asked, always looking for the most practical answer.

"I could bring your car back to campus and then when you feel better, I'll bring it back to your house," Marlee said.

"And in the meantime, you'll drive all over asking questions about Tim's disappearance?" Barry was not as out of it as she thought.

"Well, I suppose I could do that. If it would be alright with you."

"Okay, just don't wreck it. My insurance rates will go through the roof," Barry muttered.

After delivering Barry to his home and getting him settled inside, Marlee drove north of town to talk with Blake, Adam, and John. Not only did she want to talk to them about Tim's possible whereabouts, but she had questions about the fire.

The rural ranch-style house sat upon an acreage complete with a garage, a small red barn, and a leaf-barren

142

orchard. The buildings were in good repair and had been recently painted. Marlee found herself making an introduction and going through her spiel for the umpteenth time in the past few days.

"Sure, the guys are staying here. We have plenty of room in the basement, and they moved in down there," said a man in his mid-twenties who introduced himself as Ben Rikers. "When my wife and I heard about the fire, we let Blake know he and his friends were welcome to stay here. It's not ideal, but they have some privacy in the basement. They're not here right now. John and Adam are in class, and Blake is at work at Shafer Printing."

"Will they be around this evening?" Marlee asked, knowing she needed to do as much sleuthing as she could manage while she had possession of Barry's car. He would likely be feeling better by tomorrow or the next day, and then she'd be at his mercy for transportation.

"Sure, stop back around 7:00 tonight. That way, if they're going out on the town you can catch them before they leave again," suggested Ben.

"Do you have any idea what happened to their fourth roommate, Tim? He's the guy that's been missing since the fire."

Ben scratched his two-day chin stubble. "No, I don't. I overheard the guys talking downstairs, and they think he might be in hiding."

"Why would Tim be hiding? And who's he hiding from?"

"Don't know. I didn't hear anything other than that. They stopped talking about it when they heard me coming downstairs. Guess you can ask them yourself when you come back."

Marlee reappeared at the acreage that night, and this time, she brought backup. Jasmine, dressed in a leopard mini-skirt, tall black boots, and a fluffy faux-fur jacket, had rehearsed all afternoon. The questions Marlee wanted her to ask the roommates were fresh in her mind, and she was prepared to get some answers.

It didn't take a genius to know that you get more accurate answers to questions when you talk to people individually rather that in a collective. In a group, there's usually one spokesperson, and the others throw in a detail here and there. Not much nuance is gathered from a group interview. When people are separated and talked with individually, a fuller picture develops. Sometimes, the accounts between parties are so different that it's easy to spot deception.

The three guys stopped talking when they saw Jasmine's long legs walking down the stairs. The basement went silent, as Jasmine, followed by Marlee, entered the open room of the basement. There would be no need for introductions or a long preamble, as none of the guys would hear a word Marlee had to say anyway.

Marlee pulled Adam aside and led him to the far side of the basement out of earshot from the others. "Can I talk to you? It's about Tim."

He looked disappointed to be pulled away from The Jasmine Show. "What's up?" Adam asked, fidgeting with the drawstring on his sweatshirt hood.

"What do you think happened to Tim?" Marlee asked.

"I told you that night that I didn't know, and I still don't," Adam said with an air of disdain. "Why are you still asking about this? The police are investigating it."

"Yeah, they are, but I can't help but think I should do what I can. Are you doing anything to help find out what happened?" Marlee asked pointedly.

"I'm not a cop. I'm leaving it to the professionals. If I hear anything, I'll tell them," Adam said.

"Do you think Tim is in hiding?" Marlee asked, remembering her conversation with Ben earlier that day.

"Hiding? Why would he be hiding?" Adam asked with a defensive air, still fidgeting with his sweatshirt drawstring.

"You tell me. I hear you guys think it might be

possible that he's hiding out somewhere."

"Where did you hear that?" Adam demanded.

"Never mind where I heard it. I just heard it. So why do you think he's hiding out?"

"I don't think Tim started the fire. At least not intentionally. But if it was an accident or if he burned down the house when he was delirious from his fall down the stairs, maybe Tim's afraid he'll go to jail," Adam said. "That's what other people said. I don't think Tim started the fire."

"Do you think Tim might be hiding out for other reasons?" Marlee inquired.

"I don't know what it would be," Adam replied.

"He seemed genuinely surprised when he overheard me tell you that Beth Van Dam was pregnant when she died. That's when he tripped and fell down the stairs. Maybe he knows something about her death that he didn't want to reveal. Or that he felt responsible for." Marlee let those thoughts hang in the air and waited for Adam's response.

Adam did not have a reaction. "Doubtful that Tim knew anything about Beth," he said, as he walked back toward the others. Laughter rose from the other end of the basement as Jasmine flirted with John and Blake. She was doing a great job keeping them occupied while Marlee talked to the guys one-on-one.

Jasmine knew her biggest task was before her now. She needed to keep Adam and Blake entertained so that Adam would not bring up the questions Marlee just asked him. Jasmine had to keep Adam from tainting Blake's response to the questions Marlee would be asking him in a few minutes.

"So, Adam, I was just asking the guys if they thought this skirt was too short to wear in the winter. What do you think," Jasmine asked, running her long slim fingers up the side of her boot and thigh. And the worry was over that either Adam or Blake would be discussing Tim for the next few minutes.

Marlee intercepted John a few minutes later when he exited the bathroom. "John, I'm trying to find out more about Tim and what happened to him. What's your theory?"

"I don't have a theory. I just know he's gone, and none of us have heard from him since the night of the fire. I went downtown that night and was pretty sloshed when I got home. I went to bed, and the next thing I know, Blake is yelling for all of us to get out the house because there's a fire," John recalled.

"So you guys think Tim might be hiding out somewhere, huh?" Marlee asked casually.

"Well, we talked about it, but I'm not positive that's what he's doing. I don't know why he would just take off unless he started the fire, but he's not the type of guy to do that," John reported.

"Why do you say that?"

"Tim's one of the nicest guys I've ever met. He would never burn down the house, especially knowing that people were inside."

"Let's just say for argument's sake that it was an accident, or he started the fire as a result of his head injury. Where would he hide out?" Marlee asked.

"He didn't really hang out with anybody other than us guys at the house. He's nice and friendly, but doesn't really have any friends other than us. Not that I know of, anyway," John reported.

"What about high school friends or relatives? Anybody like that he might be staying with?"

"I don't think so. He didn't get along that well with his family because they screwed him out of getting the family farm. And I think Blake is the only person from high school he still hung around. That's how we got Blake as a fourth roommate. Tim vouched for him. We were a little leery of letting him room with us since he's not in college and all, but it's worked out fine."

"Do you think one of the other roommates might know where Tim is?" Marlee asked.

"No, I don't think any of us have any idea what's going on," John replied.

"Is there anybody else who might know where Tim is?"

John shook his head. "Nobody knows where Tim is. I think he's alive, but I don't know why he hasn't contacted any of us."

"Who would want Tim gone or dead?"

"Nobody!" John said, a bit more defensively than was called for.

Marlee was out of questions, so she and John returned to the group where Jasmine was still working the crowd. "I'm thinking of getting my hair cut short," she said as she whipped her long locks over one shoulder.

"No," the men chorused, still mesmerized.

The whole questioning process was repeated with Blake when he went to get a beer. He didn't have any additional information to reveal and portrayed himself just as puzzled as his roommates by Tim's disappearance.

"You used to go by 'Elvis' when you were younger, huh?" Marlee asked, wondering how the nickname came to be.

Blake chuckled. "Yeah. That was a long time ago. I did an Elvis impersonation for a school talent show in fourth grade, and the name stuck. My brother, who was a junior in high school at the time, played guitar for me. Once I started high school, I started going by my real name again. It took Tim awhile to start calling me Blake instead of Elvis."

"You and Tim have been friends a long time. Who would Tim turn to if he was in trouble? If you guys weren't around?" Marlee asked.

"Maybe his grandpa?" Blake suggested. "That's about the only person in the family that he was on good terms with."

After a few questions, Marlee realized Blake was referring to Tim's grandpa, the partially-demented man she spoke with on the phone.

"I think he's in an old folk's home now," Blake continued. "Tim goes to visit him sometimes. I went with him once."

"Do you think Tim's still alive?" Marlee asked.

"I hope so. I really hope so."

On the way home, Marlee and Jasmine interrupted each other as they attempted to tell their stories. "I think the guys, at least some of them, know a lot more about Tim's disappearance than they're saying," Marlee reported.

"I think Adam is cute. We exchanged phone numbers." Jasmine became so caught up in her role of temptress that she began to fall for it herself.

"Focus, Jazz! We're trying to find Tim, not get you a date!" Marlee barked as she wheeled Barry's car into the parking lot nearest their dorm.

"I can do both."

"Did any of the guys say anything about Tim while I was talking to each one individually?" Marlee asked.

"Not really, but right after Adam came back he looked at Blake and John and shook his head like this," Jasmine said demonstrating a sinister side to side twist.

"What did you make of it?"

"It was like Adam was telling them not to say anything," Jasmine said. "But I don't know if he meant something specific or to just generally keep their mouths shut about everything."

"You know, maybe getting Adam's number wasn't such a bad thing after all. How do you feel about worming your way into his heart and finding out all you can about Tim?" Marlee asked.

Jasmine thought for a moment. "But what if I really like him, and then he finds out I've been using him to get information?"

"You'll have to use your acting skills you learned in Theater class last semester. Do whatever it takes to make sure he doesn't find out," Marlee said.

"You don't think Adam's dangerous, do you?"

Jasmine asked. "I want to find Tim, but I don't want to get hurt in the process."

Marlee shrugged. "I hope they didn't have anything to do with Tim's disappearance. My guess is that they know Tim's hiding out and are keeping his whereabouts secret. I just don't know why they don't want anyone to find him. Blake said Tim's still close with his grandpa, so I think I'll look him up tomorrow and see what he can tell me. He's senile, so who knows how much of what the grandpa has to say will be factual."

"You promise there won't be any danger in hanging out with Adam?" Jasmine asked.

"No, I can't promise that. For all we know, Adam and his roommates could have killed Tim and disposed of his body. But I think if you can get into their inner circle, we might learn more about Tim and what happened to him."

"It sounds like a terrible idea," Jasmine said. "I'll do it."

My friends were my family; the family I created. I don't have any use for most of my biological family. Some of them are trying to kill me.

Chapter 17

After a sleepless night, Marlee got out of bed and sat at her desk. Thoughts raced through her head as she tried to comprehend what happened to two of her friends in the past few days. Beth was dead and Tim was missing. Were the two situations linked or had they occurred independently of each other?

"What are you doing?" mumbled a sleepy Jasmine as she propped herself up on her elbow and peered down from the lofted bed.

"I'm documenting everything we know about Tim's disappearance and Beth's death." Marlee was hunched over her built-in desk writing in a blue notebook.

"But the police closed Beth's case. They ruled it an accidental death. Do you think there's more to it than that?" Jasmine asked as she climbed down from her bunk with ease.

"I don't have any new information, if that's what you mean. Since so much has happened in the past few days, I thought writing everything down about Beth and Tim would be a good idea. Maybe I'll see something from the written words that I'm not seeing now."

Jasmine looked skeptical. "Like a theme might emerge?"

Marlee stopped writing and looked at her roommate with a grin. "Yeah, that's exactly what I'm thinking. Something might pop out when it's in writing. We've talked to a lot of people, and I want to keep my memory fresh as to what each of them said."

Jasmine made toast for both of them while Marlee continued to write down facts and details from the interviews they conducted. Plus, she recorded everything Officer Barry Stevens told her about the case.

"Whoa, you know what I just realized?" Marlee asked munching on her fourth piece of generously-buttered toast. Jasmine just raised her eyebrows since her face was stuffed full.

"You're going to be a busy girl if you're dating both Doug from the police department and Adam from Stairway to Hell, er, what used to be Stairway to Hell."

"I thought of that in the night. I'm like a double agent trying to find out information from the police and from a witness at the same time. And neither one knows about the other guy." Jasmine seemed so proud of herself that Marlee didn't have the heart to tell her that's not really what a double agent does.

"You should keep notes too, just to make sure you don't mix up what they tell you," Marlee said. "Be sure to write it all down right away so you don't forget anything. But don't do it while you're in their presence."

"Duh! I'm not a total door knob. Did you think I'd take out a little notebook and start writing as they were talking to me?" Jasmine was peeved, but only a little.

"I know, I know. Just thinking out loud, I guess. Let's figure out what we know now about Beth and Tim. Just talking about each of their cases should help us process what happened."

Jasmine sighed. "Why are we still discussing Beth Van Dam? I don't mean to be heartless, but she drank too much at a party, fell down, and froze to death. And she happened to be pregnant and working as a prostitute. That's all. End of story."

"Yeah, you're right. It's time to let it go," Marlee said, even though she was thinking just the opposite. In Jasmine's mind, Beth's demise was unfortunate and sad, but it had been explained, and it was time to move on. Marlee still believed there was more to Beth's untimely death, but kept that thought to herself.

The two worked in tandem to recall the information they received from legitimate sources as well as what might be considered hearsay. After they had everything recorded in the notebook, Marlee said, "Okay, let's do a recap to make sure we haven't missed anything."

"Tim fell down the stairs on Monday night and hit

his head. He was unconscious for a minute or so but then came around. He didn't think he had a concussion and refused to go to the hospital. Adam called his mom, who works in a doctor's office. She said to wake Tim up every two hours, and Adam agreed to do it. It was about 11:00 pm when we left," Jasmine reported.

"Around 4:00 on Tuesday morning, we got a call from Officer Barry Stevens saying there was a fire at Stairway to Hell," Marlee continued. "He and Officer Doug picked us up, and we went there and saw the house had burned. Three of the roommates were outside, but Tim was nowhere to be found."

"Then we talked to Adam who said he woke Tim up at 1:00 and 3:00 am, and he seemed fine both times. He said Tim wasn't in his bedroom or anywhere upstairs or on the main floor when they ran out of the house. Adam also said he wasn't able to get downstairs to the basement to see if Tim had wandered down there."

"Tim's car was parked in the driveway, but his dog was missing. On Tuesday night, we found out Rufus had been found dead. Somebody broke his neck and left him in a ditch on the edge of town," Jasmine said.

"The police said they checked with the hospital and his family but no one had heard from Tim," Marlee continued. "Barry and I talked to his sister, Pam, who said Tim wasn't very close to the family any more since she took over the family farm. Tim wanted the farm and held it against the family when they decided he was too young to take over and turned it over to Pam. She thought he still might hang out with Elvis from high school, who now goes by his real name; Blake Rikers. Then I went to talk with his parents, and his mother, who is having an affair, didn't have any information about Tim's whereabouts either. Tim's high school friend's father lives across the street so we walked over, and he confirmed that Tim and his son are roommates. Then Mr. Rikers told us the roommates from Stairway to Hell were all staying at Blake's cousin's place outside of town. I went to the cousin's place, and he said to come back later when the guys were home from work and classes. He also said he overheard them say they thought Tim was hiding out somewhere."

"That's where I come in," Jasmine said, rubbing her hands together in anticipation of telling her part of the story. "We went to the place the roommates were staying, and I diverted their attention while you asked them questions one by one. I wore my slinky, leopard skirt and black boots with..."

"Your wardrobe is not pertinent to the story," Marlee interrupted. "When I talked to Adam, he said he'd heard from someone that Tim might be hiding out, but he didn't know or wouldn't say anything else about it. He didn't think Tim's fall down the stairs had anything to do with him hearing that Beth was pregnant. Adam also said Tim might have started the fire accidentally, and he's in hiding because he's scared of going to jail. Now, John said he was drunk when he got home that night and didn't see Tim at all. And then I talked to Blake, and he said Tim's grandpa was the only person in the family he had regular contact with any more. I talked to him on the phone. His name is Edgar, and he lives in an old folk's home because he's senile. None of the roommates gave me any other theories on what started the fire or where Tim could be."

Jasmine sniffed, still perturbed about what Marlee said about her wardrobe when they went to visit the displaced roommates from Stairway to Hell. "And we still don't know what or who started the fire. Luckily, Tim's body wasn't found in the house, so we know he was alive when he left."

"But we don't know where he is now. That's the mystery," Marlee said.

"So, where do we go from here?" Jasmine asked.

"I want to talk to Grandpa Edgar. He's senile, according to Tim's sister, but I'd like to see if he has theories. Maybe he'll be coherent when I talk to him and maybe he won't, but I need to at least try," Marlee said.

They both jumped as the phone rang. "You answer

it," Marlee directed Jasmine. "And if it's Barry or Doug, tell them I'm in classes, and you don't know when I'll be back."

Jasmine answered the phone and it was, in fact, Barry. He was feeling better and wanted Marlee to drive over and return his car. With some hesitation, Jasmine relayed the information Marlee told her.

"Barry wants you to call him the minute you get home. He's feeling better and wants his car back. He wanted to know where you parked, and I told him I didn't know. I think he was going to get somebody to bring him over and pick up his car if you weren't around," Jasmine reported.

Marlee slid the notebook under her mattress just in case someone walked in and started snooping around while they were gone. "He must have an extra set of keys. I better get out of here with his car before he starts scouring the parking lots. I really like having my own wheels."

"It sure beats walking everywhere," Jasmine agreed.

Marlee found Grandpa Edgar in the second nursing home she looked. Golden Arms was a single-level facility built in the shape of an L. If she didn't know better, Marlee would have thought it was a motel. She parked the car, and feigning confidence she didn't possess, she marched up to the front desk. Introducing herself to desk staff as his granddaughter, Marlee was shown to Edgar's room.

"Edgar, it's your granddaughter, Marlee," said the orderly in a soothing tone. He sat in a padded easy chair facing the television, his twin bed in the corner of the room.

"I don't have a granddaughter by that name," Edgar said. Marlee felt bad for what she was doing, but thought it was necessary.

"Oh, Grandpa. You remember me, don't you?" And

then in a whisper to the orderly, "He must be having a bad day. I'll just sit with him for a while."

The orderly nodded with a knowing look and left the room. As soon as she left, Marlee wasted no time. She pulled up a hard-backed chair so she could face Edgar. She kept her explanation simple, not knowing if Edgar would understand who she was and what she was doing.

"Tim? Yeah, he was here a couple days ago," Edgar said as he sipped from a cup of coffee resting on an end table. "Why?"

"Did he say anything about a fire? About his rental house burning down?" Marlee questioned.

"Nooooo, I think I would have remembered that," Edgar said with some hesitance. "What happened to his house?"

Marlee ignored the question, knowing she had limited time before Edgar faded or the staff discovered she was not a relative. "Did Tim say where he was going or where he had been staying?"

"Nooooo, he really didn't say."

"What did the two of you talk about?" Marlee asked.

"The weather and how we're both ready for spring. And how the days are getting longer and there's more sunlight. And he asked about the key to the old shed," Edgar said.

"What old shed?"

"The old shed on the edge of the farm. I always kept it locked after the accident."

"What accident? What happened?" Marlee asked, but it was too late. Edgar began to fade.

"Accidents can happen anywhere. The lady across the hall had an accident at supper," Edgar said, his eyes wandering.

"What about Tim? Did you give him the key?"

"What key?" And Edgar was gone. No telling when he would return. For now, Marlee had to make do with what little the old man shared with her. Whether or not it was factual was up for debate. And even if what Edgar said was true, he may have confused Tim with someone else or the locked shed could have been torn down twenty years ago.

"Thank you, Edgar," Marlee said as she left the room. He was back to gazing at the television although it was doubtful he could recall what he saw five seconds ago.

Driving out to the farm, Marlee decided she needed to ask Pam a few more questions. Specifically, she wanted to know if there was a locked shed, and if they could go look in it. It was possible Edgar's account had been true and rational, but it could just as easily be false.

When Marlee arrived at the farm, there was no one in sight. She pounded on the door, but no one answered. She even went back to the car and honked the horn, thinking Pam might be taking a mid-morning nap or in the back part of the barn. Still no answer. She decided to look around the outbuildings to see if there really was a shed.

The barn was larger than the house and was flanked by two smaller buildings. One building housed a John Deere tractor while the other smaller structure held gardening tools, a lawn mower, two bicycles, and other items. Both were unlocked, and neither looked as though they held a clue to Tim's whereabouts.

She pulled her crocheted scarf tighter around her neck to keep out the brisk, icy breeze. Marlee took off at a steady pace, hoping to find the locked shed soon. She walked and walked, keeping the fence around the front of the property within her eyesight. Finally, she had to turn and walk behind the tree belt. That's when she saw it. A rickety old building set far enough beyond the house that no one would know it was there unless they went looking.

Marlee approached the structure, careful not to make noise as she walked in the snow. If Tim was inside, she didn't want to give him advance notice of her arrival. As she neared the side of the shed, a strip of a tattered curtain blew out of the broken window and glass crunched beneath her feet.

As a kid, I found peace and comfort at the farm. Spring was a particularly fun time there with planting crops and the birth of baby pigs. Those memories will always hold a special place in my heart. I'd hoped those fun times would continue, but I was wrong.

Chapter 18

The shed was more of a shack, barren of paint and with a broken window. Why it was kept locked was a mystery, since it didn't appear to be of any value. She crept closer, trying not to be creeped out by the howling wind and the eeriness of the setting. The door was ajar, giving doubt to Grandpa Edgar's assertion that the shed was locked. More of his demented thinking, Marlee guessed.

She pushed open the door and gasped. Tim was on the floor, and he was a bluish color. Marlee raced to him and felt for a pulse. He was ice cold to the touch. Even though she knew he was dead, she ran as fast as she could back to Pam's house. Again, she knocked and knocked, but there was still no answer. She hopped in Barry's car and sped down the road to the nearest neighbor. Through tears and babbling, Marlee was able to communicate that an ambulance and the police were needed at Pam's farm.

After the neighbors placed the calls to the officials, Marlee called Barry. "You need to get to Pam DeWitt's farm right away. Tim's dead. I found him in a shed on the edge of the property!"

Against the protests of the neighbors, Marlee went back to Pam's farm alone. She wanted to be there when the police and the ambulance arrived so she could take them directly to Tim. Nothing could be done to bring the student back to life, but she wanted to honor him by being there when the authorities arrived.

Sirens were heard in the distance within minutes, and then they rolled into the farm yard. Marlee directed them to follow her to the shed. In rambling and sometimes incoherent sentences, she told the police officers what little she knew of Tim's demise. Once they arrived at the shed, she was not allowed to go within several feet of the structure since the cops were roping off the surrounding area to secure the crime scene.

Marlee felt shock when she learned of Beth Van

Dam's death. She also experienced shock when she learned about Beth's life as a prostitute. But nothing prepared her for the feelings that overcame her after she found Tim's lifeless body. She began shaking uncontrollably, and the ambulance attendants placed her in the back of their vehicle. Marlee knew what she saw and was clear on why she had come to the farm, but none of that could be communicated through words.

"Give her time. She's in shock," an EMT said to Barry as he opened the door to the ambulance and climbed in beside her. He placed his arms around her in a big bear hug, not asking any questions at this point.

When she was able to talk again, Marlee spit out bits and pieces of the story. Barry listened quietly, letting her tell her story in her own way. Since he was not on duty until that evening, he could take on the role of friend rather than investigator. Soon, a responding officer approached Marlee and asked if she was able to answer some questions.

They sat in the front seat of the patrol car while Officer Dawn Frentz asked questions. The car held a faint smell of cigarette smoke and vomit from previous drunks, criminals, and suspects. The distinct smells made Marlee want to puke, but she did her best to hold up. She told everything about talking to Grandpa Edgar at the Golden Arms Home that morning and then coming to Pam's farm to look for the shed.

"When I touched him, he was cold," Marlee said, her voice barely audible as she thought how helpless her friend looked as he lay on the floor of the shed. "I knew he was dead before I pushed up his coat sleeve and felt for a pulse. His face was an odd color. A weird shade of light blue. And he was in a position that I've never seen anyone in before. His leg was twisted behind him and his neck was angled in a strange way." She realized as she relayed the information that she had stopped using Tim's name and just referred to him as "he".

"Do you know where his sister, Pam is?" asked

162

Officer Frentz as she jotted down notes in her notepad.

"I knocked when I first got here and then again after I found the body. Tim's body. There wasn't any answer, and I didn't see any sign of Pam," Marlee said, consciously using his name now.

After a few more questions, Officer Frentz ended the interview. "Do you know how he died?" Marlee asked. She went on to tell the officer about Tim's fall down the stairs on Monday night, even though she was sure all law enforcement personnel in the area already knew the details leading up to Tim's disappearance.

"We won't know until the coroner makes a ruling. There may be an autopsy to determine what happened. We won't know for a while," the officer replied.

In her mind, Marlee replayed what she saw when she walked in the shed door which was ajar. She didn't see any blood and did not notice any gunshot or stab wounds. Tim was clad in his heavy winter coat, sweatpants, and tennis shoes. The hood to his coat was pulled up over his head, obscuring much of his face and neck. There were no signs of bruises on what little of his face was exposed.

Could it be another case of a college student freezing to death? Beth had frozen after she had too much to drink and then fell down as she walked home from a party. At least that was the conclusion of the coroner and the cops. Tim may very well have perished after wandering out into the cold due to his head injury.

After the police allowed Marlee to leave, Barry drove her to Fryin' Pan for a meal and a chance to talk. She held her head in her hands, not believing the events of that morning. "I knew Tim would be found, but I thought he'd be alive. And I never thought I'd be the one to find him."

"So Tim's grandpa tipped you off about the shed and that Tim had asked for the key recently?" Barry asked, even though Marlee had already briefed him on her conversation with Grandpa Edgar. She realized Barry was checking to see how reliable of a witness she really was.

"Yes, he said Tim asked for the key to the shed.

163

Edgar said he kept it locked since the accident but when I questioned him, he began to fade. I asked when he had the conversation with Tim and a few other questions, but Edgar was completely out of it. I wasn't even sure that there was a shed on the farm, but thought it was at least worth checking out," Marlee said as she sipped her hot tea.

"Why would Tim want to get inside a locked shed? It looked like it should have been torn down years ago."

"I thought the shed was in poor shape too. And why would he need a key to get in if the windows were broken? What could have been in the shed that he was looking for? Or was it merely a place to hide out?" Marlee wondered. She thought back to the shed, trying to recall what was inside. Try as she might, Marlee could not recall anything other than Tim's body lying on the floor.

"I'll go in to work early and see what I can find out about any accidents that may have happened at the shed," Barry said. "Of course, it could just be the rambling of an old man."

"Seems like more than coincidence that Grandpa Edgar told me about the shed and then that's where Tim was found. At least some of Edgar's story is on-target. We just don't know how much of it. When we were at the shed, did any of the cops on duty tell you anything?"

"Nothing other than what you've told me. It didn't appear to be a death from a beating or a shooting. Not much could be determined, and I suspect we won't know until after the autopsy," Barry said. "Did you see anything that would suggest the cause of Tim's death?"

"No, I didn't. And another thing that's really bothering me is that his dog was found dead outside of town. Did someone take Tim and his dog from Stairway to Hell and then kill Rufus and bring Tim out here?"

"Or maybe Tim just wandered out here, still delirious from his fall down the stairs. That could happen. I've heard of people doing strange things when they've suffered a head injury," Barry reported.

Barry dropped Marlee off at her dorm and went

home to catch a few hours of sleep before he reported for work. She had the unenviable task of breaking the bad news to Jasmine.

"Tim's dead?" Jasmine's jaw dropped and the tears began to roll. "How do you know? What happened?" She sank onto her desk chair to steady herself as her legs began to wobble.

Marlee relayed the story of finding Tim's body, her interview with the police, and her talk with Barry. She felt her own legs begin to go weak and slumped in her chair. The roommates faced each other, both without words to describe their feelings. This was the second death of a friend within the past week. Nothing in the college brochure could ever prepare them for the tragedy that befell two of their college friends.

Once again, Marlee and Jasmine turned to the notebook to record the new information about Tim. The notebook was becoming not only a source of factual information, but a catharsis in dealing with the trauma of two deaths. After discussing and then writing down everything they could think of pertaining to the events of that day, Marlee closed the notebook with a thud.

"I wonder if the cops will come to the same conclusion with Tim as they did with Beth." Marlee said.

"What was your gut feeling when you saw Tim?" Jasmine asked. "Did it look like foul play or another case of exposure to the elements?"

"There were no obvious wounds, but that doesn't automatically make it an accidental death. Any number of things could have happened," Marlee replied. "His leg was twisted and his neck was at an odd angle."

"Was there anything to indicate that Tim took his own life?" Jasmine asked.

"No! I mean, I don't think so. Why would Tim commit suicide?"

"I don't think he would, but if he was out of his mind from head trauma, who knows what he might have done. And if Tim started the fire, he might have felt so

165

guilty about it that he killed himself," Jasmine added.

"Arson is a serious felony, but no one was killed. Even if he set the fire on purpose, I think Tim would be given some consideration for his head injury. Barry said he's heard about people doing all kinds of weird things after they hit their head. The cops and courts would have to cut Tim some slack if he set the fire. There's a difference between knowingly and intentionally starting a fire versus setting a fire when you're not in your right mind," Marlee said, ticking off the reasons in support of Tim's innocence.

"Yeah, I suppose. But maybe he heard about the fire and remembered he set it. And then he didn't know if everyone got out or not. Tim might have thought he killed his roommates. He's such a kind-hearted guy that I don't think he could stand knowing he killed someone."

"True, we don't know what Tim knew about the fire. Maybe he didn't know anything. It could have happened after he left the house," Marlee said. "Until the fire investigators determine the cause of the fire, we won't know whether it was intentional or accidental. And even then, we may not know the actual cause."

"Of all places, why would Tim go to that old shed?" Jasmine mused.

"I wondered the same thing. It didn't appear to have heat or electricity. The window was broken out, so there wasn't much difference between the temperature inside the shed and outside. The roof and walls blocked some of the wind, but not much," Marlee said.

"I wonder if his sister would have let him hide out at the farm house if he asked. Even if there was some bad blood between them," Jasmine said.

"The riff seemed to be one-sided, according to Pam. Tim was mad at her and their parents over Pam taking over the farm. It didn't seem like any of them were holding a grudge against Tim. In fact, Pam said she offered to turn the farm over to Tim after he graduated from college."

"So he could have stayed with Pam or the

166

parents?"

"I think so. The only thing holding him back was his ego. He made it clear that if he couldn't have the farm then he didn't want much to do with the rest of the family. Grandpa Edgar was the only one he associated with very much," Marlee said. "I get the feeling that Tim felt he and his grandpa were both forced into things they didn't want to do. Tim was forced to go to college, and Grandpa Edgar was taken off the farm and put into an old folk's home."

Barry called while Marlee and Jasmine were trying to make sense of Tim's death and his life. There was no verification yet, but the dispatcher at the police department remembered something about a child falling off a ladder and dying about ten years ago. "I'll do some digging to see what I can find out," Barry said.

"I'm going to the library. They have old newspapers on micro fiche, and I bet I can track down the accident Barry talked about." Marlee grabbed her coat and was out the door. The library was a quick ten-minute walk from her dorm, and she made it in record time. The wind had let up and, the temperature seemed a few degrees warmer than it had in the past week.

Once in the campus library, Marlee sought out a staff member from the archives. Her name tag revealed that her name was Blanche. She was in her fifties and wore her gray hair in an unflattering Pilgrim cut. Blanche showed Marlee to the micro fiche readers and gave her a refresher course on how to use the machine.

Before Blanche could leave the room, Marlee asked, "How long have you lived here in town?"

"I lived here all my life except for the two years I was in the Peace Corps in the '50s," Blanche said.

"The Peace Corps? That's really cool. One of my professors told me about her experiences in the Peace Corps. She said it changed her life. The reason I asked you about living here is, I wanted to talk to someone who might remember an accident at the DeWitt farm outside of town. There was an accident, maybe about ten years

167

ago, in an old shed on the edge of the property and someone may have died," Marlee said.

"The DeWitt farm?" Blanche asked. "Yes, I remember it well. It happened in 1977. That's the same year I got married, so that's why I remember the time frame so well. Billy DeWitt died, but it was no accident."

Everybody wants to hear family secrets. Especially when it's about someone else's family.

Chapter 19

Blanche was not used to someone hanging on her every word, so she took her time telling the story. Working in the archives section of the library was a thankless job, but appealed to her introverted nature. Since her husband's death, she had no one to talk to at home and very little human connection at work. It wasn't until Marlee asked Blanche about the incident at the DeWitt farm that she realized just how much she missed interacting with people.

"It was at Easter," Blanche said, now sitting at the table next to Marlee. "We had a lot of snow that winter, so everyone was in high spirits about the nice spring weather. Edgar and Ethel were still running the farm and were in good health. It was a Sunday, and they had their two adult kids out for lunch. Both of the kids were married and had kids of their own. Pam and Tim are Bernie and Nicole's children, and Billy belonged to Art and Lola."

"So how do you know it wasn't an accident?" Marlee asked, trying to get to the heart of the story.

Blanche would not be rushed. She continued her telling of the story as if Marlee had not just interrupted. "After lunch, the kids were outside playing. Edgar always told them to stay in the yard where the adults could see them. They were not supposed to play in the buildings because of all the machinery and dangerous tools. Edgar was afraid they might get hurt and only allowed them to go in the barn and the other buildings when he or another adult were there."

"So they went into the shed?" Marlee would not give up. The suspense was killing her.

"From what I heard, the kids played Frisbee in the yard until they got bored. Then, as kids will do, they decided to do something they shouldn't. They went into the barn and messed around with the tools and machinery. To their surprise, none of the adults even noticed. That's when Pam had the idea to go to the shed on the other side of the tree belt. She was the oldest of the grandkids, so she was the boss. They let themselves in to the unlocked shed and explored. The shed is small, but it held a lot of junk. Things that would appeal to kids. Stuff like old trunks with clothes from early 1900s, boxes of letters, and albums of family photos. It would be like opening a time capsule. There was a ladder in the shed, and Pam dared Billy to climb to the very top of it and touch the ceiling. He got to the top and Pam shook the ladder. Billy fell off, broke his neck, and died."

"Pam intentionally killed her cousin?" Marlee was incredulous. "Did she go to juvenile detention?"

"No, she insisted it was an accident. She said Billy climbed up to the top of the ladder even though she told him not to. Then he lost his balance and fell. Tim tried to tell the adults that Pam caused Billy's fall, but they didn't believe him since he was quite a few years younger than his sister. They thought he either made it up or just didn't understand what had happened. It was ruled an accident, and to this day, Tim is the only one in the family who believes Pam killed their cousin," Blanche reported.

"How do you know all of this?" Marlee asked, wondering if Blanche was just a lonely old lady who enjoyed spinning a tale for anyone who would listen.

"Because Billy's parents got divorced shortly after he died. Billy's dad, Art, and I were married at the end of that year," Blanche said.

"But why do you think Pam killed Billy? You said nobody believed Tim."

"Tim's parents and grandparents didn't believe him, but Art did. Art told me he believed Pam got away with murder," Blanche said.

"But they were all just kids. Why would Pam kill her cousin?" Marlee asked, seriously starting to believe this woman was out of her head.

"Because it was well-known among the family that the farm would go to Billy. Pam was the oldest, but Billy was the oldest boy. Edgar was old-fashioned and thought the land should only be passed on to the boys. Pam wanted to make sure Billy wouldn't get the farm, so she killed him."

"What about Tim? Wouldn't the land have been passed down to him since he was a boy?" Marlee questioned.

"Ordinarily, it would, but he was a lot younger than Pam and Billy, and the farm needed taken over while Tim was still in high school. Plus, Pam made sure everyone saw Tim as unstable. She set him up time and time again to look bad in front of his parents and grandparents. They loved him, but didn't think he would be able to manage a farm."

"Why didn't Tim's dad or Billy's dad take over the family farm?" Marlee asked.

"Tim's dad didn't have any interest in farming or country life. He wanted to work in an office where he wouldn't get dirty. Art suffered from severe asthma and allergies, so he couldn't be outside for extended periods of time. The grandkids were slated to take over, and it was known that Billy would be the recipient of the farm since he was the eldest boy. That's just how a lot of traditional families do things," Blanche stated.

"Pam was jealous and wanted the farm for herself," Marlee added.

"Yes. She always loved the farm, and it's really a shame that she wasn't even considered a viable candidate to take it over until Billy died and Tim was thought to be incompetent," Blanche said.

"So Billy's father believed Tim. Did he try to talk to Tim's parents and the grandparents about what he thought really happened?" Marlee asked.

"Yes, he did, but none of them believed him. It was a huge blow-up in the family, and Art was basically shunned."

"Did he think Pam really wanted to kill Billy or that she just did a reckless thing that resulted in Billy's death?

173

I mean, kids do dangerous and stupid things all the time. Sometimes somebody gets hurt. That doesn't mean they intended to kill," Marlee said.

"Oh, no. Pam intended to kill Billy. Tim told Art that she tried to shoot Billy with a bow and arrow in the barn that day but missed him by an inch. On another occasion, she tried to push him into the artesian well." Blanche was adamant in her claims.

"Blanche, I need to tell you something, and you have to promise not to tell anyone about it until the information is released in the news," Marlee whispered, looking around to make sure no one was standing behind them. Blanche nodded, not breaking eye contact.

"I'm sure you know that Tim is missing. His house burned down and everyone has been looking for him," Marlee said, not relishing what she was about to disclose to Blanche.

"Yes, it's been all over the news."

"Tim was found dead this morning. At the old shed on the edge of the DeWitt farm," Marlee reported.

Blanche gasped, one hand covering her mouth and the other hand clutching her chest. "What happened?"

"The police don't know yet. I went out to the farm after someone mentioned the old shed to me. I walked around to the building and found Tim lying there on the floor. I felt for a pulse, and he was ice cold. So I went to the neighbor's farm, and they called for an ambulance and the cops." Marlee said.

"Why didn't you have Pam call from the farm house? It would have been much quicker," Blanche said. The look in her eye suggested she already knew what Marlee was going to say.

"I knocked several times, and no one came to the door. I even honked the horn in case Pam was sick or taking a nap. The house was locked, so I drove to the neighboring farm," Marlee said.

"Well, that tells you everything you need to know," Blanche said, her face taking on a hard look.

174

"What do you mean, Blanche?" Marlee asked.

"Pam killed her brother so he wouldn't be able to take over the farm," Blanche said as matter-of-factly as if she had just recited a recipe for peach cobbler.

Marlee sighed, not trying very hard to hide her disbelief. "Oh, come on, Blanche. Do you really believe that? Pam already had control of the farm, and it didn't seem to me like anyone was trying to take that away from her. Plus, you said it yourself that Tim's family didn't think he was competent enough to run the farm. What motive would she have for killing him? She already had the farm."

"You don't know just how devious Pam is. I dealt with her for a few years while Art and I were married. She comes across as a nice, hard-working person, but I assure you Pam is as cold-blooded as they come." Blanche was now on her feet and speaking in a loud tone. "There's no way Pam isn't involved in this. She might have everyone else bamboozled, but I won't be fooled!" With that declaration, Blanche marched out of the room and slammed the door behind her.

For a full minute, Marlee sat in her chair with her mouth open, not fully believing what just happened. Blanche seemed so convinced that Pam was capable of murder in order to keep control of the family farm. Was it possible that the calm, unassuming farmer killed both her cousin and her brother to gain and keep control of the farm?

She continued to scan through micro fiche, now focusing on April of 1977. The newspaper printed scant information on William (Billy) DeWitt's death other than an obituary identifying an accident leading to his demise. There was no mention of an investigation or any suspicion about cause of death. *An obituary? That's it?* Marlee thought. *Maybe Blanche is batshit crazy and came up with this theory on her own. Maybe she was never even married to Billy's father.*

Marlee scrolled through more micro fiche looking for applications for marriage licenses from late 1977.

Blanche was true to her word, on the marriage anyway. A little more digging found a small wedding announcement for Art and Blanche. Marlee then dug into divorce records from earlier that year and found that Art and his first wife indeed divorced soon after Billy's death. A wave of sadness came over Marlee as she thought about the unhappiness the DeWitt family suffered with Billy's death and the dissolution of their marriage. At least Art had somewhat of a happy ending in that he married Blanche.

I wonder what happened to Billy's mom, Marlee thought as she continued to scroll through newspaper articles. *Did she stay in town or move away? Was she even still alive? Did she believe Billy's death was an accident?* Marlee jotted down her thoughts as fast as they raced through her mind. She needed to find out more about Billy's death and what had become of his mother. Luckily, Marlee had a good source of information working at the police department.

Marlee went to the bank of pay phones in the library lobby and called Barry at his home. A drowsy-sounding roommate answered and said Barry was sleeping until he went on the night shift and was not to be disturbed.

"It's an emergency!" Marlee insisted.

A scuffle ensued as the phone receiver was put down and Barry was summoned to the phone. "It's your girlfriend," said the man who answered the phone.

"What do you want now?" Barry growled, knowing it was Marlee.

"I need two things. First, can you give me a ride out to Pam DeWitt's farm? I want to see if she's home now, and I want to talk to her. The second thing is, can you track down Lola DeWitt? She's the mother of the kid that died in the accident in the shed back in 1977." Marlee then went on to detail her conversation with Blanche at the library and what she confirmed herself through the old newspaper articles.

"Really? I never heard anything about a young girl

killing her cousin. There are a lot of stories floating around down at the cop shop about mysterious deaths, but this never came across my radar. I'm headed to work in a couple hours. How about if I pick you up on my way to work and you can borrow my car?" Barry asked.

"Barry, you're the best!" Marlee said, and she meant it. Just not in a lovey-dovey kind of way. She pranced back to her dorm room, excited with all the new information she learned and anxious to report to Jasmine.

As Marlee burst through the door, ready to report her findings, the phone rang. Jasmine answered and after a brief conversation said, "I have a date tonight. Adam's picking me up, and we're going out to eat."

"Are you afraid to go out with him? On your own, I mean?" Marlee asked, realizing she pushed her roommate into spending time with Adam, who may or may not be dangerous.

Jasmine didn't answer immediately, but her discomfort was visible. She shuffled her feet and wrung her hands. "No, I'll be okay."

"I'll have Barry's car tonight. How about if I follow you to make sure you're not in danger?" Marlee asked.

The smile on Jasmine's face said it all. "Yeah, that's a good idea. I'm sure he's harmless, but I'd feel a little better if someone knew where I was with him. He might suggest we go out to the bar afterward or back to the place where he's staying. I'd feel a lot safer knowing someone was keeping an eye on us."

With their plan firmly in place, Marlee and Jasmine settled in for a quick nap before the evening events began. Jasmine crawled up to her lofted bed while Marlee pulled a blanket over her as she loafed in her reclining lawn chair. A pounding on the door woke them a short time later.

"Barry, what are you doing here? I thought you said you'd come by in two hours?" Marlee asked rubbing her eyes.

"It's been two hours since I talked to you. Come on,

I need to get to work," Barry said impatiently.

Jasmine was scrambling out of bed. She needed to get ready for her date in a hurry and didn't have time to waste making small talk with Barry.

"I'll be right back, okay? Don't leave until I get back," Marlee directed as she left the dorm room.

Marlee and Barry talked over each other in the short time it took them to drive to the police station. "What kind of read did you get on Pam? Does she seem like someone who would kill to keep control of the family farm?"

"She seemed really laid back and a salt-of-the-earth type to me, but you can never tell. We had a kindly grandma smother her husband of over fifty years in his recliner right after I started here."

"Did you hear anything about Tim's cause of death? Any theories floating around even though the autopsy isn't done yet?" Marlee asked.

"Just the most obvious one which is that Tim wasn't in his right mind after hitting his head and he wandered out to the farm and froze to death. Other than that, I haven't heard any other ideas, but I was only at the station for a little bit after I dropped you off," Barry reported. "It will be the only topic everyone's talking about tonight, and there may even be new developments."

"Will you call me right away if you find out anything?" Marlee asked.

"Will you be home? I thought you needed my wheels to go out investigating again," Barry said with a laugh.

"Well, I won't be out all night. I should be back by midnight or 1:00 for sure. Just call anytime if you find out something," Marlee directed. She hadn't had a decent night's sleep in several days and doubted that Barry had slept well either, since she kept calling and waking him.

Marlee put the pedal to the metal as she gunned Barry's car back to the dorm. She jogged in from the parking lot, which she never did, and burst into the room.

178

No one was there. She checked the communal bathroom and called out for her roommate.

It wasn't intentional, but Marlee failed to keep her promise to her roommate. Jasmine had left on her date with the sketchy Adam, and Marlee had no idea where they went.

My roommates were all quite the ladies' men. Each weekend meant different girlfriends in the house. After a month, I stopped asking their names. No point getting to know someone if you'll never see them again.

Chapter 20

"Hello, I need to speak with Officer Barry Stevens. It's an emergency!" Marlee screeched, pacing as far as the spiral cord to the wall phone would allow.

"You're turning into the little girl who cried wolf," Barry grumbled. "Not everything that pops into your mind is an emergency."

Marlee detailed the plan she and Jasmine cooked up to get closer to the guys from Stairway to Hell. "We were trying to find out what they knew about Tim. Now that Tim's dead, I'm worried that one of his roommates might know something about it. Jazz left on a date with Adam before I could get back here to follow them. We both think Adam is kind of creepy, and she didn't want to be alone with him. I need your help!"

"I'll do some checking and call you right back," Barry assured her.

Her nerves were on edge as she paced around the small dorm room. If Jasmine got hurt carrying out their plan to find out more about Tim's disappearance, she would never forgive herself. It had, after all, been her idea, and Jasmine just went along with it to help.

Marlee's heart jumped into her throat when the telephone rang. Barry, true to his word, did some record checking.

"It's not good," he reported with a solemn tone. "Adam has a pending charge against him for attempted rape in Brown County."

"What?" Marlee shrieked. "We have to find them. Jasmine's sassy, but she's not very big. I don't think she could defend herself very well against Adam. Please help me find them!"

"Already on it. I ran Adam's name to get the make and model of the car registered to him and the license plate number. We should have him located within the hour. Since you said Jasmine thought they were going out to eat, officers are checking all the parking lots for the restaurants and fast food joints in town."

"Can you have someone go out to the house where Adam and his roommates are staying now? He might have taken her back there, especially if the other roommates aren't around." Marlee was beside herself with worry about her friend.

Barry tried to calm Marlee, but he was just as concerned as she was about Jasmine and Adam's date. He rattled off the description and tag number of Adam's car, and Marlee jotted it down on a greasy napkin left over from a McDonald's bag.

"I'll call in every so often," she promised before hanging up. Marlee ran out the door and got into Barry's car and tore off to find her friend. She cruised around the downtown area, thinking they went straight to a bar for something to eat. Then she cruised the campus parking lots, knowing that there was little chance Adam would chose a campus activity for a first date.

Marlee sped down the main highway leading through town. She was deep in thought and didn't see the flashing lights behind her until the police car sounded its siren. "Dammit!" *Of all times to get busted for speeding,* Marlee thought. She briefly considered outrunning the cops and then turning herself in later after Jasmine was safe and sound. Sensibility prevailed, and she pulled to the side of the road.

A self-assured officer in his early forties strode up the passenger side of the car and motioned for her to roll down the window. Marlee complied and produced her driver's license when asked.

"Step out of the car, Miss and have a seat in the patrol car," the officer stated as he held on to her driver's license.

"I know I might have been going just a smidge over the speed limit, but I have a good reason. My friend..." She was cut off by the officer giving her a stern look and raising his hand to silence her. It was clear she would not be getting any breaks from this hard-ass cop.

Marlee slid into the passenger seat of the cop car and marveled at all the devices, radios, and other crime-fighting tools. The officer picked up the radio receiver and rattled off some jargon. Then he handed the receiver to her. "Just push this button in when you talk," he said.

With a confused look, Marlee did as directed. "Hello?"

"It's Officer Stevens," said Barry with an air of cockiness. "We've located your roommate and her date."

"Is she alright?" Marlee asked. Her heart was beating like a drum, and she held her breath as she waited for the answer.

"Jasmine is fine. They're at Bubba's Pizza eating supper. His red Buick Skylark is in the short-term parking lot near a light pole," Barry reported.

"Thanks, Barry! Uh, I mean Officer Stevens," Marlee said, a wide grin spreading across her face, relieved that her roommate wasn't being attacked and butchered out in an abandoned house. "I'll keep watch on them for the rest of the night."

"Fine. Check in later," Barry said.

"You're free to go," the cop said with a slight smile playing at the corner of his mouth. "I heard you were a firecracker. Barry needs somebody like you."

"No, we're just friends. We have a class together," Marlee mumbled realizing that all of Barry's coworkers at the police station must think they were an item. That was her original intent when she kissed Barry in front of his cop classmate, but now this rumor was taking on a life of its own.

"Uh huh," said the officer. "Have a nice night. If you need anything, just call us."

Marlee got back in her car and drove to the short-term parking lot to keep tabs on Adam's car. She parked a row over and a few cars away so she could see if Jasmine and her date returned to the vehicle. Wherever they went after their meal, Marlee was sure to follow.

The wind had picked up, making it cold sitting in the car. She started the vehicle and turned the heater on full blast for a few minutes, then repeated the process every so often. Marlee wanted to keep warm, but if she became too warm, she might fall asleep, given her lack of sleep the past several days.

Making mental notes became a way to keep alert. She thought about all the things she would add to the notebook when she returned to the dorm. Additional entries would include Jasmine's date with Adam, her disappearance, and the cops tracking them down. Plus, she planned to document Adam's pending charge for rape. Then she needed to write down everything that Blanche from the library said about Pam killing her cousin Billy.

A light snow began to fall, but with the wind, it was turning into a mini-blizzard. Marlee kept her eyes focused on Adam's car, and after what seemed like hours, he and Jasmine returned to his vehicle. They were walking hand-in-hand, and he opened the passenger door to let her in. *"Hmmm... very polite for a rapist,"* Marlee thought as she started the car and followed them out of the parking lot.

She had watched enough cop shows to know if you're following a car that you shouldn't drive right behind them. That would alert the driver's suspicion. She lagged a couple cars behind Adam and changed lanes once. She even passed them, her scarf draped up around the side of her face, so he wouldn't recognize her. Tailing Adam wasn't as difficult as she thought it would be, especially since he just drove a few blocks to the only movie theater in town. She parked in the adjacent Burger King lot. Jasmine and Adam walked into the theater, again holding hands. And Marlee watched as they purchased tickets, popcorn, and pop before walking toward the back of the building. Movies tended to last around two hours, including the previews, so Marlee knew she had plenty of time to go on another caper before they returned to their car.

The snow and wind made driving in town tricky,

but it was downright nasty outside the city limits without the protection of buildings. Marlee drove slowly with the car lights on bright, until she reached Pam DeWitt's farm. The lights were on in the big farm house, so she suspected Pam was now home. The wind had whipped the already-existing snow and the newly-fallen snow into peaked snow banks reaching nearly two feet. Instead of testing the metal of Barry's car, she parked outside the driveway to the farm and walked in.

Pam flung the door open before Marlee knocked. "Tim's dead!" she wailed as she pulled Marlee into an awkward embrace.

Marlee waited for Pam's crying to subside before she expressed her sympathy regarding Tim's death. They made their way to the large kitchen table and sat down. "I'm the one who found him," Marlee said, watching Pam's expression. Surely the police told her who found Tim's body and where it was located.

"Yeah, I know." Pam grabbed a handful of tissues and blew her nose with a honk. "The police said he'd been dead for a long time before he was found. He was right here under my nose, and I didn't even know it."

"I'm so sorry, Pam. It must be a really tough situation to handle." Marlee could feel the emotion welling up in her chest and in her eyes. She fought to gain control of herself. She didn't come out here just to express sympathy, although that was the role she intended to play. Marlee's main objective was to find out what Pam knew about Tim's death and also what she had to say about Billy's accident ten years ago.

"I came out here this morning and knocked on your door but there was no answer. Where were you?" Marlee tried to keep her tone even and not full of judgment.

"The hogs were running low on feed, so I went to the grain elevator to order more for delivery. Then I ran a couple other errands and met a friend for coffee. When I got back here, an ambulance was just pulling out of the driveway, and there were cops all over. I had no idea what happened." Pam used the wad of tissues to dab the tears running down her face.

"Why would Tim go to the shed?" Marlee asked.

"I don't know. We always kept it locked. My cousin died there. We were horsing around, and he fell off the ladder and broke his neck. Since then, the shed stayed locked, and we never kept much in there except some old junk. It had gone to ruin in the past couple years. Now I wish I'd talked Grandpa Edgar into demolishing it."

"How would Tim have gotten in?" Marlee asked, wondering if Grandpa Edgar's claim of Tim coming to him and asking for the key was legitimate.

"The key is still here in the entry way," Pam said pointing to a wooden wall hanging with a series of hooks, each holding a key. "Tim must've had his own key."

There was a light knock at the door, and then Pam's mother, Nicole, and a man in his forties entered the house. They carried with them a paper sack of groceries and a twelve-pack of Coke. Pam got up from the table and hugged them both, introducing them to Marlee as her parents.

"Yes, I met Nicole yesterday," Marlee said as she shook hands with them both. "I'm so sorry about Tim. I know we were all hoping for a much different ending than this." She held her breath after she spoke, never sure of what to say to people who just lost a loved one. Everything seemed so trite and pointless, yet Marlee knew she needed to say something to show her sympathy. Tim really was her friend, but she could not think of a way to express how she felt. They hadn't known each other that long, and their encounters had either been in class, at parties, or on campus talking about their shared class or upcoming parties. She doubted his parents cared to hear about any of that.

"Thank you. We're so glad Tim had you as a friend," Nicole said, wiping her red eyes with the sleeve of her coat. "It's such a shock. I thought we'd find him soon, and he'd be fine." She dissolved into sobs and collapsed into a kitchen chair. Her husband, in a trance, stood behind her and rubbed her shoulders.

Marlee had several more questions to ask, but she also had a level of common decency that knew sticking around would be inappropriate. She gave her condolences again and walked through the snow drifts to her car.

Glancing at her watch, she could see that she'd spent more time at the farm than intended. She revved Barry's car and took off toward the movie theater. Luck was on her side, as Adam's car was still parked in the same spot. She sat and waited. And waited. *If they decided to go to a second show I'm going to lose my mind,* she thought as she drummed her fingers on the steering wheel.

Luck was still on Marlee's side, because she woke up when her head hit the steering wheel. It was the same time Adam and Jasmine backed out of the theater parking lot. "Damn, I almost lost them," Marlee chastised herself, realizing Jasmine's safety depended on her.

Adam drove to Blake's cousin's acreage and held Jasmine's hand as they walked inside. Marlee parked the car on the outskirts where it wasn't visible from the house. She pulled her coat and scarf tighter and ventured to the house and found a window to the basement which wasn't covered with a curtain. Peering inside, she could see Adam and her roommate sitting on an orange-and-brown plaid couch, each holding a can of beer and chatting. Hard rock music was playing in the background, and even though Marlee recognized the drum beat, she couldn't place the song. Jasmine appeared relaxed and happy. She smiled and then reached over and touched his knee as they talked. Marlee was happy her friend was having a good time, but would she be this at ease if she knew about his pending rape charges? Who knew what tricks Adam had up his sleeve to entice his victims?

Even though she felt like throwing up a little, Marlee continued to peer through the basement window as Jasmine and Adam kissed. His hands slid all over the back of her sweater and eventually he stood up and took her hand. Adam helped Jasmine from the couch and led her out of Marlee's eyesight. She froze, not knowing what to do next. If she did nothing, Jasmine could be Adam's next victim. If she interrupted them, then their cover was blown. Jasmine seemed to be consenting to everything that was happening between herself and Adam right now, but what if she changed her mind when they got to the bedroom? Would he attack her?

Marlee took a deep breath and knocked on the door. She knew what she had to do, not just for Jasmine's sake, but for the sake of the whole case. The door was flung open by Blake after two knocks.

"What's going on?" he slurred, several beers into his usual Friday night routine.

"Not much. Just wondering if I could come in and chat with you guys for a bit," Marlee said as she rubbed her mittened hands together even though they weren't even that cold.

He motioned for her to come in and led the way downstairs. A Krokus cassette was playing, and John was sprawled in a recliner watching the television with the volume turned down. "Want a beer?" he asked.

"You bet," Marlee said, glancing around looking for Jasmine. "What's going on around here tonight?"

"Nothing. Blake and I are just watching *Hangin' with Mr. Cooper*. Adam's got a hot date back in his room." John flopped into the other recliner after he handed Marlee a can of generic beer.

"Is Jasmine here by any chance?" Marlee asked in her most innocent voice.

"The chick in the mini-skirt that was with you the other night? Yeah, she's with Adam in his room. Why?" Blake asked.

"I thought she might be here. I need to talk to her immediately." Marlee stood up and placed her opened beer can on the floor. "What room is she in?"

"Wait. You can't just go barging in. Who knows

188

what's going on in there," Blake said.

Marlee disregarded Blake's objections and knocked loudly on a closed door. No answer. This time she knocked hard enough to make the door rattle on its hinges.

"What?" growled a male voice from the other side of the door.

"I need to talk to Jasmine," Marlee yelled. "It's an emergency!"

Rustling sounds were heard before the door burst open. Adam stood in the doorway, his eyes ablaze and his shirt partially unbuttoned. "What the fuck do you want?"

"It's a life or death situation! I need to talk to my roommate right now!" Marlee insisted as she shoved by Adam and found Jasmine sitting on the floor, crying.

"Jazz, are you okay?" Marlee rushed to her roommate's side and helped her to her feet. "Did he hurt you?" She gave a death glare to Adam, who had now buttoned his shirt.

"No, I'm fine," Jasmine insisted although she continued to cry.

"We're leaving. C'mon," Marlee said to her roommate as she led her out of the bedroom and outside to the car. None of the guys stood in their way as they left the house, although they all stared.

Once safely in Barry's car with the doors locked, Marlee asked, "What the hell happened? What did he do to make you cry?"

"Adam didn't hurt me. He said I was beautiful, and it caught me off guard. No guy has ever told me that before," Jasmine said.

Marlee was dumbfounded. Her roommate was drop-dead gorgeous, and to find out that Jasmine had never had her beauty commented on was unbelievable. "So he didn't hurt you? He didn't try to attack you?"

"No! Adam is a perfect gentleman," Jasmine said, drying the last of her tears.

"Maybe not a perfect gentleman," Marlee said with

a frown. "When you left the dorm before I got back, I was a nervous wreck. I called Barry, and he ran a check on Adam and his car. Turns out that he has a pending charge for attempted rape."

"Rape? You're kidding, right?" Jasmine scoffed. "He's one of the nicest, most considerate guys I've ever met. Barry must have his records mixed up. It was probably somebody with the same name."

"I don't think so, Jazz. Barry seemed pretty confident that Adam was charged with rape and is out of jail on bond until his trial." It was difficult, but Marlee tried to be sympathetic when relaying the news. She felt in her heart that Adam was a dirtbag, but she didn't want Jasmine to feel even worse about the whole situation.

"I don't care what you say. I don't believe it," Jasmine said, her arms crossed in front of her in defiance.

"You don't have to believe me, but just promise you won't go anywhere alone with him unless you tell me. Please?" Marlee begged.

"Fine." Jasmine wouldn't even look at Marlee and had shortened her answers to one word, so Marlee knew her roommate was pissed.

Taking a deep breath, Marlee changed the subject. "When I went to the library I talked with a lady who told me all about the accident in the shed at the DeWitt farm."

"Really?" Jasmine turned toward Marlee, now with rapt attention. "What did she say?"

As they drove back to the dorm, Marlee revisited her conversation with Blanche and the claims that Pam was responsible for her cousin's death and maybe even the demise of her brother. "I did a little fact-checking, and what Blanche said about being married to Billy's dad checked out. I just don't know what to believe about Billy's death."

"You're shitting me! I can't believe all this. Ten days ago I couldn't name anyone who died except my grandparents, and now you're asking questions about the deaths of two friends plus Billy. I can't get my head around all of this," Jasmine said as she shook her head back and forth in an attempt to rattle some of the facts into place.

"I don't know what's going on either. I went to talk to Pam tonight while you and Adam were at the movies. She seemed pretty torn up about her brother's death. Then their parents showed up, and I left. There was no way I could bring up Blanche's accusations while they were in so much pain. It's going to be tough, but I need to confront Pam with Blanche's claims. Based on the way Pam was acting tonight, I don't think she had anything to do with Tim's death. But who knows? She might have killed her cousin and her own brother just to keep hold of the farm."

"My date tonight wasn't all talk and smooching. I asked Adam some questions about Tim, and he was very forthcoming. He said Tim was determined to take over the farm when he graduated college and that he and Pam argued about it last week," Jasmine reported.

"Really? What else did he have to say?"

"He doesn't think Tim started the fire or even knew about it. Adam thinks Tim was lured out of the house by Pam. Adam called her that night to tell her Tim had been knocked out, so she was aware of his head injury. She might have seen this as the perfect time to do away with her brother and keep the farm for herself, but do you really think Pam is that evil?" Jasmine asked. "It would take a heartless person to kill their own sibling, don't you think?"

"Yeah, it would. But Blanche is convinced Pam killed her cousin, Billy, and when I told her about Tim's death, she immediately suspected Pam. Plus, you just said Adam thinks Pam lured Tim away from the house the night he hit his head. Maybe she's responsible for the fire," Marlee said.

"Could Pam actually kill Tim and hide his body in the shed, and then act like nothing happened?" Jasmine arched her eyebrow, her skepticism evident.

"We just don't know. She might be somebody who seems perfectly normal on the outside, but in reality, she's a cold-blooded killer. And I'm not going to rest until I figure out what happened."

When I think back, there were plenty of people who would benefit from my death. And not just my family.

Chapter 21

Jasmine and Marlee collapsed on a pile of blankets on the floor in their dorm room. Both were fully clothed, including their coats. They were both out within seconds. Marlee didn't even hear the phone ring. Jasmine shook her shoulder and mumbled something incoherent.

"What?" Marlee sat up and grabbed the phone receiver that Jasmine held in her direction.

"Can you pick me up at the station? I'm off duty now," Barry said, fatigue creeping into his voice.

"On my way," Marlee said, already on her feet and ready to go.

She gave a brief explanation to Jasmine, who was already back asleep. Marlee picked Barry up and told him everything that occurred with Jasmine's date with Adam and her own conversation with Pam. Plus, she relayed Jasmine's comments to her. Barry didn't have anything new to report. The main theory at the police station remained the same: Tim wandered out to the family farm, delirious from being knocked out, became confused, and froze to death.

"The results from Tim's autopsy should be in tomorrow, even though it's a Sunday," Barry reported as he dropped Marlee off in front of her dorm. "I'll let you know what I hear about it."

The next morning came way too soon, as Marlee found herself still dressed and clad in her winter coat lying on the floor. Jasmine had migrated to her lofted bed where she snored softly. A wind-up alarm clock rang, but neither roommate could locate the offending gadget.

"Did you set the alarm?" Marlee growled. She wasn't a morning person to begin with, and her lack of sleep these past few days had turned her into a major grump.

"No, did you?" Jasmine snarled back. If not cheerful in the morning, at least Jasmine was sociable, but the lack of sleep was catching up to her too.

After Jasmine found the alarm clock, she silenced it and threw it against her pillow. "I don't know how it got turned on," she grumbled as she fell back asleep. It was nearly one o'clock in the afternoon when they woke again.

"Shit! We missed class!" Jasmine shouted, slithering out of bed.

"Isn't it Saturday?" Marlee asked, hoping, but not sure.

"Well, it's too late now to go to class." Jasmine poked her head out the door and asked someone in the hallway who confirmed that it was indeed the weekend.

"Hallelujah!" Marlee yelled, even though she wasn't particularly religious.

A knock on the door preceded the unlocked door being flung open. "Wakey-wakey!" called out Kristie as she stood in the doorway with her hands on her hips. "What do you think you're going to accomplish if you stay in bed all day?"

Jasmine and Marlee exchanged looks. They both wanted to punch their dorm neighbor in the face, even though it wasn't her fault that she hadn't been kept up to date on their investigative efforts. "Hey, Kristie," Jasmine said.

"Have you two been avoiding me lately?" Kristie seemed hurt that her friends hadn't been including her in activities. If she only knew the nature of the activities her dorm neighbors had been involved in.

"No, we've just been really busy," Marlee said. "How about you? Have you been avoiding us? We knocked on your door a couple times to see if you wanted to hang out." She thought turning the tables might get Kristie off track, even if it was a lie.

"No! I guess I've been busy too. We haven't even had a chance to talk about Tim DeWitt's death. Can you believe there have been two student deaths in the past week and that we knew them both?" Kristie shuddered as she spoke.

"It's horrible," Jasmine said, glancing at Marlee for guidance on how much to share. They were obligated to keep their alliance with Barry Stevens a secret, but the sources of all the bits and pieces of information they received via the police department were murky at best.

"Have you heard anything on what caused his death, Kristie?" Marlee asked.

"No, just that he was found frozen out in the country somewhere. That's another odd thing, both Beth and Tim were found frozen to death."

"You're right. There's just too much going on to comprehend," Jasmine agreed.

"Why were you two sleeping so late? And why are you dressed and wearing coats?" Kristie asked.

"We didn't want to say anything to anybody just yet. We thought we would wait and see if anyone noticed. For the past couple weeks, we've been getting up really early and going to the gym to work out. When we got back this morning, we were both really cold and tired so we stretched out to rest for a bit and overslept." Marlee could feel her neck and face growing hot as she spun the lie to her friend.

"Yeah," Jasmine chimed in. "And we're entering a body-building contest in April."

Kristie and Marlee both turned to stare at Jasmine. "Um, okay," Kristie finally uttered, suppressing a laugh. Marlee gave Jasmine a death glare so she wouldn't try to improvise any more of the story. A body-building competition was an unrealistic explanation for why the two roommates had been so busy. Neither possessed the physique that would be favorable to extreme muscle building, especially within the next two months. Jasmine was tall and willowy with almost no body fat. Marlee was short and stout with a doughy middle.

When she couldn't take it anymore, Kristie finally gave a chuckle and said, "Well, I better let you two get back to pumping iron. Let me know when the competition is held, and I'll be there to cheer you on."

After they heard Kristie's door close next door, Marlee whispered, "What the hell were you thinking, Jazz? You're terrible at lying!"

"I was just trying to add in some detail to your story. Besides, how believable is it that we're getting up early to go to the gym? That doesn't seem like a story anyone would believe."

"Sooner or later, we'll have to tell Kristie that we backed out of the body-building competition. Let me handle the excuse for that, okay?" Marlee was afraid Jasmine would dig them into a bigger hole with one of her ever-expanding stories.

Before long, they were able to laugh at their feeble attempt at throwing their friend off the real story. The wall phone interrupted their laughter as they took turns striking different muscle woman poses.

Marlee answered the phone and listened without saying much. When she hung up, there was plenty to report to her roommate. "That was Barry. Tim's autopsy is finished, and they think the cause of death was from a head injury. But get this, the medical examiner doesn't think the injury that killed him is from the fall down the stairs. There was another head injury more on the top of his head. And it looks like it was intentional rather than accidental."

"Intentional? So, what does this mean?" Jasmine asked.

"It means the death is being ruled as suspicious, and the police are now looking for Tim's killer." The news came as a shock to both roommates, and they sat down on the floor.

"Somebody actually killed Tim? It wasn't an accident? Somebody wanted Tim to die?" Jasmine was in shock and could not wrap her mind around the facts.

"It's horrible that Tim is dead, but now to find out that somebody killed him..." Marlee let the sentence hang as she struggled to find words.

Taking a deep breath, Jasmine crossed her legs

and lifted herself up off the floor. "Do the police have any suspects?"

"None that Barry knew of. He'll do some asking around today about Pam's involvement in Billy's death. At this point, we don't know if the story Blanche told has any factual basis or if she's just some weird old cat lady who likes to spread gossip," Marlee said.

Jasmine strode over to Marlee's bed and retrieved the notebook on Beth and Tim's deaths from under the mattress. "Let's update the notebook." Jasmine, who was usually the one to fall apart, was composed and focused on the task at hand. Marlee on the other hand, had a spinning head and a mind racing for answers.

Upon updating the information in the notebook, Marlee ripped a page out of the notebook and wrote MOTIVES at the top. "In order to figure out who did it, maybe we need to determine why someone would kill Tim."

"Good idea. I think money is a typical motive," Jasmine said.

"Yes, that's always a consideration. Revenge is another one," Marlee reported, thinking back to her criminology class and their discussion on why people kill.

"I think love could be a factor too."

"How so?" Marlee asked, puzzled as to why someone would kill another person if they truly loved them.

"It could be because of betrayal. A wife comes home and finds her husband in bed with the babysitter. The wife flips out and kills them both because she loved the husband and hated the babysitter."

Marlee jotted down Jasmine's contribution. "Maybe Tim had something that someone else wanted or he had information someone didn't want him to make public. I think Pam killing her brother to keep the farm might fit in here."

"What about Tim's roommates? What might be their motivation for killing him? I'm not saying any of them did it, but if one or more of them did, why?

"Hmmm," Marlee said as she chewed on the end of the pencil. "Any of the above reasons, I suppose. It might have to do with the fire. Tim knew who set it and why, and the killer was afraid he would turn them in."

"Other than one or more of the roommates killing Tim because of the fire or Pam killing him to keep the farm to herself, who else would want him dead?" Jasmine queried.

"No one that I can think of. I think the Pam theory and the roommate theory are both a bit of a stretch. Since the coroner ruled the death suspicious and not a homicide, maybe someone struck Tim with an object, not meaning to kill him. It would still be homicide, but it wouldn't fall under first-degree murder." The more Marlee thought about Tim's death, the more confused she became.

"Did Tim or his family have a lot of money?" Jasmine asked.

"I don't think so. I'd say they were middle-class just based on their homes, cars, and clothes. Why?"

"Maybe somebody was blackmailing Tim, and when he didn't pay they killed him," Jasmine suggested.

"Do you even know what blackmail is?" Marlee was skeptical that her roommate knew half the terms she threw around.

"It has something to do with money. I know that much," Jasmine sniffed, peeved that she'd been called out.

"Here's an example," Marlee said, getting ready to repeat what she learned in class earlier in the semester. "I steal fifty dollars from Kristie, and you find out about it, and you threaten to tell Kristie or turn me in to the cops if I don't pay you half to keep quiet."

"Can you think of anything Tim would've done that could be used against him by a blackmailer?"

"No, unless he cheated on a test and somebody found out. Even so, I have a hard time believing someone would kill another person over that," Marlee said.

"So unless some other motive comes to the surface,

our most likely suspects are Tim's roommates and his sister," Jasmine said.

"I guess so. The one thing I know for sure is that we need to start all over questioning each of them." Marlee called Barry and arranged to borrow his car again that night while he was on duty.

"Who do you want to talk to?" Barry asked.

"Jazz and I are going to talk to Tim's roommates and Pam. Right now, we think those are the most likely culprits, although I sort of doubt any of them killed Tim. At least I don't think they intentionally killed him," Marlee said.

"You two need to realize that this case is dangerous. Tim was killed. He didn't just die from exposure to the cold. Keep in mind that whoever wanted Tim dead doesn't want to be found out. They will go to whatever lengths necessary to remain in the clear. If you and Jasmine question the wrong people, they may do away with both of you." Barry was stern in his lecture and Marlee took offense. She didn't need some guy taking a paternalistic role in a misguided attempt at protecting them. She just wanted updated information on the case and unlimited use of Barry's car.

Taking a deep breath to calm her nerves, Marlee said, "You're not trying to tell me what do, are you, Barry?"

He broke out into laughter. "As if anyone could tell you what to do. Look, I'm not trying to control you. I just want you and Jasmine to be aware of the potential danger, especially since the guy Jasmine went on a date with last night is charged with attempted rape."

"I'm not letting her out of my sight if they go out again," Marlee said.

"What do you mean? Is she thinking of seeing him again? Didn't you tell her about his rape charge?" Barry was livid.

"I told her, and I'm sure she won't go out with him again. I just meant that after last night, I'm keeping an eye on Jasmine no matter who she dates." Marlee wasn't sure if Barry would buy her backtracking excuse, but he didn't challenge her.

They ended their conversation with the agreement that Barry would pick up Marlee and Jasmine at their dorm and then turn his car over to them after he was dropped off at the police station. After showers and a change of clothing, the roommates walked over to the Student Union for some food. Both were starving, and they heaped their trays with pasta, French fries, grilled cheese sandwiches, tomato soup, and chocolate cake.

After eating like pigs, Jasmine and Marlee waddled back to their dorm room and loafed around until Barry came to pick them up. "I want you two to be careful," Barry said before getting out of the car and turning the wheel over to Marlee. "I'm serious. If anything happened, I don't think I could live with it."

"Easy on the drama," Marlee teased. "We won't do anything reckless. And we'll call in to leave a message for you here and there." Barry nodded, although his face was lined with worry. He knew damned well they would do whatever they pleased, regardless of the danger level.

"What should we do first?" Jasmine asked.

Marlee glanced at her watch. It was nearing five o'clock, and even though the campus library didn't close for several more hours, she thought Blanche might be off duty soon. Before they went inside, Marlee had a firm chat with Jasmine. "You're a shitty liar, so don't try to spin a yarn. Just go along with what I say and don't add anything."

Jasmine nodded her assent, but she was anything but happy about it. She had been nearly as involved in this matter as her roommate, yet Marlee seemed to think she was the lead detective on the case. She had to admit that she was a horrible liar, so Marlee did have a point.

Blanche was just walking out of the back exit from the library when Marlee and Jasmine spotted her from the parking lot. Marlee jogged up and reintroduced herself to Blanche, who had cooled off since their last talk. "Can we take you out for a beer or a cup of coffee?" Marlee asked.

"Sure," said Blanche, her eyes growing wide with glee. "Where should we go?" The wheels in Blanche's head were turning as she thought about the various choices.

"How about the Student Union?" Marlee asked, remembering that she was low on cash and had a meal card. "Unless you want a beer."

They agreed on the Student Union, and Marlee waived Jasmine over from the car and made introductions. "I was telling my roommate here about our conversation. We just had a couple other things to ask you about Tim."

"I'll tell you what I know, but you probably won't believe me. The cops thought I was lying when I told them about Pam killing Billy. Everyone just wants to stick their heads in the sand," Blanche said with a touch of bitterness.

"We want to hear everything you have to say," Jasmine said, assuring Blanche that they were on her side.

They settled in at the Student Union with hot chocolate and cinnamon rolls for each of them. "Pam could lie her way out of anything," Blanche said as she chewed her roll. "She puts on a good show and has everyone fooled."

"Did you like Pam when you first met her?" Marlee inquired.

"I sure did. She was nice, friendly, and seemed like the type of person everyone would want as a friend or in their family. My husband, Art, was fooled by Pam too, until Billy died. He thought she knew more about Billy's death than she let on. Of course, Tim always maintained that Pam shook the ladder Billy was standing on and caused him to fall and break his neck. I wasn't around during any of this, mind you. Art and Lola were in the process of getting divorced when Billy died, but no one in the family knew it. They had to stay together for a bit after his death for appearances," Blanche said, stopping for another bite of cinnamon roll.

"When did you and Art become involved?" Marlee

asked in a non-judgmental tone, assuming there was some overlap between Art's first marriage and his relationship with Blanche.

"Oh, we went to high school together. We dated for a couple years, then he dumped me after graduation. That's when I went into the Peace Corps. He was married by the time I got back. About a year before Billy died, Art looked me up and said he and Lola were getting a divorce. He said he'd never forgotten me and wanted another chance."

"And?" Marlee and Jasmine chorused, on the edge of their seats as if they were watching an episode of The Young and the Restless in the dorm dayroom.

"Like an idiot, I agreed. I knew he was married and that there was a strong possibility he wouldn't get divorced, but I loved him. Since the day we broke up, I'd dreamed of getting back together. It was a dream come true, and I wasn't about to let it pass me by. We were seeing each other while he was getting his things in order to leave his wife. Then Billy died. I'd never seen someone so devastated. Art thought it was his fault for not keeping an eye on Billy while the cousins played on the farm. He knew how dangerous it could be, but assumed Pam would be sensible since she was the oldest."

"When did Art start to suspect Pam?" Marlee asked.

"Everyone thought Tim was either confused or lying when he said Pam dared Billy to climb to the top of the ladder and then shook him off. The family, the police, everyone thought it was just an unfortunate accident where a boy fell and broke his neck while playing. But Tim insisted that what he saw was real. At first, I think Art was just so grief-stricken that he would have listened to any theory just so he could place the blame for Billy's death on someone. Then everything started to make sense. Art laid out the whole case for me, and I believed it too. Pam, even at age seventeen, knew she needed to get rid of Billy if she wanted to take over the farm."

"I don't doubt you, Blanche," Marlee said, gently easing into a counter argument. "But Pam killing her younger cousin for the farm sounds like something out of the 1800s."

Blanche nodded. "I know. I thought the same thing when Art told me, but primogeniture is a very real thing in this day and age."

"Primo what?" asked Jasmine.

"Primogeniture is the inheritance of land by the eldest male in the family. Land was traditionally passed to the eldest male, leaving the other males in the family to find other means of making a living. And girls had no inheritance rights at all pertaining to the land. Times have changed, but in the DeWitt family, Billy was the rightful successor to the family farm. By killing him, she made sure she would have control of the farm, at least until Tim came of age. But Tim was seen as mentally fragile and delusional by the family because of his claims of how Billy died. Pam killed two birds with one stone, if you'll forgive the poor pun."

"If the family still saw Tim as unstable, why would he be a threat to Pam's control of the farm?" Marlee asked.

"Because it was agreed when Pam took over that once Tim graduated from college, he would get a chance to be in charge of the farm. If it didn't work out, then Pam would be put back in control. After Tim graduated, Pam would be working for him if she chose to stick around. For the past five years, she's been making all of her own decisions without any interference from anyone. When Tim took over, she would either have to work for him or find another place to live and work. She had a very strong motive to kill Tim," Blanche said. Whether or not this tale was true remained to be seen. What was true was Blanche's belief in it.

"Couldn't Pam just keep working to discredit Tim? I mean, she could surely say and do plenty of things to make the others in the family doubt Tim's competence. No one wanted to see the farm go under, so if Pam was doing a good job, and Tim was still seen as unstable, then Pam would be the obvious choice," Marlee said.

"But Grandpa Edgar had always insisted that Tim be allowed to operate the farm when he graduated from college. He and Tim's parents, as well as Billy's parents, thought if Tim worked hard enough to get a degree, then he deserved a chance to run the farm. I don't think anyone thought he would succeed, but he had to be given the chance. With their relationship with Tim on shaky ground, everyone knew he would cut all ties with the family if he wasn't given the opportunity."

"You think Pam was threatened enough to kill her brother?" Jasmine asked. "Why wouldn't she just let him have his chance and then when he failed, she could take it over again."

Blanche croaked out a laugh. "Because that's not how Pam works. She's a hard worker, but she doesn't have much business sense. I think the farm is in quite a bit of debt. Tim would have his work cut out for him trying to pull the farm out of debt. Pam's territorial. If she wants something, she'll do whatever it takes to get it. Or keep it. I think the rest of the family would have been a lot easier on Tim these past few years if Pam hadn't kept everything stirred up. Of course, it was in her own best interest. If everyone thought Tim was unstable, then no one would believe Pam caused Billy's death. She's been a conniver since she was a little kid. At least that's what my husband always said."

"When did your husband pass away?" Marlee asked, sensing that Blanche wanted, and perhaps needed, to talk about her husband.

"About a year ago. He battled cancer for a few years before it finally got him. Things just haven't been the same since," Blanche said with a saddened expression that nearly put Jasmine in tears.

"Does his family still include you in things like Thanksgiving?" Marlee asked.

"No, he was cut out shortly after Billy's death

because he was so vocal about Pam's involvement. I was never included either because I was on Art's side. Plus, they all saw me as a homewrecker since Art and Lola got a divorce."

"Where's Lola now? Did she believe Tim's story too?" Marlee questioned.

"She's around town. Even though the divorce was amicable, she flipped me off the last time I saw her. Real mature, huh?" Blanche said with a touch of bitterness. "I don't know for sure if she believed Pam killed Billy. Art told me Lola didn't buy the story at first, but then started to think there might be more to it."

"Do you think she'd talk to us?" Marlee asked.

"She might. Just make sure you don't mention my name. She hates me even though their marriage was over before I came back into the picture. The divorce was just a formality, but I understand she needs someone to blame, and I'm it." Blanche was very matter-of-fact in her words, not showing any disdain for her deceased husband's first wife.

Marlee and Jasmine, sensing there was not much else they could learn from Blanche, took down Lola's contact information and went on their way to find her.

"Blanche said Lola works at the courthouse, which is usually an eight-to-five job, I think. Let's spin by her place and see if she will talk with us," Marlee suggested. They drove to an apartment building in a newly developed part of town and found Lola's name listed on the mailbox inside the lobby. They walked down the hall to 9A and knocked, waiting patiently for Lola to answer.

No one answered immediately, but after some rustling and clatter, they heard a female voice call out, "Wait a minute, I'm coming." The door was pulled open, and a woman with a stained horse t-shirt and a plaid skirt peered out.

After Marlee stated their reason for the visit and identified themselves as Tim's friends, Lola invited them in. "I just got home from work and was changing into my lounge clothes," she said with a bit of embarrassment. "If you'll excuse me for a minute, I'll be right back."

Lola returned, now wearing gray sweatpants and frumpy slippers. "Okay, so what do you want to know?" She tried to put on a cheerful façade, but Marlee could feel the sadness that spread over Lola as she prepared to talk about her son, who had died ten years ago.

"Do you think it was completely accidental?" Jasmine blabbed out. Marlee glared at her, sending her the message to shut up.

"What?" Lola asked, more surprised than taken aback.

Marlee noticed Lola didn't seem offended or shocked, so she continued with Jasmine's line of questioning. "I suppose you've heard about Tim DeWitt's death." When Lola nodded, Marlee continued. "We heard that your son, Billy, died in the same shed where Tim was found. We did a little asking around and heard that Tim had accused his sister, Pam, of daring Billy to climb to the top of the ladder and then shook him off."

Lola took a deep breath, taking time to formulate her words. "Tim always said Pam killed Billy. That she dared him to climb up the ladder and then moved it around so he'd fall off. Tim said it was a long time before Pam would let Tim come to the house for help. I lost track of who said and did what then because we were trying to save Billy's life even though we knew he was already dead. After that, I kind of went into a fog. I didn't care about anything in the world if Billy wasn't in my life. He was my only child. Then I started to think about what Tim said, and it made sense. Billy's dad and I were going through a divorce at the same time, so everything was a mess."

"So, what do you think now? Was Billy's death an accident or did Pam plan it out?" Marlee asked.

"You know, I saw Pam downtown at a bar one night. It was about a year after Billy died, and I was newly divorced. I was spending too much time drinking, and that night was no exception. She went to the bathroom, and I confronted her. Pam denied everything, saying Tim was mistaken and had a nervous breakdown. She was so calm and convincing when she talked, she made me doubt what Tim said. I never talked to her after that, but there's always been something in the back of my head. It's a feeling more than anything. Maybe she dared Billy to climb the ladder and then she made him fall off. Whether she intended just to scare him or actually kill him, I don't know. I'd like to think it was accidental, but a little voice inside my head says otherwise."

"And her motive for killing Billy?" Marlee asked even though she already knew the answer.

"To gain control of the farm, of course. Neither of Edgar's two sons wanted to operate it, so it was going to one of the three grandkids. By eliminating Billy and making everyone think Tim was nuts, she made herself the only choice to run the farm. She'd have everything she ever wanted: the farm and complete control of it."

After leaving Lola's apartment, Marlee and Jasmine drove to the acreage where the Stairway to Hell guys were staying. They were almost there when Marlee realized that they should have called Barry to check in. He would be livid when he found out they went out to confront a man charged with rape. If he ever found out. There was no reason to tell him if the topic never came up.

Adam was home, and he answered the door when they rang the bell. He glared at Marlee as he opened the storm door to let them in. Without a word, he walked downstairs and they followed. Flopping down on the couch, he picked up the remote control and began flipping through stations.

"So, you're probably wondering what we're doing back here," Marlee said as an ice breaker.

"I don't really care what you two are doing. You're both dead to me," Adam said.

Marlee couldn't help herself as she broke out into laughter. "That's a bit dramatic, don't you think?"

He shrugged without offering additional

information. Jasmine sat in one of the recliners and Marlee followed suit.

"What do you know about Tim's feud with his family over the farm?" Marlee asked, knowing full well that Adam wouldn't tell them anything.

"Not much. He was on the outs with them over the farm, especially his sister," Adam said as he tried to appear intent on a show he was watching. "Why?"

"We're wondering if Pam could have had something to do with Tim's death," Marlee said, hoping Adam would relate his theory now as he had with Jasmine the previous night.

"You think Tim's sister killed him?"

"We don't know. Do you have any ideas who might have hurt him? The coroner ruled the death suspicious. Tim's head trauma was not caused by his fall down the stairs," Marlee said.

They now had Adam's attention. He muted the television and met their eyes. "Really? Tim had another head injury? An injury from something other than his fall down the stairs?"

Marlee and Jasmine nodded without saying a word, giving Adam time to process the information. "Holy shit. Who would have done this?" he mumbled more to himself than anyone else.

"There's more," Marlee said. "Tim's cousin Billy died in the same shed on the farm where Tim was found. It happened years ago when Billy, Tim, and Pam were playing. Did Tim ever talk to you about that?"

Adam didn't speak for a whole minute. "Now it makes sense," he said. "It all makes sense."

*Of course, I wasn't the only one in the
family with a target on my back.*

Chapter 22

"What makes sense?" Jasmine gasped, out of air from holding her breath.

"Tim never came out with the whole story, but he hinted around that there was an incident when he was a kid. Sometimes when he got really drunk he'd make comments about his sister wanting him out of the picture. I thought it was just sour grapes from losing the farm to her. He had a tendency to ramble on about things when he had too much to drink. Lots of people say stupid stuff when they drink, so we always just let it go," Adam said.

"What about Blake? He and Tim have been friends since they were little kids. What did he have to say about Tim's ramblings?" Marlee asked.

Adam shrugged. "Nothing that I can remember. He seemed as confused as John and me when Tim took off on one of his tangents."

"Nothing about Pam killing her cousin, Billy?" Marlee pressed.

"No, Blake never mentioned anything about it to me. Of course, we don't always get along that well. He stays out of my way, and that's how I like to keep it."

"Did Pam ever come over to Stairway to Hell?" Marlee asked.

"Sure, she stopped by a couple times. She'd ask Tim his opinions about what to plant the next spring or about the hogs. He never had much to say, so they were short conversations," Adam replied.

"Did Tim talk much about his Grandpa? Or did Grandpa Edgar ever come visit him?" Marlee asked.

"Yeah, Tim talked about Grandpa Edgar all the time and how he really wanted Tim to run the farm. He thought his grandpa would have stood up for him with the family if he hadn't become senile in the past few years," Adam said.

"How did Pam and Grandpa Edgar get along? Did

Tim ever say anything about that?" Jasmine asked.

"Tim said their grandpa wanted Pam out. He didn't agree with some of her ideas about expanding the livestock part of the farm. But Pam stuck to her guns and then Grandpa Edgar started to go downhill, and then it became a non-issue. Without their grandpa in his corner, there was no way Tim was getting the farm," Adam reported.

"Now, I need to switch topics to something a bit more sensitive," Marlee said.

"More sensitive that murder?" scoffed Adam.

Marlee nodded. "We found out that you were charged with attempted rape."

Adam started laughing. "I don't have to rape anybody. The ladies love me."

Marlee sighed, disappointed that yet another male didn't know that rape was about power, not access to sexual partners. "You know, many rapists are married or have girlfriends. That isn't what rape is about. It's about controlling another person."

"Whatever," Adam said with a wave of his hand and a chuckle as if he'd never heard anything so silly. "I'm not a rapist. The charge is bogus. And that's all I'm gonna say about it. My lawyer told me not to answer any questions." He stood up, signaling that it was time for them to leave. "I need to get some things done, so..."

"Now what should we do?" Jasmine asked once they were back in the car driving toward town.

"Let's go to Pam's farm. I don't know what to say, but we could at least drop by so you can pay your respects," Marlee said.

"Okay," Jasmine said. "I didn't know Tim hardly at all, but I can talk about meeting him recently at the house party and how we visited him at Stairway to Hell after Beth died. Then I can mention..."

"Less is more, Jazz. No need to say too much. Just say you knew him from college and leave it at that," Marlee said, afraid her roommate would again try to cobble together an unbelievable story.

Inside Pam's house, the three sat around the kitchen table. Photo albums and pictures of Tim were scattered about on the table. Pam looked ten years older than the last time Marlee saw her. An opened can of beer sat before her and multiple empties were strewn about the kitchen. Marlee wasn't sure she had the nerve to ask Pam about Billy's death and Tim's claim that she had killed him. Even though she felt uncomfortable doing so, Marlee finally broached the topic.

"Pam, I heard that the old shed where Tim was found was the site of another family tragedy," Marlee said gently, hoping to ease Pam into a conversation on the topic.

"Yes, it happened years ago. Sometimes it seems like yesterday," Pam said as she recounted playing in the shed with her brother and cousin. "I'll never forgive myself for not watching Billy more closely. I told him not to climb all the way to the top on the ladder, but he wouldn't listen. I turned my back for just a minute, and he made it all the way to the very top. That's when he lost his balance and fell on the hard cement floor."

She felt like a shit-heel for doing so, but Marlee had to follow up that bit of the conversation. "We heard Tim blamed you for Billy's accident. Actually, we heard Tim accused you of shaking the ladder to make Billy fall off."

The silence in the house seemed to last a life time as everyone waited, plotting out their next move. After a minute, Pam spoke. "Tim told everyone that I killed Billy. He blamed me, even though Billy was fourteen, and I was only seventeen. Tim said I dared Billy to climb to the very top and then I shook the ladder to make him fall. Tim was always a troubled child, and it just got worse after Billy died. I think he wanted someone to blame, and I was the only person there other than him."

"Forgive me for asking about this, but why would

Tim want your family to think you intentionally caused your cousin's death?" Jasmine asked.

"I don't know that he had an ulterior motive. I was six years older than Tim, so it's not like we competed against each other like some siblings do. I think that Tim either dreamed that I hurt Billy, or he convinced himself that's what he saw. Tim really believed what he told everyone. He was never the same after that."

"Did Billy's parents believe it was accidental, or did they place the blame on you?" Marlee asked.

"Unbeknownst to the rest of the family, Art and Lola were going through a divorce at the time Billy died. They stayed together for a few months after his death, but then they went their separate ways. Tim talked to Art and spread his messed-up theory, and then Art began making claims that I killed Billy to get control of the farm. His second wife believed him and was shooting her mouth off about it too. It still makes me mad, but I try not to hold a grudge. Art was hurting and trying to deal with his grief any way possible," Pam said.

"Did Tim receive counseling or psychiatric help?" Marlee asked.

"Mom and Dad took him to a counselor a few times, but he wouldn't open up to her. He refused to participate in any kind of testing, so it was impossible to diagnose him," Pam stated.

"How could he be so messed up as a kid, yet functional as an adult, if he didn't receive therapy?" Marlee asked.

"Oh, Tim was still messed up. He just got a lot better at hiding it. He knew better than to bring up Billy's death to Mom and Dad and the other relatives. Tim kept all of us on the outskirts of his life. Like I said before, he showed up for the major holidays to eat, and then he would leave immediately. It was like he couldn't stand to be around us," Pam said with a hint of sadness.

"But I understand you stopped by Stairway to Hell to talk to Tim about crops and the animals," Marlee said.

216

Pam squinted. "You sure seem to be hearing a lot of information about our family."

Marlee nodded. "I just can't get my head around the fact that Tim is dead. I keep talking to people about him, and information keeps coming up."

Pam nodded. "Yeah, I tried to include Tim in some of the decision-making for the farm. Like I said before, I told him he could take it over when he graduated college. I was going to step back and let him run the whole thing."

Jasmine sensed an opportunity to dig into another area. "What were you going to do if Tim took over the farm?"

"He still had another year before he graduated, so I hadn't made any firm plans. I thought maybe I'd stay at the farm with Tim and help him. Then I got the sense that he didn't want me anywhere near him when he took over, so I'd thought about going back to school myself. I wanted to stay around the area in case Tim couldn't handle the farm, and I had to step back in and take over," Pam reported.

"What did you want to study if you went to college?" Marlee inquired.

"Either Biology or Animal Science. Maybe I would have double-majored in them," Pam said as she continued to sift through family photos. "The funeral home asked us to bring in some pictures of Tim throughout his life. They are making a photo display to show at the lunch after the funeral."

"When are the services?" Jasmine asked. "Is there anything we can do to help?"

"No, everything is being handled by the funeral home and our church. The funeral will be Wednesday at 10:00 am at St. John's Catholic Church. If you could pass the word on to his friends from college, that would be a big help. I've met his roommates from the house, but not any of his other friends," Pam said.

"Of course, we'll let everyone know the time and location of the funeral, and we'll be there for sure," Marlee said.

"Pam, are you staying out here alone? Are your parents or friends staying with you while you go through this terrible time?" Jasmine asked.

"No, I prefer to be alone. Mom and Dad are having enough trouble handling their own grief. They don't need to deal with me too. One of my best friends lives in Minneapolis, and she's coming for the funeral and will stay a few days," Pam said.

Jasmine and Marlee were silent on the drive back to the dorm. Conflicting stories, swirling emotions, and obscure facts fused together to create uncertainty in the roommates. "I just don't know who or what to believe," Jasmine said, breaking the ice as they walked into their room.

"Clear as mud, isn't it?" Marlee joked, although neither of them was in the mood for humor. "I'm going to call Barry to see if he found out anything new." She placed the call and detailed her and Jasmine's conversations Blanche, Lola, Adam, and finally with Pam.

"Thanks a lot for checking in," Barry said dryly.

"No problem," Marlee chirped, choosing to ignore his sarcasm. "So, as you can see, we've had a fairly productive evening thus far. How about you?"

Barry went on to detail the minutiae of his evening, conveniently leaving out anything to do with Tim's death investigation. "I better get back to work. I have more paperwork to fill out from a drunk driving arrest earlier tonight."

"Oh no you don't! What did you find out about Tim's death? Or Billy's?" Marlee asked.

"Oh, that. I talked to Smith, one of the guys who's been here for quite a few years, and he was on the scene after Billy died. He said it was a suspicious case, and he thought Pam was involved, but without evidence nothing could be done. Some of the other officers at the scene thought the same thing."

"So, Pam was under suspicion? Why didn't the

cops listen to Tim when he said Pam caused Billy's fall?" Marlee asked.

"Apparently, Tim went into shock at first and wasn't able to talk about it. By the time he did talk, Pam had spun the story her way, and she already planted seeds that Tim was unstable. Anything Tim had to say to their parents fell on deaf ears. The parents defended Pam and supported the instability claim against Tim when the police questioned them later," Barry reported.

"Did he think the parents really, truly believed Pam, or were they just protecting her since she was their daughter?" Marlee asked.

"He seemed to think they found Pam's story believable and that Tim was mistaken or had somehow dreamed up his version of events."

"Why did the police feel compelled to rule it an accidental death right away? Couldn't they have ruled it suspicious or inconclusive and left the case open until they knew for sure that Tim was telling the truth?" Marlee asked.

"Remember, there was no evidence to suggest Pam or anyone else caused the accident. By looking at it, it seemed like just an unfortunate accident of a kid playing recklessly that ended in tragedy. It was just a gut feeling Smith and some of the other officers had that Pam was responsible. And Tim wasn't seen as a reliable witness."

"I wonder how many cases of homicide go undetected or unprosecuted because they look like accidents." Marlee said, more to herself than to Barry.

"Many more than you would think possible. I can think of at least six cases around here where someone died in a so-called accident but most likely another person had something to do with it. It's especially unsettling if the person in question had something to gain from the victim's death," Barry said.

"Like Pam getting control of the family farm?" Marlee asked.

"Exactly," Barry replied before ending the

conversation.

As she filled Jasmine in on the details of her conversation with Barry, Marlee jotted down details of their conversations in the notebook. It was turning out to be a handy reference since so much had happened, first with Beth's death, and now with the death of Tim. Plus, they were learning more and more about the death of Billy which happened ten years ago. All three cases were intertwined, and Marlee began thinking about breaking them out into separate parts to keep the stories straight.

"Jazz, I just don't get it. Could Pam really have killed her cousin and then her brother to keep the farm to herself? Does she seem that cold-blooded to you?"

"No, but I bet a lot of people are able to get away with crimes because they don't seem like the type."

"We talked about this in criminology a couple weeks ago. There's no one type of person who is a murderer or a thief or any other type of criminal. You can find some similarities in the way they think or carry out their crimes, but just to look at someone you can't tell if they're deadly. You could be a murderer. I could be a murderer. You just never know," Marlee said.

"Do you think you could ever kill someone?" Jasmine asked.

Marlee laughed until she realized Jasmine wasn't joking. "God, no! I couldn't do it even if I was really mad at someone. How about you?"

To Marlee's surprise, Jasmine replied in the affirmative. "My best friend in high school was beaten up by her boyfriend. He broke her nose, her arm, and some ribs. Sheryl was in the hospital for nearly a week. I didn't even recognize her the first time I went to visit. I think I could kill the bastard that did that to her. Or if I knew someone was going to harm my family, I could kill them."

"Remind me to never get on your bad side," Marlee said as she made toast for them. After a few pieces of hot, buttery toast, they were ready to check out for the night. It had been a long evening of investigating and asking questions.

Marlee was dog tired, but she couldn't fall asleep. Facts about Tim and Billy's death kept surfacing, then she would think of additional questions to ask Pam, Tim's roommates, and others. After an hour of tossing and turning, she finally fell into a fitful sleep. Her brain continued to churn the information she had taken in during the past several days. When she woke the next morning, her blankets were all tangled up around her and the pillow had fallen out of the lofted bed onto the floor. Marlee was just as tired now as she had been when she went to bed last night. "That was pointless," she though grumpily as she grabbed her towel and toiletries and stumbled toward the shower.

When she exited the communal bathroom, freshly showered, with her towel wrapped around her, Marlee felt awake and ready to take on the day. Entering her room, she was greeted not by Jasmine, but by Barry.

"Morning!" he said with a smirk.

"How did you get in here so early? The doors are supposed to be locked!" She pulled her towel tighter, self-conscious about how much skin was showing.

"I flashed my badge, and they let me right in. Just got off duty a bit ago and thought I'd come over and tell you something I found out," Barry said.

"Spill it," Marlee said as she pulled her blue fluffy robe around herself and cinched it tight.

"It seems Pam's name came up in another death," Barry stated.

"Whose death? Where?" Marlee asked.

"It was her grandma's death five years ago. Out at the farm," Barry said.

No matter where you go, there will always be somebody spreading gossip and lies with just enough truth mixed in to make the story believable.

Chapter 23

"Her grandmother's death? Really?" Marlee exclaimed.

"Pam was the one who found Ethel DeWitt at the farm. Grandpa Edgar was over at the neighbors' having coffee. He hadn't been tested for dementia yet and was still driving. The family just chalked his behavior up to typical forgetfulness that comes with old age. Pam said she stopped out to visit her grandparents and found her grandma collapsed on the upstairs bathroom floor." Barry rattled off the details of this additional tragedy that occurred at the DeWitt farm.

"What caused her collapse?" Marlee asked.

"She went into a diabetic coma because of low blood sugar. No one was around to help her, and she wasn't able to get her insulin shot. According to the report I saw at the station, Pam said Grandma Ethel was already gone by the time she found her," Barry reported.

"That sounds plausible. Why did the cops have doubts?" Marlee asked.

"Because of Billy's death five years prior. It just seemed odd that Pam was at the scene of yet another unexpected passing of a relative. Everything could have happened just as she said. There was no evidence of foul play on Pam's part, and it was deemed a death due to natural causes," Barry said.

"Was anyone in the family suspicious?" Marlee asked.

"There were questions by Billy's father, Art, but nothing was ever pursued. I guess everyone just accepted it," Barry reported.

"And then Billy's father died just last year. How did he die? Was Pam a suspect in his death too?" Marlee's imagination was running away with her and she knew it, but was unable to jump off this high-speed train of thought.

"Naw, he died from a long-term illness," Barry replied. "There wasn't anything fishy about his death."

Barry went to the dorm lobby and waited while Marlee got dressed. They drove to a greasy spoon and ate a hearty breakfast of scrambled eggs, hash browns, sausage, and toast. Pop refills were unlimited, so Marlee also drank four Diet Pepsis, and Barry gulped down at least that many glasses of Mountain Dew.

After their meal, they discussed the latest developments regarding Tim's death. "What caused the blow to Tim's head? Has the coroner figured it out yet?" Marlee asked.

"Not exactly. It was a blunt instrument, so it could have been a baseball bat or a tire iron. Anything with a bit of weight to it like that could be the weapon," Barry said.

"Were there any bats or tire irons in the shed?"

"No, there isn't anything in the shed that could be the weapon. And based on the angle of the blow and the location of the wound on Tim's head, he could not have hit himself. The cause of death was changed to homicide," Barry said.

"So, it's official. Someone killed Tim, but we just don't know who. That's really scary when I think about it. I might have talked to the killer." Marlee shuddered as she gave this some serious thought. "Who do you think did it?"

"My money is on Pam. It's just too much of a coincidence for her not to be involved. She had motive because she wanted to keep the farm for herself. She had means because there are all types of blunt instruments on a farm. And Pam had opportunity. Tim was killed on the family farm where Pam lived sometime after the fire at Stairway to Hell. Like I said, just too many coincidences to be believable."

"Okay, I know anyone can be capable of about anything, but does Pam strike you as a killer? I mean, I get that she had motive and could have done it. But does your intuition tell you she's involved?" Marlee asked.

"Intuition is useful, but I look at the evidence.

Besides, she might be a psychopath, like Dr. Eisner talked about in criminology at the beginning of the semester. She might be capable of distinguishing between right and wrong but not have any empathy for others," Barry said as they both reflected on the lecture in criminology.

"If Pam is guilty, then we need to believe she lured Tim out of his house and set the house on fire. Then she took him somewhere, probably her house. At some point, she killed him and stashed him in the shed. And if that's all true, then there's a good chance she killed Billy and maybe even her grandmother. It would take quite a bit of cunning and criminal intelligence to pull these off. I don't think Pam's stupid, but she's not exactly a genius," Marlee said.

"So, who do you think killed Tim?" Barry asked, trying not to roll his eyes but not trying very hard.

"I don't know who killed Tim, but I think his roommates know a hell of a lot more than they've told the cops or me, and I still think Beth Van Dam's death might be a key component in this too," Marlee said.

Barry didn't even try to hide his disdain. "Are you kidding? You still think Beth was killed? Come on, it was an accident, and you know it! If there was something suspicious about her death, the coroner and detectives would have found it. And why would Tim's roommates kill him? Because he was late with his rent check this month? Because he ate some food that belonged to one of the other guys?"

"I may not be a cop, but my theories are just as credible as yours!" Marlee exclaimed as she slammed down the last of her Diet Pepsi. "I know the outcome of the investigation into Beth's death, and I don't know why I think her death is fishy or why Tim's roommates would want to kill him. All I know is that I can feel it."

"Are you saying you have ESP?" Barry frowned and tried not to roll his eyes again.

"No, I don't have any special powers. I'm just telling you I can feel that there's more to Beth's case and

Tim's case than meets the eye. Call it what you want," Marlee said.

"But as an officer of the law, I can't base my decisions on feelings. It's all well and fine to have feelings, but unless there's proof to back it up, then those feelings mean nothing. I can't go into court and testify what my feelings were. The judge and the jury want evidence," Barry said in a gentler tone.

"You don't have to talk to me like I'm nine years old. I know feelings are not evidence, but I also know your brain picks up a lot more than what your senses tell you. I've taken enough psychology to know that we pick up on subtle cues that we can't even identify," Marlee said, proud of herself for standing up to Barry, who seemed to be turning into a bully when his views on police work were challenged.

"Hmmm, I don't know that I buy into psychology," Barry said.

"It's a social science, and it's one of my majors. There are a number of world-renowned theorists who studied psychology and have expanded the field into what it is today," Marlee said.

"It's Head Shrinking 101 as far as I'm concerned. Give me a bloody knife or a gun at the crime scene any day," Barry said. It was obvious they weren't going to agree on the debate, so Marlee dropped it. For about a minute.

"Duh! A weapon at the scene with the culprit standing there waiting to give a confession is the dream scenario, but how often does that happen?" Marlee asked, not pausing to give Barry a chance to answer. "Not very often, I bet. That's why you have to rely on feelings and intuition too."

Barry was tired of arguing too, and it was his turn to let the matter drop. He drove her back to the dorm and dropped her off. "Let me know if there are any updates, okay?" Marlee asked and he agreed.

After giving Jasmine a brief update, Marlee

226

realized she still had time to prepare for her classes on Monday. Pulling her backpack from the bottom of a heap of dirty clothes, she looked at her day planner. It was then she realized she had a paper due the next day in her social problems course. "Dammit!" she yelled. Marlee was good at scheduling and rarely forgot anything, but the drama of two deaths in the past week had put her into a tailspin.

"How am I going to get this paper done before class tomorrow morning?" She rummaged through her notes, reminding herself of her topic and headed off to the library. Her class was at 9:00 am the next day, and she finished late that afternoon with hours to spare, wondering why she'd been so worried.

Trudging back to the dorm, Marlee bumped into Barry on his way to the library. He motioned her over, and Marlee thought he was going to apologize for his asinine behavior at breakfast that morning. Instead, what he had to say was better. Much, much better.

Barry was upbeat, almost giddy, as he reported his news. "I found something out about Beth Van Dam this afternoon. It doesn't change the ruling in her death, but it's very interesting. Turns out, she wasn't a prostitute after all."

"How do you know?" Marlee nearly shrieked until she realized she was in a public campus building and people were turning to look at them.

"Detective Barkley went to the Moon Glow Motel and put the pressure on Robbie, the manager. He backtracked on the story he told you about Beth meeting clients there. When Barkley threatened to arrest him for providing false information to the police, Robbie admitted he was paid to tell that story to the cops or anyone else that asked."

"Why? Who paid Robbie to say that?" Marlee asked.

"They haven't gotten that out of him yet. They took him down to the station for additional questioning and are hoping he gives up the person who hired him," Barry said.

"If Beth's case is closed, then why did Detective Barkley even go to the Moon Glow to confront Robbie?"

"Through his work on another case, he found out the story of Beth working as a hooker was false. He had to talk to Robbie anyway on this other case, and Beth's name came up."

"Barry, why did you say that this new information doesn't change the ruling on Beth's case? It seems to me that it blows the case wide open," Marlee said. Seeing Barry's blank look, she continued. "Tim and his three roommates each told me that Beth was a prostitute. Maybe they're the ones who started the story and paid Robbie to tell it to the police."

He gave a deep sigh. "I know you want there to be more to Beth's case. That's why I was anxious to tell you this bit of news. But it doesn't change anything. What motive would Tim and his roommates have for saying Beth worked as a hooker? Maybe they heard it from someone else and just took the story at face value. There's no reason they would pay a motel clerk to fabricate a story about Beth. No reason at all."

Marlee smiled. "What if I told you that I can just feel the guys from Stairway to Hell are mixed up in this somehow?"

"I'd say, show me the evidence," Barry said, his old skeptical self returning.

"I'll do that!" Marlee said with more confidence than she felt as she continued her walk back to the dorm.

228

I never thought about it before now, but I guess you can be a victim and a criminal at the same time.

Chapter 24

Jasmine wasn't in the dorm room when Marlee arrived, and she was disappointed not to have her roommate there to discuss the latest news in both Beth and Tim's cases. Since she couldn't talk about it, she did the next best thing. By the time Jasmine returned from the library at 6:30, Marlee had updated the notebook. She also put together a timeline for both cases and was in the process of synthesizing all the comments people had made to her about the cases. Marlee had a separate sheet of paper which set forth the information about Billy's death at the DeWitt farm ten years ago.

"I take it you didn't get your paper done," Jasmine said as she unpacked her backpack and began putting books on her desk.

"Nope. Finished the paper. Then I decided to bring the notebook up to date, and I'm putting together timelines," Marlee said, showing her finished work to Jasmine like a proud kindergartener hungry for praise.

Jasmine peered over her roommate's shoulder and took in the latest news. "Wait! Beth wasn't a prostitute?" Her long, boney fingers grasped Marlee's shoulder in a death grip.

Struggling away from her roommate's clenches, Marlee detailed her conversation with Barry and her suspicions regarding the guys from Stairway to Hell. "Each one of them told me they heard Beth was working as a hooker. Why do that unless they have something to hide?"

"Exactly! There's no reason to say that unless they were intentionally spreading a rumor. Do you think they're the ones who paid the motel clerk to confirm it?" Jasmine asked.

"I don't know. There are several possibilities. Only one of them could be involved or two or more. Or they all might be in on it. What I don't get is why any of them would do it. What would they have to gain other than trying to throw the cops off the trail of a death investigation? That suggests they had something to do with Beth dying, or they know something very important about it."

Shaking her head, Jasmine tried to wrap her head around the latest news regarding Beth. "Did you ever talk to her dirtbag boyfriend again? You know, they guy who hit on you when you were there asking about Beth?"

"No, I never went back. That guy gave me the creeps, but that's not why I didn't go back. It just didn't seem like there was anything new in Beth's case that involved him. Maybe it's time to go chat with him again. This time I'm taking someone with me!" Marlee said.

"Oh, no! Not me. I don't want to be used as bait again," Jasmine said.

"Not you, Jazz. I'll take Barry. Maybe Barry can get that slimeball to answer some questions. He'll probably call tonight, and I'll run the plan by him," Marlee said.

"You two seem to be getting pretty cozy," Jasmine teased.

"Not at all. We're strictly co-investigators working on the same cases. Besides, he doesn't think psychology is a science. How could I ever date someone like that?"

"I don't know," Jasmine continued in a sing-song voice. "You spend a lot of late nights and early mornings together. If I didn't know better..."

"Very funny. I have no attraction to Barry, and the feeling is mutual. But if I ever became a cop, I wouldn't mind working with him. We make a good team. That's all," Marlee said, and she meant it. She finally felt comfortable around Barry knowing that he was no longer pining for her. In fact, she had a friend that she was thinking of setting up with him.

When Barry called that night, he didn't have anything else to report on any of the cases they'd been discussing. "I mentioned your theory about the Stairway to Hell guys to my sergeant, and he laughed at me. Then he said he'd think about it. You might actually be on to something."

"Jazz and I were talking, and she suggested that I go back and talk to Eddie Turner, Beth's icky boyfriend. I wondered if you wanted to go along," Marlee said letting the idea hang in the air while the cop thought it over.

"Yeah, sure. Tomorrow is my day off. I'll call you after I have some sleep, and we can put together a plan. Maybe my sergeant will have more thoughts on the Stairway to Hell guys by then."

After they finished their call, Jasmine continued with her teasing. "Sounds like you have a date!"

"Only if the date includes confronting liars and sleazebags," Marlee said with a smile, already anticipating what she was going to ask the Stairway to Hell guys and Eddie Turner. It was time for some serious answers, and she meant to get them one way or another.

The two went upstairs to the dorm cafeteria and were soon joined at their table by Polly and Kristie. "Hey, strangers! Haven't seen you guys around much," Polly chirped in a way that made Marlee want to slap her even before she sat down.

"We've been around, just busy with classes and such," Jasmine said.

"And such? Ooh, that sounds interesting," Polly said as she leaned in, always ready for the latest gossip. "Does 'and such' involve guys?"

"Yes, it does, Polly. Jazz and I have been dating twin lumber jacks, and we've been out on the town with them for several nights."

Polly's jaw dropped, figuring she would need to work a lot harder to get the scoop on her neighbors. "Really? How did you meet these guys?"

"We went roller skating one day, and they were there. They came up to us and asked us to couple skate," Jasmine added, jumping on board with the developing story.

"I didn't know there was a roller rink in town.

Actually, I didn't know people roller skated anymore," Polly said.

"Roller skating is making a comeback," Marlee assured her nosy neighbor. "How about you? What have you been doing?"

The only thing Polly loved more than collecting information was spreading gossip. "Did you hear about Janice from third floor? The one who fell down the stairs at Stairway to Hell at their party right before Christmas? She's pregnant!"

Marlee and Jasmine both raised their eyebrows as Polly continued with the lowdown on the impregnated dorm mate and the possibilities as to the paternity. "It could be anybody. Janice is such a slut."

"That's a bit harsh, Polly," Jasmine chided. She didn't really know Janice, but neither did Polly.

"Well, that's just what I've heard," Polly said defensively. "Everyone says it about her."

"I never heard anything like that, and it doesn't matter anyway," Marlee said. "If she's pregnant, I'm sure everything will work out just fine. And if she's not, then I don't want to be somebody spreading gossip about it." She gave Polly a pointed look. It shut her up for thirty seconds, which was a new record.

Although Marlee tried to steer Polly's gossip toward Tim and his roommates, she appeared not to know much. Either that, or she was protecting Blake Rikers, whom she had a crush on since she spent an evening at his house. "I already told you everything I know about Beth, the party, and Blake. I only know Tim from parties at his house and have no clue how he died. Why are you so interested anyway? You didn't know Tim or Beth much better than I did."

Marlee didn't answer. She knew anything she said or did would be exaggerated and then Polly would pass it on to whomever was available to listen to her poison. They made small talk until they finished their meals.

Seething inside, Marlee complained to Jasmine on

the walk back to their room. "Polly can be such a bitch. And she does it for no reason whatsoever. I think she feels bad about herself, so she goes out of her way to bring others down to her level."

"Did you learn that in one of your psychology classes?" Jasmine asked.

"No, my mom explained it to me when I was a little girl. Somebody who's mean to others is upset with their own life, not everyone else's."

"That makes total sense. Your mom sounds like a wise lady," Jasmine said.

"She is," Marlee replied. "She understands how people work."

"Polly can be nice if she wants something, but most of the time she's a super-shitty friend. I don't want anything to do with her any more. She's getting worse," Jasmine said. "And Kristie hates being her roommate. She barely talked tonight at supper."

"I don't like Polly at all, and I'm going to take a stand. I'm not hanging out with her any more even though I know it means walking to the bar and to parties from now on," Marlee said.

"We'll walk together, because I'm not hanging out with her anymore either," Jasmine said with a nod in solidarity. "And Kristie will walk with us too."

Marlee smiled as they walked back to their room, knowing her true friends were with her and that she would always have to deal with gossip mongers and hate spreaders like Polly. Jasmine and Marlee spent a quiet night in their room reading and preparing for the next day's classes.

The next morning, Marlee and Jasmine woke up on time, ate some toast, and made it to their first classes. It felt wonderful to be prepared and on time, and Marlee vowed to keep this trend going, no matter what developed in Beth and Tim's cases. She engaged in her classes, ate a quick lunch at the Student Union, went to the library to study, and then attended her criminology class in the afternoon.

After criminology, Marlee and Barry met at the coffee shop on the corner of campus. "Anything new with your sergeant? Has he considered that maybe the Stairway to Hell guys had something to do in Beth's death?" Marlee asked as she sipped her hot chocolate.

"No decisions yet, but he called me in to talk about it some more. I think he believes there's merit to your theory about Tim and his roommates," Barry said. Marlee smiled at him, knowing it had to be hard to admit he was wrong, and she was right. He was an eight-year veteran of the police force, and she was a sophomore college student. Still, he handled it well, acknowledging her theory.

"Each one of the Stairway to Hell roommates told me that they either knew or had heard that Beth was a prostitute. Obviously, we can't talk to Tim about it, but the other three are still around. How do you think we should go about questioning them?" Marlee asked.

"I've been thinking about it, and it seems like you and your roommate got a lot of information using the tactics you devised," Barry said.

"You mean having Jazz dress in a miniskirt and flirt with the guys while I pull one aside at a time to question them?" Marlee asked. "You want us to do that again?"

"Yes, but with me in the room while you talk to them individually. That way I can make sure you're safe and also ask questions," Barry said.

"You don't need to worry about me. I think Jazz is more in need of protection than I am," Marlee said. "She handled those guys just fine last time, but I'm kind of worried about her now. Especially since we found out about Adam's rape charge. Plus, if the other roommates are involved in Tim's death, and maybe Beth's too, then I think Jazz needs someone to keep an eye on things."

"Jasmine seems very strong to me. I don't think you give her enough credit," Barry said.

236

Marlee glared at him. "But you think I need someone to watch over me? Are you kidding?" She envisioned herself ten times more able to take care of herself than Jasmine or any of her other female friends.

"No, that's not what I meant. Jasmine comes across as harmless and flirty. They'll see you as a threat because you don't play around," Barry said.

At that point, she felt closer to Barry than ever before. "Thanks," she said as she blushed. Marlee didn't need to be complimented on looks, but she did want to be recognized for her street smarts and ability to get shit done. Barry just accomplished both of those things and had managed to dig out of the hole he worked himself into during their previous conversation.

"So, what should I ask them?" Marlee asked. "I thought I'd start out with some chit-chat like before and then ask how they knew Beth was a hooker. After they told their story, I'd hit them with the fact that I knew Beth never worked as a prostitute and that they'd lied to me."

"Sounds good to me," Barry said. "It might hamper the interview if I sit in, but I want to be able to hear what's going on. We'll get you fitted with a wire so I can sit outside and hear what's going on. If any of them threaten you or Jasmine, I'll be able to intervene. Doug will help, and I'm sure he'd be happy to help Jasmine get wired up too."

"What's Doug's deal? Jasmine likes him," Marlee said, stating the obvious.

"Doug's a nice guy, but he's not single. Not yet. He's going through a divorce, and it should be finalized by summer. I hope he told Jasmine about that. They would be good together, but I don't want him to lie to her about his wife and his son," Barry said.

"Wow, you're actually ratting out your friend to make sure he does the right thing by Jasmine? That's cool," said Marlee.

Barry looked at the floor, embarrassed by the positive affirmation. "I don't know if Doug told her about his situation yet, but I'm sure he will in due time. He likes her too. And I'm not ratting him out by saying this!"

"No, of course not," Marlee said, backtracking so as not to offend the officer with the medium-sized ego. "I was just impressed that you told the whole story about Doug. A lot of guys would say their friend is the best person in the world even when he's a serial killer."

Barry broke into a hearty laugh. "I'm sure Doug's not a serial killer, unless you count hunting pheasants."

"Is he trying to fix things with his wife? Is he seeing anyone else?"

"Doug's been a mess since he found out his wife is a drug addict. The only time I've seen him come to life in the past six months was when he was around Jasmine. I know for a fact that he and Margo are not getting back together. The only reason they aren't already divorced is that they've been fighting over custody of their son," Barry said. "He's not seeing anyone else either. I'm sure of it."

They finished their discussion about meeting with the Stairway to Hell roommates that night. Marlee walked back to the dorm and explained the whole process to Jasmine.

She took a deep breath and waited before she answered. "I'm in, and I know exactly what I need to do!"

If a lie is repeated often enough it becomes a fact.

Chapter 25

"What are you guys doing in there? Are you having a party? I can hear guys' voices," yelled Polly through a closed door as she feverishly knocked.

Marlee, Jasmine, Barry, and Doug all held their breath until the pest from next door went away. "Keep your voices down," Marlee chastised. "Or else Miss National Enquirer will be over here." The guys both nodded, unaccustomed to the acoustics of dorm living.

After both Marlee and Jasmine were wired, the two police officers tested the wiring ability by having them speak. Once it was determined that the wires were in place and functioning, the group drove in two separate cars to the acreage to talk to the guys from Stairway to Hell. Marlee parked one car in front of the house, and she and Jasmine walked up to the front door. Barry and Doug hung back in the other car, listening to every conversation the women would have.

The smell of pizza wafted from the house as the front door was opened. Blake's cousin let Marlee and Jasmine inside and motioned for them to go downstairs. "Guys! You've got company," he yelled past them.

The scent of pizza intensified as they walked downstairs. In the corner of the living room was a toaster oven and the wrappers from two frozen pizzas. The oven dinged just as the girls descended into the main room. John and Adam stood up from their chairs, paper plates in hand. Blake remained seated, still working on a slice left on his plate.

"What do you two want?" growled Adam as he sliced the pizza into six pieces with a jack knife that he folded up and placed in his pocket after wiping it clean.

Marlee took a deep breath, knowing she needed to lie her ass off and make nice with these guys. "We're here to apologize. I acted like a jerk when we were here the other night. I don't know what to say other than I'd been drinking, and I was jealous of all the attention Jasmine was getting. I'm sorry and wanted to let you guys know that it's not how I really am."

Jasmine nodded along. "And I didn't mean to get so emotional. I was having a good time with you guys and then everything just went wrong." She looked sad, and Marlee had to admit that her roommate was getting much better at lying. It was an uncomfortable silence as the guys grabbed more pizza and flopped back down into their chairs.

John was the one to finally break the ice. "Grab a beer from the fridge and sit down." Marlee knew this was guy speak for "all is forgiven." She grabbed cans of beer for herself and Jasmine, and they settled in on the couch. A basketball game was on the television, and she feigned interest until her eyes felt as though they couldn't stay open any longer. At least Jasmine cared about sports and was able to carry on a conversation that held the guys' interest. She wore stirrup pants and a long sweater, but was no less captivating than the last time she was at the house. When Jasmine spoke, the guys listened.

It was during one of Jasmine's comments that Marlee pulled Adam away from the rest of the group. "Why did you tell me Beth was a prostitute? I know for a fact that she wasn't," Marlee hissed as she maintained eye contact with Adam.

He looked shocked then dropped his gaze as only someone caught in a lie would do. "I didn't pay her for sex, but I heard other guys did."

"Who?' Marlee asked pointedly.

"I don't know of anyone specifically. It was a rumor going around," Adam said.

"If it was a rumor, why would you tell it like it was a fact?" Marlee asked, challenging him.

"I didn't. I mean, I don't know. I heard it at the bar from some guys I was talking to. Beth walked by, and they all commented that she was a hooker. I didn't ask for any details. Just took them at their word," Adam said.

242

"Who were these guys?" Marlee asked.

"Don't know. We didn't exactly introduce ourselves," Adam said.

"Had you seen them before?"

"Once or twice, I guess," Adam said.

"So, you'd remember them if you saw them again?" Marlee pressed on.

"Maybe. I don't know. I was pretty drunk," he said.

"Yeah, right. You're full of bullshit!" Marlee exclaimed, not caring how this made Adam feel.

"Screw you! You don't know anything about me, and you come in here throwing around all kinds of accusations against me and my roommates. Who do you think you are?" Adam shouted.

"You're very defensive for someone who says he doesn't know anything about Tim's death or Beth's. I think you guys are in it up to your eyeballs and so do the cops. It's only a matter of time before they come here and haul you guys down to the cop shop to answer some questions!"

"That would take proof, and the cops don't have evidence that me or my roommates did anything illegal," Adam retorted.

"An arrest and conviction take proof, but anybody can be questioned about their knowledge or involvement in a crime. Better get your story ready because I'm sure the cops are dying to hear it," Marlee spat back at Adam.

Adam stood up and flipped her off with both hands before storming past the rest of the group. He went into a bedroom and slammed the door. At least she wouldn't have to deal with him contaminating her upcoming talks with his two remaining roommates.

Jasmine was working her magic and had Blake and John entranced with a story detailing a mix-up with a class assignment. The guys hung on her every word, enchanted with telling of a tale that had happened to all of them at least once.

Marlee crooked a finger at John, motioning him to follow her to the far corner of the basement. She was impressed that people would agree to speak with her about personal matters even though she had no authority to be doing so. It was a classic example of people obeying those they believed were in authority. But why the guys from Stairway to Hell would think she had any more authority than any other student was beyond her.

John leaned against the wall, and Marlee stood inches away from him. "How did you find out Beth was a prostitute?"

"Adam told me. Why?" John asked, not missing a beat.

"Adam? How did he know?" Marlee asked.

"I didn't ask, but I guessed somebody he knew was a customer," John replied.

"When did he tell you about Beth's occupation?"

"It was a few weeks before she died. Less than a month, anyway. Why all the questions about Beth working as a hooker? I thought her case was closed."

"It was, but it was just determined by the cops that she really wasn't a prostitute and that someone paid others around town to spread the lie. Do you know anything about that?" Marlee asked.

"No, how would I?" John scoffed.

Marlee shrugged and changed her line of questioning. "Did Tim ever tell you anything about his sister and how she took over the family farm?"

"Sure, we all heard about it. When Tim got drunk he told the story of his sister taking the farm away from him. I don't know if it was true or not, but Tim was really pissed about the whole thing," John said.

"Did he mention anything else about Pam?"

"Just that she was evil and had the whole family wrapped around her finger," John recalled. "He hated her and was counting the days until he could take the farm away from her."

"But he still had at least a year or two before graduation," Marlee said, recalling a conversation she had with Tim in a 200-level class taken almost exclusively by sophomores.

"Oh, no. He was graduating in May. Tim took a heavy course load every semester and during the summer too. He was set to graduate after just three years," John said.

"So, Tim really was counting down the days until he was finished with college and able to take over the farm," Marlee said more to herself than to John. During all the questioning of people and uncovering new evidence, Marlee never thought to determine Tim's graduation date. This fact placed Pam back at the center of the controversy, especially since she told Marlee that Tim had a year left before graduation.

"Yeah, and I guess Pam was none too happy about it," John said. "I heard them arguing on the phone one day when I came home early from class. He said something like 'I'm taking over in May, and there's nothing you can do about it.' When Tim saw me standing there, he hung up the phone and tried to play the whole thing off like it was a joke. He only talked about the issue with Pam and the farm with me when he was really blitzed. When he was sober, he never even mentioned his family."

"Did Tim ever say anything about an accident at the farm when he was just a kid? A cousin of his died about ten years ago when the cousin, Tim, and Pam were playing," Marlee explained.

"He said something about a cousin being killed and Pam knowing all about it, but that's all he ever said. That was one night right before he passed out on the couch," John said. "Did Pam kill their cousin?"

"Tim made claims to that effect, but Pam was never charged. Everyone seemed to think it was just an accident," she said, hoping she wasn't providing John with too much information. Since they had a good dialog going, Marlee hoped to get more details by providing him with some details he might not have otherwise known.

John was dumbstruck. His mouth hung open and his eyes bulged as he digested the news Marlee just dropped in his lap. "Are you kidding?"

"No, Tim told several people that Pam dared their cousin to climb to the top of a ladder and when he did, she shook it and he fell. Billy broke his neck and died. It all happened in the same shed where Tim's body was found," Marlee said.

"No, he never said any more about it," John replied.

"Surely, Blake must have brought it up. He and Tim have been friends since they were little boys. They lived right across the street from each other growing up. Even if Blake didn't know about it at the time it happened, I'm sure he would have heard something as he got older from his parents or the neighbors," Marlee said.

"Blake never said anything about a death at Tim's family's farm. Either he didn't know or was keeping it to himself."

"Maybe Tim asked him to keep it quiet, and they just talked about it between the two of them. Or maybe Tim didn't talk about it at all except when he was really drunk," Marlee suggested.

John shrugged. "I don't know. I just don't know. This is all news to me." He sat quietly and then put his head in his hands. "What do you think happened?" he finally asked.

"I'm trying to figure out what happened. That's why I keep coming out here to talk to you guys. You weren't just his roommates. You were his best friends. In order to find out more about the crime, I need to have a better understanding of Tim, and you guys are the best resources," Marlee replied. "Do you really think Beth died because she drank too much and then fell down and froze to death?"

"Well, yeah. Sure. I mean, that's what the cops think, right?" John asked.

"But what do you think happened? Just between you and me, do you think there's more to her death than that?" Marlee asked.

246

"It's possible, I suppose," John said.

"Did you know that the autopsy revealed that Beth was pregnant?" Marlee asked.

"No, I didn't. Do they know who the father is?" John asked.

"Yes," Marlee said, bluffing, not even knowing if the paternity of a fetus could be determined after death.

John looked at Marlee with a forlorn expression. "Was it Tim's baby?"

Have you ever played the game Two Truths and a Lie? The first person in the group makes three statements and the others try to guess which one is the lie. Everyone takes their turn, and it's a lot of fun trying to separate truths from lies. I've been lied to and deceived so much in real life that I always assume people are lying whenever their lips are moving.

Chapter 26

Marlee did her best to hold her composure and not show any shock or emotion. "Do you think Beth was carrying Tim's baby?"

"I don't know. I just wondered," John said.

"So, they were seeing each other? Beth and Tim?" Marlee asked.

"Nothing serious, at least not on Beth's part. I just think they got together when they were drunk. She stayed over a few times in Tim's room, and they seemed pretty cozy before they went to his room," said John.

"Could Tim have anything to do with Beth dying, especially if he knew she was pregnant with his baby?" Marlee asked.

"No, he's not a typical college guy. He would love to have a family, especially since he was moving out to the farm after graduation. A wife and a baby by his side while he was running his grandparents' farm would be a dream come true for Tim. If he knew Beth was pregnant, he would have asked her to marry him right away. He was really traditional like that," John said.

"What if somebody else was the father?" Marlee asked. "What would Tim think of that?"

"Tim would have stepped up and married her, or at least been involved in the baby's life if he was the dad. If he wasn't the baby's father, he would have hoped for the best for Beth and the baby, and that would be all. Tim wouldn't be so jealous over Beth's involvement with another guy that he would kill her, if that's what you're getting at," John said.

"How long had this thing with Tim and Beth been going on?" Marlee asked.

"They were together for a couple months. He even met her parents. After she died, he told me her mother asked him to be a pall bearer at Beth's funeral. As far as I know, he agreed. But then there was the fire, and Tim disappeared, so I don't know for sure what happened," John said.

"Tim knew Beth's parents? They must have been fairly close if they were meeting each other's parents," Marlee observed.

"Beth introduced them when her mom and dad came to town one weekend. I don't think she planned it. Tim just happened to be around when they were visiting. They liked him right off the bat. Tim was more serious about their relationship than Beth was. In fact, I think she's the one who wanted to go from being in a relationship to just being friends," John reported.

"How did Tim handle the movement from boyfriend-girlfriend to just friends?" Marlee asked.

"He tried to play it off like it was no big deal. Tim was a man of few words, as you know. But it bothered him. He liked Beth, and I think he'd envisioned their relationship going in a different direction. Maybe even marriage some time down the road," said John.

Marlee was shocked. She never thought about any of her friends or classmates being at the marriage stage. Sure, she had friends from high school who were already married, but most of the college crowd seemed to be all about partying and sometimes classes. "Tim was serious enough about Beth that he considered marriage?"

"He never came out and said it, but he danced around the subject a few times. We all teased him about it, and he didn't deny it. He really liked Beth, loved her, even."

"Had Tim ever been that serious about anyone else?" Marlee inquired.

"No, I don't even remember him seeing any other girl other than just once or twice. This was a big deal for Tim. It wasn't even so much what he said, but just the look he had on his face every time Beth was around or we brought up her name," John said. "He thought a lot of her."

"What did Beth think of Tim?" Marlee asked.

"She seemed to be having a good time without any attachment. Beth was always up for a good time, but I don't think she wanted to be held back. A steady boyfriend would be too much for her. She was all about having fun and enjoying the moment. I talked to her at a party one time at Stairway to Hell, and she was bitching about her sister who was only a year older than her. The sister just got married and was moving to her husband's farm up north. She was really critical of the whole thing, but I don't know if it was the marriage, the living arrangements, or the sister that had Beth the most upset."

"Could you ever see Beth marrying Tim, having a baby, and living on a farm outside of town?" Marlee asked.

"Hell, no!" exclaimed John. "Not that she ever told me, but if I had to guess, I think Beth would leave the area as soon as she got her degree. I could see her moving to Minneapolis or Chicago and spending the rest of her life in a big city."

Marlee agreed. "I can't picture her as a farm wife either."

Marlee was pleased with the information she had extracted from John. She was happy that this discussion ended on a much more positive note than her talk with Adam. After their discussion, Marlee asked John to send Blake over to talk with her.

Blake caught her by surprise as he bounded over seconds later. "What are you doing?" he asked as he saw her standing there.

She hadn't yet decided what type of interview tactics to use on this guy. With Adam, she had been confrontational and aggressive, but with John she took an approach as if they were two colleagues sharing information. Blake wasn't as cooperative as John, yet not as combative as Adam.

"So, what can you tell me about Beth Van Dam working as a prostitute?" Marlee asked, jumping right into the topic she most wanted to discuss.

"I never paid her for sex," Blake said with an air of

indignance.

"No, I didn't mean that. I meant, what had you heard about Beth working as a hooker?" Marlee said, clarifying her position with the hopes of putting Blake more at ease.

"Not much, just that was a prostitute and worked out of the bars and out of the truck stop on the edge of town," Blake replied.

"How did you hear about it?" Marlee asked.

"Everyone knew about it. I don't remember how I first heard about it," Blake said.

"The police thought Beth was a hooker, but now they've found out that she wasn't. Somebody was paying people around town to spread that lie about her," Marlee said, intentionally leaving her comments open-ended.

"Who would do that?" Blake furrowed his brow.

"That's what I'm trying to find out," Marlee said.

"Why are you asking around about Beth and Tim? It's not like you're a cop or anything," Blake said.

"I knew both of them, although not very well. And it really chaps my ass that they both died and nothing is being done about it," Marlee said.

Blake raised his eyebrows and looked directly at Marlee but didn't offer any additional information.

"What did you know about the relationship between Beth and Tim?" Marlee asked.

"I think 'relationship' is overstating what was going on. They were just getting together once in a while. It wasn't anything serious," said Blake.

"Really? I heard Tim thought about marrying Beth before she broke it off with him," Marlee said, not naming her source of information.

Blake burst out laughing. "I don't know where you're getting your facts, but Tim wasn't all that interested in Beth. Sure, they slept together a few times, but she didn't mean anything to him. I know she wanted to sink her claws into Tim and would do whatever it took," commented Blake.

252

"So, you're saying that Beth was the one who wanted a relationship, not Tim?" Marlee asked, confused by the conflicting information she was receiving from Tim's roommates.

"Yeah, Tim was just using Beth for sex," Blake said.

"That doesn't sound like the Tim I knew. It doesn't sound consistent with anything I've heard from anyone else either," Marlee said, letting the implication hang in the air.

"I'm not lying. Why would I?" Blake asked defensively.

Marlee shrugged, not baiting him any further.

"Maybe the other people you talked to didn't know Tim as well as I did," Blake said. "Of course, his family wouldn't know much about his sex life."

"Were there other women Tim was seeing at the same time?" Marlee asked.

"Probably. I didn't keep track of everything he was up to. I've got my own life," Blake sneered.

"But you seemed to know quite a lot about Tim and Beth. How is that?" Marlee asked.

"Why do you care? Did you have the hots for Tim?" Blake asked.

Marlee started laughing. "No, I didn't. I'm worried that his death and Beth's aren't being taken seriously enough by the police or anyone else. Don't you want to find out what really happened?"

"What does it matter? They're both dead, and they aren't coming back. What are you getting out of all of this?" Blake accused. "I think you just like the attention."

"Yep, you have me all figured out. I'm asking all these questions just so I can get attention for myself. That's my only motive," Marlee said, not trying to hold back the bite of sarcasm as she glared at Blake. "And what happened between you and Beth on the night of the party when she died? People saw the two of you walking upstairs together."

"We're done here. I'm not talking to you any more,

you psycho bitch!" Blake said as he stormed off.

"That was uncalled for," Marlee thought as she pondered Blake's accusations about her involvement. She only wanted to get to the bottom of what really happened to Beth and Tim. Why would anyone ever think she was only asking around to get attention for herself? But maybe she was. Who was she, a sophomore college student, to think she could figure out both mysterious deaths when a trained police force was working on them? Did she really think that her involvement was essential to getting to the bottom of both cases?

Marlee sat in self-reflection for a few minutes, deciding if she had the best of intentions in nosing around these cases or if she was doing it to fulfill some need of her own. *I'm only trying to help*, she thought, reassuring herself that her motives were pure.

She walked down the stairs and retrieved Jasmine. Only John was in the basement living room chatting with her. "Ready to go?" Marlee asked. John waived good bye as they left. The other two roommates were likely just waiting for them to get the hell out of their living space.

They left the home and met Barry and Doug at the pre-established location. They each ordered up gigantic burgers with an overflowing portion of fries and dug in. Marlee chugged a Diet Pepsi as she crammed the salty fries in her mouth. She was so excited about what they learned from the Stairway to Hell guys that she talked with her mouth stuffed full of food. "They certainly don't have their stories straight. Each one of them has a bit of a different story to tell. And Blake and John's stories actually contradict each other."

"Maybe it was intentional," suggested Doug in a rare moment of speech.

Everyone turned toward him for clarification. The upside of talking very little is that when Doug did speak, they all hung on his every word.

"What do you mean, Doug?" Jasmine asked, smiling as she talked to her cop crush.

"Maybe they all decided to tell you a different story to keep you guessing. You know, give three different stories, some of them bogus and some true. You don't know what's true so you check into everything, which is a huge waste of time," Doug said.

"That makes a lot of sense," Barry said, nodding in agreement.

"I can't figure out if the Stairway to Hell guys are all working together to stump us, or if they are working independently and don't know for sure what each one is saying to us," Marlee said.

"Or maybe a bit of both," Doug added.

Again, everyone turned and waited for him to expand on his thought. "They may all think they're working together, but one or two might be telling their own versions, true or false," he stated.

"But they would have to know if they have an agreed-upon story and one of them deviates from the script that we'll figure it out eventually, and the cops will know about it," Marlee said.

"Jasmine, your microphone was kind of muffled, so I couldn't always hear what you were saying. Did you find out anything of importance while you were talking to the guys?" Doug asked. Now that he'd broken the ice by talking there was no shutting him up.

"Not really. The guys are planning to stay at Blake's cousin's house for the rest of the semester and find a new rental this summer. Nobody knows anything else about the fire. They lost almost everything they had, which wasn't much. Their landlord helped them in finding some towels and bedding at the second-hand store. A campus group gave clothes and money to replace their books for classes. None of the guys had anything else to add about Tim or Beth. Adam was really defensive when I brought up the subject, but John and Blake didn't object to talking about it," Jasmine reported.

"You know who else I'd like to talk to?" Marlee asked. "Blake's cousin. He may have overhead something

255

or have some suspicions of his own he would be willing to share if anyone asked him. I also want to talk to Grandpa Edgar again at the nursing home, and I'm going to pay another visit to Eddie Turner's place."

"Eddie Turner?" asked Doug. "Is he the slimy boyfriend at the trailer park?"

"That's him," Marlee said. "He's a real creep, but I think he might have some more information. If I catch him when he's drinking, he might be willing to talk."

"From what you told me earlier, it sounds like Eddie's always drinking," Jasmine said.

With the plan set in place for the next day, the foursome departed the Fryin' Pan, and Barry dropped off Marlee and Jasmine at their dorm.

"Tomorrow's the day we find out what happened to Beth and Tim," Marlee said with confidence. "I can feel it in my bones!"

Television and movies tend to portray murder as premeditated, but most are the unintentional consequence of a fight or a poor decision. Premeditated murders are planned, and every effort is made to conceal the identity of the killer. The deaths resulting from a bad decision tend to leave clues all over the place.

Chapter 27

Classes were an inconvenient necessity the next day. Marlee made it to every class, but learned absolutely nothing. She was present in body, but not in mind or spirit. As soon as her last class finished, she rushed from the building and back to the dorm to call Barry.

He picked up on the first ring and agreed to join her in talking to Grandpa Edgar at the old folk's home. Barry knew that Grandpa Edgar had said that Tim had come to see him and asked for the key to the shed at the farm. The point of this visit was to determine if that actually happened, and if so, when. After all, Tim could have asked his grandfather for the key months or even years earlier. Senility had a way of playing with the memory, making what happened years ago seem like a recent event.

It was mid-afternoon, and Grandpa Edgar had just woken from his nap. Marlee saw that as a positive sign. The rest may have allowed him to refresh a bit. She recalled her last visit with him when he began to fade after a short conversation.

"Hi!" Marlee said cheerily as she walked into the old man's room. He was sitting in a recliner by the window looking at the snow-covered ground. He turned when she and Barry walked in and gave a smile of recognition. "This is my friend, Barry, and we came to visit you." Edgar made an attempt at getting up to shake hands with Barry, but the cop strode over and grasped Edgar's hand so the old man didn't have to get out of his chair.

"We came to talk to you about your grandson, Tim," Marlee said. "Tim DeWitt." Grandpa Edgar nodded his head in recognition, and Marlee continued. "Did he ask you for the key to the shed on the farm?"

"Yes, he wanted the key because he knew I always kept it locked."

"When did he ask you for the key?" Marlee asked,

not sure if Edgar would be attuned to time frames.

"Not that long ago. Maybe a week," Edgar replied.

"Was there snow on the ground when he asked you for the key?" Marlee inquired.

"Hell yes, there was snow on the ground! I just said it was last week," Edgar barked.

"Why did Tim want to unlock the shed?" Barry asked, noticing the old man's irritation with Marlee.

"He didn't say. Just knew I had the key and wanted in," Edgar stated, now calm.

"Did Tim ever talk to you about his sister, Pam, being responsible for Billy's death at the shed?" Marlee asked. She knew she might be pushing it with the old man, but his time of lucidity was limited and they needed to find out what he knew.

"Tim always said Pam killed Billy. Nobody believed him. We all thought he'd snapped when Billy died, and it was just his imagination playing tricks on him. But he stuck to the story, and it never changed one bit in the way he told it. I started to think maybe he was telling the truth," Edgar said.

"What do you think of Pam running the farm?" Barry asked.

"I thought one of my sons would follow in my footsteps, but they had their own interests. When I had two grandsons, I hoped one of them would take over. Since Billy was older, it was naturally his birthright. But then he died, and Tim wasn't old enough to take over when I retired. So, Pam's parents talked me into letting her run the operation," Edgar reported.

"Are you happy with what she's done?" Barry asked.

"She's done okay, for a girl. I just don't like the idea of a woman running the farm. Everybody says I'm old fashioned, but it's just the way things were when I was younger," Edgar said.

"What did you think of Tim running the farm when he graduated college?" Marlee asked.

"I think he will do a great job, if the cops ever find him. The only problem will be getting Pam uprooted from the place. She won't leave without a fight," Edgar said, either unaware that Tim had been found dead or had forgotten it.

Marlee and Barry looked at each other. Their shared glance confirmed that neither thought they should bring up Tim's death. If Edgar already knew, then he had forgotten. If he didn't know, then the family or his doctors made the choice not to tell him. Either way, it wasn't their place to update the old man about his grandson's death.

"What do you think Pam would do if someone tried to take the farm away from her?" Barry asked.

"She would do whatever it took to stay there," Edgar said as he gazed out the window.

"Does that include killing someone?" Marlee asked.

"Pam is capable of about anything. After all, she killed my Ethel in 1982. That was her first step in getting control of the farm," Edgar said bitterly.

"She killed your wife?" Marlee asked.

"Damn right. She knew what time Ethel ate breakfast and when she took her insulin shot. Pam locked her in the bathroom while I was gone, and she went into diabetic shock. Then she died. It was all part of Pam's plan to get the farm. Tim and I talked it over, and we think that's what she'd done. We were talking about it the last time he was over here. She came to visit me that same day, just after Tim was here. It was all I could do not to accuse her, but Tim said he was working to prove Pam's guilt, so I stayed quiet," said Grandpa Edgar, a tear forming in the corner of his eye.

"I bet Pam overheard the conversation between Tim and Grandpa Edgar," Barry said as they walked to the car. "That goes a long way in explaining why Tim died shortly thereafter."

"If we can take Grandpa Edgar at his word. I know

he thinks he's telling us the truth, but his time frames and some facts might be out of whack. With dementia, it can be difficult to determine what's accurate and what isn't. From what I learned in my psych class, people often remember things from years ago, but have trouble recalling recent events," Marlee said.

"You're just pissed because it's looking more and more like Pam is the culprit, and you've been focused on Tim's roommates as the killers," Barry said with a little swagger as he opened the car door.

"I'm not pissed!" Marlee shouted. "It's just that a senile old man might not be the best historian. Granted, he seemed lucid today, but who knows if he was accurate about his dates and times. Pam might have come to visit him days after Tim was there. She might be completely innocent of everything. I have a hard time believing she killed her cousin to gain control of the farm when her grandparents retired. Then Pam killed her grandmother to hurry along their departure from the farm. Then when her brother starts making plans to take over the farm after his graduation, he dies mysteriously too."

"You don't think three deaths linked to one person in a family is more than a coincidence? Especially if that person has a motive for the deaths?" Barry asked, incredulous.

"It sounds really bad when you put it that way," Marlee said with a laugh. "But let's keep in mind that Billy's death was ruled an accident and the grandma's death was due to diabetic shock. Tim's death is the only one that has been ruled homicide, and there's no proof that Pam was involved."

Barry gave her a hard look as he backed out of the parking lot, and they continued back into town and to the trailer park where Eddie Turner lived. He parked across the street, and they engaged in an argument before Marlee exited the car. Barry thought he should be involved in the interview, but Marlee knew the aging rocker would be put off by Barry's presence. Better to let Eddie think she was there by herself.

She could hear Whitesnake music blaring from inside as she pounded on the door. Eddie flung the door open and motioned her in with a fling of his head. He was dressed much like before, dirty and scruffy. He held a drink in his hand, and the whole trailer reeked of booze and cigarettes.

"I see you couldn't stay away," he said with a sneer, an unlit cigarette hanging from the corner of his mouth. "Come on in and take a load off."

Marlee paid particular attention to her surroundings. She chose the chair that was located furthest from Eddie and closest to the door in case she needed to run. "Have you been over to a college party house called Stairway to Hell?" she asked, jumping right into the heart of what she wanted to know.

"Sure, who hasn't? Everybody knows about that place. They throw some of the best parties in town. Threw, I mean. Not any parties happening there now since the whole fucking place burned to the ground." Eddie chuckled as he lit his cigarette and blew the smoke directly at Marlee.

"What have you heard about the fire? I know that you're in with everybody around town. I just thought that if anyone knew what caused the fire, you would," Marlee said, playing to Eddie's inflated ego.

"Want a beer?" he asked, grabbing a can of generic beer from the refrigerator and handing it to Marlee.

She took the can, popped the top and took a sip. She vowed not to say anything until he spoke. Eddie walked around the kitchen and finally settled in his worn recliner.

"Yeah, I've heard some scuttlebutt about the fire," he said, not offering any details.

"So, what did you hear?" Marlee was on the edge of her seat and ready to ring Eddie's neck. She wanted answers, and she wanted them now.

"I heard Tim DeWitt's psycho sister did it."

"But why? What would be her motive?" Marlee asked.

"Like I said, Pam's a psycho. I never heard why she started the fire, just that she did it," Eddie said, not divulging anything further.

"Who told you this?" Marlee persisted.

"Just overheard it at a bar downtown. Don't know who said it," Eddie replied evasively.

She was exasperated. Knowing that Eddie had more information on the fire than he was willing to divulge, she changed her course. "I'm sure you heard about Tim being missing," Marlee said and Eddie nodded. "He was found dead on his grandparents' farm. Have you heard anything about that?"

"I heard that sister of his has killed before. She killed a cousin just to get her hands on the place," Eddie said as he puffed out more smoke. "Psycho. From what I hear, she probably killed Tim too."

"Do you believe that, or is it just idle gossip around town?" Marlee asked. She'd never been able to figure out if there was fact to the allegations against Pam or if it was just small-town gossip.

"There might be some truth to it. A lot of people talk about her cousin and how she killed him. I can't tell you anything about it for sure. I met Tim at the party house awhile back, but didn't really talk to him. But from what I hear, that whole family is really fucked up," Eddie said.

"What else have you heard?" Marlee asked, leading him wherever he wanted to go with his story.

"Just that the cousin was killed and the rest of the family covered it up. That's fucked up!"

"It's not normal, that's for sure," Marlee agreed with Eddie, anything to get him to keep talking. This part-time employed aging band member seemed to have his ear to the ground. "Did you know Tim and Beth were seeing each other for a while?

"Didn't know, didn't care," Eddie said, doing his

best to exhibit nonchalance. "I told you before, Beth and I would hit it and then she'd go do her thing, and I'd do mine. We didn't have some big love affair where I was jealous if she was with another guy."

"Yeah, I remember. But did you know about Beth and Tim?" Marlee persisted.

"Sure, I knew they were together for a bit. Beth told me about it. Not that I cared, but she liked to talk. Sometimes I actually listened, but usually I didn't," Eddie said with a laugh.

"What else did she say about Tim and the guys at Stairway to Hell?" Marlee asked.

Eddie shrugged and stared at Marlee. "How about you and me go in the back and talk it over in there?"

"No thanks. I need to be on my way," Marlee said, springing to her feet and making her way toward the door. "See you around."

She hurried to the car and gave Barry a full report. "Eddie said he heard Pam killed Billy and Tim to get the farm. He also thought she started the fire at Stairway to Hell but didn't know the reason."

"Wow, you got a lot of information," Barry said admirably.

"And I might have gotten more if Eddie hadn't suggested that we go into his bedroom for further discussions," Marlee said, making a gagging sound. "He is honestly one of the grossest guys I've ever met!"

"So, he implicated Pam in Tim's death and the fire?" Barry asked. "Did he have anything to say about Beth?"

"He knew Beth and Tim were together for a while, and he didn't care. How he got the rest of his information, or misinformation, I don't know."

"And he hit on you," Barry said with bitterness. "Do you want me to go in there and punch him?"

"No, if I thought he needed punching, I would have done it myself. But thanks for the offer," Marlee said.

Barry drove around town aimlessly, as if he wanted

to talk about something but wasn't sure how to broach the topic. Marlee wanted to ask him to spill it, but was afraid he was going to profess his love for her, and she didn't want to deal with that mess. Barry cleared his throat and when Marlee looked at him he said, "Do you know any college girls you could introduce me to?"

She broke out laughing, but then stopped when she saw the hurt look on Barry's face. "Yes! I do, I was just laughing because I wanted to introduce you to my neighbor in the dorm. Her name is Kristie, and I think you two would get along great. She was with me that day I first talked to you over at Stairway to Hell. The morning Beth was found."

He relaxed after their discussion and drove Marlee back to her dorm. "So, you're not hurt or jealous, are you?" Barry asked, a bit of hope in his voice.

Marlee, not usually one to indulge the male ego, made an exception this time. "It will be hard to see you two together, but I think we all know it's for the best," she said with a sigh as she got out of the car and walked to the dorm. She smiled as she turned away from Barry, knowing she had done a good thing. Marlee made him feel better about himself and potentially had set up a date for her friend. Nothing was going on in her own love life, but at least she was helping out some friends.

Jasmine was asleep when Marlee walked into the room. She needed Jasmine's help and didn't want to wait around, so she slammed the door twice and rattled around until her roommate sat straight up in bed.

"What the hell are you doing?" she yelled.

"Oh, Jazz! You were asleep. I'm sorry. I didn't even see you up there," Marlee lied, hoping Jasmine would now get out of bed and listen as she talked about Beth and Tim's cases. "How about if I make us some ramen noodles?"

"Ramen noodles would be good," Jasmine conceded as she maneuvered her way out of bed and on to the floor. "And maybe some toast."

266

Minutes later, they were feasting on a late-night supper of nothing but carbohydrates and fat. "This is delicious. I could eat this for the rest of my life and never get tired of it," Jasmine said, cramming a second piece of buttered toast into her mouth.

"Me too!" Marlee agreed as she twirled noodles around the tines of a plastic fork and shoveled them into her mouth. "Who needs fancy dining? I think the main food groups should be toast, noodles, Pop Tarts, Diet Pepsi, beer, bananas, and chicken sandwiches."

"I would take out the pop and add in cheese and bacon," Jasmine said.

"I deny your omission of Diet Pepsi but will gladly accept your additions. Cheese and bacon make everything better," Marlee said, and they clinked together their aluminum glasses of Tang instant orange drink.

After updating Jasmine on the new case information and reviewing the old details, Marlee asked, "Do you think Beth's death was accidental? And who do you think killed Tim? Barry and I have been arguing over whether Pam was involved in Tim's death or if it was his roommates."

"Maybe you've been looking at the cases all wrong," Jasmine suggested. "What if they are linked in some way that you haven't even considered?"

"Such as?"

"Okay, this is far-fetched, but let's say Tim was dealing drugs and Pam was his supplier. The tension between them was fabricated as a cover. Beth found out about the drug dealing, and Tim killed her to keep her quiet. Then he was overcome with guilt, and Pam killed Tim to make sure he didn't talk," Jasmine said.

"Um, that's really out there. No one ever mentioned that drugs were involved in either Beth or Tim's deaths," Marlee said as she mentally sifted through all the information she had taken in during the past few days.

"That was really more of an example than an actual

theory." Jasmine pushed down the lever on the toaster. "It's not that I think this happened, but maybe something no one has thought of yet is the reason for both of the deaths."

"That's a good point. We've been under the assumption that if Pam killed Tim that it was because she wanted to keep control of the farm. And if his roommates killed him, it was to keep Tim quiet about Beth and what happened to her at Stairway to Hell. Maybe none of these things are involved. If that's the case, then who might have killed them?" Marlee asked.

"Assuming, of course, that Beth's death wasn't an accident," Jasmine said.

"I don't know, Jazz. I just feel like there's much more to Beth's death than her getting really drunk and falling down and freezing to death outside a party house. Maybe it's just because I knew Beth and thought of her as a friend. I've asked myself if I would feel the same way if the victim had been someone I didn't know."

"And?" Jasmine asked.

"With everything else being the same except that I didn't know the victim, I'd still feel the same way. It's a feeling in the pit of my stomach that Beth didn't die accidentally. I realize the autopsy didn't show anything suspicious other than too much alcohol in her system, but maybe somebody forced Beth to drink a lot more alcohol than she wanted. It would be a good cover since Beth was a party girl and loved to drink. Who would ever consider that she was held down and forced to consume more than she wanted?" Marlee asked, setting forth her thoughts on Beth and the tragedy that befell her.

"How would someone force her to drink too much? Hold her down?" Jasmine asked.

"Maybe. Or they could have used a beer funnel and held it in her mouth while they poured in a bunch of beer or hard alcohol," Marlee said, thinking back to the beer bongs she had seen at various parties.

"But who would do that? And why?" Jasmine

asked.

"I don't know who, but it must have been to keep Beth under control. Maybe they didn't intend for her to die. The intention might have been for her to get so drunk she would pass out," Marlee said.

"For what reason?" Jasmine asked, still playing devil's advocate.

"If she was passed out, she couldn't talk. Maybe she had information that somebody didn't want her to tell. Or somebody may have thought they could take advantage of her sexually if she was passed out and unresponsive," Marlee said, cringing as she imagined what Beth might have endured before she left the party.

"Whatever the intent was, Beth still left the party. Somebody lost track of her, and she wandered off. They must not have looked very hard for her since she was passed out in the yard," Jasmine said.

"Or, they could have seen her wander outside and fall down and realize that soon she wouldn't be a problem anymore. I guess that idea only holds water if they were trying to keep her quiet about something," Marlee said.

"So, it had to be someone at the party who caused Beth to die, if it wasn't an accident," said Jasmine.

"Let's make a list of everyone we can remember from the party that night," Marlee suggested, and her roommate nodded. After half an hour, they had a list of over fifty people. Some of them were named and some were merely described by appearance or their class/dorm affiliation with Marlee and Jasmine.

"Now let's cross off the people we absolutely know couldn't have hurt Beth," Jasmine suggested.

They crossed themselves off the list along with their neighbor Kristie. When they got to Kristie's roommate Polly, they hesitated.

"Polly's a gossip and a back-stabber, but I can't envision her killing someone, can you?" asked Marlee.

"No, but the intent may not have been to kill Beth. Maybe the idea was just to get her really, really drunk,"

Jasmine said.

"I can see Polly thinking that was funny or a good way to get revenge on someone," Marlee said.

"Me too," said Jasmine. Polly remained on the list as they sorted through the remaining names. "Other than us and Kristie, anyone could've been involved," Marlee said, dejected as she looked at the remaining forty-seven names on the list.

"What about Eddie Turner? Do you remember seeing him there?" Jasmine asked. "He told you he'd been to parties at Stairway to Hell. I never met him and don't know what he looks like, but you would remember him, right?"

Marlee thought for a moment before answering. She consumed several alcoholic beverages at the party that night, but she wasn't drunk enough to forget someone like Eddie Turner. "I'd remember him for sure. I think it's time to do some investigation into Mr. Turner and his connection to Stairway to Hell."

Never underestimate a disgruntled neighbor. If you want to know the unvarnished truth about anyone, ask around the neighborhood. They know the whole story and aren't afraid to dish the dirt.

Chapter 28

Marlee hitched a ride to Pam's farm with a friend from the dorm who was driving that direction. She didn't know how she'd get home, but that was a problem for another time. For now, she had information she needed to verify with Pam before things went any further.

Pam trudged toward the house from the barn just as Marlee was knocking on the front door. "Hello, again," she called out without much enthusiasm. The stress of her brother's death weighed on the ordinarily rough-and-tough farm gal, and it showed. Her pony tail was in disarray, she had bits of food stuck to her coat, and there was a rip in her stained jeans.

"Forgive me for just stopping in again, but I had a few more questions for you," Marlee said. "I'm still trying to make sense of what happened to Tim."

Pam nodded and motioned for her to enter the house. After hanging her coat up in the entry way, she turned and gave Marlee a hard look. "Why are you asking so many questions? Even more than the police. You don't have any authority in this investigation, do you?"

"Well, no..." Marlee stammered trying to articulate why it was important that she be involved with the investigation. "Tim was my friend, and I want to make sure whoever killed him gets punished for it." After speaking the words, Marlee regretted them. What if Pam was the one who killed Tim? Bumping off Marlee might be the next thing on Pam's to-do list since the nosy student was asking so many questions.

Pam's look softened, and she nodded. "I've talked to you more about Tim than I have the cops. It was ruled a homicide, but they don't seem to be working very hard at solving it. The detective that was out here yesterday kept saying I had a motive. I didn't handle it very well. I started crying and then told him to get out."

Marlee realized it might be a good time to change

tactics. "Pam, did you go to school with Eddie Turner?" It had just occurred to her that Pam and Eddie Turner were about the same age.

"Sure did. Up until he dropped out toward the end of our junior year. Actually, I don't know for sure if he dropped out or was kicked out. Eddie missed so many days of school that it was kind of startling when he would show up in class. He was a real trouble-maker."

"Do you associate with him any more now that you're adults?"

Pam snorted. "I see him around here and there, but we don't hang out. I've seen his band's poster up around town, but I don't know much else about him. He was bad news in high school. Dealt drugs, stole anything that wasn't nailed down, picked fights, and always had a different girlfriend. No clue what those girls saw in him. He was in legal trouble too, as a kid. I remember the cops bringing him home more than once."

"You saw the police bring Eddie home? Did he live on your street?" Marlee was ecstatic, hoping Pam might be a gold mine of information when it came to Eddie Turner.

"Sure. His mom is Lettie Rikers. He's Blake's half-brother. I thought you knew."

"No, it never came out in my discussions with Blake or anyone else. Are the two of them close?"

Pam thought for a minute, sipping a cup of coffee she'd just poured. "I don't know how they are now, but Blake used to idolize his older brother. They were several years apart in age, just like Tim and me. Blake looked up to Eddie and wanted to be just like him, even started acting and dressing like him when he was in middle school."

"Was Blake a trouble-maker too?"

"Not that I knew of. Tom Rikers kicked Eddie out of the house after he dropped out of high school. The two of them got into fights all the time, and I think Tom was relieved when he could finally kick his step-son out of the house."

274

"Wow. Eddie sure has had a tumultuous life," Marlee said, information swirling around in her brain. "Luckily, Blake didn't follow in his older brother's footsteps."

"Eddie never finished high school and even though Blake finished, he didn't show any interest in college. They were both geniuses and could've gone on to do about anything they wanted for careers. Instead, Eddie is in a band, and Blake works at a printing company," Pam said. "Not that there's anything wrong with either of those jobs, but it seems like a waste of potential. I had to work hard for my grades. Eddie was lazy and couldn't stick to anything. He and Blake acted like they were smarter than everyone else. I remember how Blake used to put Tim down when they were kids. And Tim was no dummy."

Pam didn't have any additional information about Tim's death, and Marlee was in a rush to get to a phone to call Barry. She stood up and as she grabbed her coat off the back of the chair she remembered she'd hitched a ride out to the farm. It was one of the warmer days that week, but still bitingly cold. "Uh, Pam? Would you be willing to give me a ride back to the dorm? Or even just the edge of town? I caught a ride out here."

"How did you plan to get home?" Pam asked as if Marlee's lack of forethought was the stupidest thing she'd ever heard.

Marlee shrugged her shoulders and did her best to look helpless. Pam gave in and drove her back to the dorm, letting her off right in front of the building. "Let me know what else you find out, okay?" Pam asked, her voice tinged with hope.

"It's an emergency!" Marlee yelled into the phone as she waited for Barry's roommate to summon him. She twirled the phone cord anxiously as she waited. And waited. And waited.

"What is it now?" growled an out-of-breath Barry.

"I have big news," she said getting ready to recap

her conversation with Pam.

"So, do I," Barry interrupted. "I'll be over to your dorm room in a few minutes." The phone clicked, leaving Marlee to wonder about the origin of Barry's big news, doubting it could top hers.

The first full minute of their conversation consisted of both talking and no one listening, convinced their information was the most important. "Stop," Marlee said, holding up her hand. "Go ahead." Sometimes it was easy to be the bigger person when you had earth-shattering news.

Barry didn't hesitate. "Eddie Turner has a criminal record in several states! He's been charged with everything from burglary to assault."

"Why didn't the cops know this before?"

"Because all of our records systems are separate from each other. Not just between states, but even within South Dakota. Remember when we didn't know about Adam's attempted rape charge in Brown County? There's no central cataloging office that keeps track of someone's criminal offenses," Barry reported.

"So, there's not much deterrent to committing crimes if every offense is treated like it's your first time, as long as it's in another county or state," Marlee said, disgusted with the lack of oversight in the criminal justice system.

"Not exactly. When someone comes before the judge to be sentenced, the probation office does some snooping around to find out what crimes they've been accused of or convicted of in all the other areas where they've lived."

"Doesn't sound too hard to pull the wool over the probation officer's eyes. If I was Eddie, I'd just lie about where I lived and where I traveled," Marlee said.

"I think he got away with a number of things for quite a while doing this, but now it's catching up to him," Barry said. "So, what's your big news?"

"Pam went to high school with Eddie and said he

either dropped out or was kicked out during junior year. And, Eddie and Blake Rikers are half-brothers. Eddie and Blake lived right across the street from Pam and Tim until Eddie's step-dad kicked him out of the house after he left high school. Pam also said that both Eddie and Blake are geniuses and thought it was a waste of potential that they never went on to college or became professionals." Marlee paused to take a breath. "And, Eddie probably has a juvenile record since Pam saw the cops bring him home more than once. She said he was always in trouble and skipped a lot of school."

Barry slid into one of the chairs by the desk, and Marlee slunk into her reclining lawn chair. They were both silent as they processed the information on Eddie Turner and what impact, if any, that it might have on the case.

"You said Eddie's actions are finally catching up to him? What did you mean?" Marlee asked.

"Eddie is under suspicion in multiple counties in Nebraska, Iowa, and Minnesota. They're all related to passing bogus twenty-dollar bills," Barry said.

"Weren't you and Doug doing a stakeout on some people you thought were involved with funny money here in town?" Marlee asked, remembering the night the two cops picked her up as she was walking from the truck stop back to the dorm.

"Yeah, but Eddie's name never came up. It was a couple other scumbags from around town," Barry said.

"If they're scumbags, then Eddie probably knows them, and I bet they're working together." Marlee said. Barry nodded, still in thought.

Marlee, with some difficulty, leaped out of the beach chair. "I think I know what happened! I think I know who killed Beth and Tim and why!"

How many criminals does it take to pull off the perfect crime? If more than one person's involved, then it's no longer perfect.

Chapter 29

Marlee and Barry shouted over the top of each other as they drove to Eddie Turner's trailer. "We need a firm plan in place when we question him. Otherwise, he'll try to baffle us with bullshit," Barry said.

"I think we just see where the conversation goes and only reveal what's absolutely necessary," Marlee argued as they pulled into the trailer court. "Besides, I have a plan." She jumped out of the car before Barry had it in park, and she marched toward Eddie's front door.

Eddie Turner jerked open the door before Marlee was on the front step. "I see you came back to take me up on my offer," he said, his voice dripping like slime as he puffed on a cigarette. "Who's this?" he growled when he spotted Barry walking behind Marlee.

"This is my friend, Barry. We wanted to chat with you a bit," Marlee said, not waiting to be invited in. She confidently pushed her way past Eddie and stood in the living room, hands on hips.

Eddie seemed more curious than offended and allowed Barry to enter the home as well. The three stood in a circle, each waiting for the other to begin.

"We know about the fake money scheme you've been running in town and all over the Midwest," Marlee accused.

"Who told you that?" Eddie asked, neither confirming nor refuting their claims. "Are you cops?"

"Hell, no we're not cops," Marlee said with disdain. "We found Beth's diary. She spelled out everything about the counterfeit money. We want in."

Barry and Eddie both looked at Marlee in surprise. Neither expected this pronouncement from her. Eddie finally laughed and blew a cloud of smoke upward. "Sure, you want in. How do I know you won't run to the police?"

"Why would we tell the cops anything if we're making money? I have a lot of school bills to pay, and

Barry wants to quit his job working for a carpenter. That takes money, and if we can get in on your money scheme, then we wouldn't have to worry so much about funds."

"What else was in Beth's diary?" Eddie asked, thinking over Marlee's claims.

"She wrote about Stairway to Hell and how you and the guys there are printing fake money and passing it all over. Beth wrote how your brother, Blake, was the brains behind the whole project, and you followed his directions," Marlee said, baiting Eddie.

"Bullshit! That bitch! I don't take orders from anyone. Blake does what I say. Where's Beth's diary? Hand it over!" Eddie shouted.

"We didn't bring it with us," Barry said, jumping in on the diary story. "We're not that stupid."

Eddie let out a long breath. "Okay, fine. You two want a beer?"

"Sure," said Barry and Marlee shrugged. Eddie sauntered into the kitchen and clanking and rattling was heard as he rustled around in the refrigerator for beer.

Barry turned around and mouthed, "What are you doing?"

Marlee merely smiled, but the smile didn't last for long. Eddie reappeared with only one can of beer. And a gun aimed right at them.

Marlee shrieked, moving out of the direct aim of the gun.

Eddie just laughed. "You think I don't know he's a cop? I've seen him around town in his little uniform directing traffic and catching stray dogs. How stupid do you think I am?"

Neither Barry nor Marlee responded to Eddie. It didn't seem like the type of question he really wanted answered. He motioned for them to sit side-by-side on the filthy couch while he lit another cigarette and opened his can of beer. Eddie seemed to be stalling, trying to figure out what to do with his two prisoners.

"Eddie, just let us go. We won't say anything, and

280

you don't have to cut us in. We'll just go away and keep our mouths shut," Marlee said, Barry nodding vigorously.

"Not until I have that diary. Where is it?" Eddie guzzled beer while moving the gun back and forth between them.

"It's in Marlee's dorm room," Barry blurted. "We'll go get it and bring it back to you."

"Nah, I think Miss Marlee and I'll go get the diary, and you can wait here," Eddie said as he set down his beer can and rummaged in a drawer all the while waiving the gun in their general direction. "Here," he said, tossing Marlee a roll of duct tape. "Tape him to the chair."

Ten minutes later, Marlee was driving Barry's car back to her dorm room. It would have been a normal drive except for the chain-smoking psychopath sitting next to her. "Do you mind putting out that cigarette? Barry will be really mad that you smoked in his car."

"How about I put a bullet in your head? How would Barry like that?" Eddie snarled.

"Never mind," Marlee said under her breath. She had no idea what her next step should be. There was no diary, so she had nothing to present to Eddie. She was also worried about bringing the gun-toting Eddie into her dorm and endangering her friends, especially Jasmine.

Marlee drove well below the speed limit, taking her time getting to the dorm, hoping a plan would pop into her head. Luck was not on her side. Her mind was as blank as when she'd left Eddie's trailer.

They walked toward the dorm from the rear parking lot. Eddie walked behind Marlee with his gun tucked inside his ratty coat. "Don't even think of doing anything funny," Eddie hissed. "One screw up, and I'll shoot you then I'll shoot your little cop friend." Marlee nodded that she understood, all the while her mind was racing.

Marlee and Eddie walked down the hallway toward her room. She desperately hoped no one would see them, thus bringing about the possibility that they too would be held at gun point. As she was fiddling with the key to unlock her dorm room, Kristie from next door poked her head out of her room.

"Hey, Marlee whatcha doing? Oh, I see you have company," Kristie said, looking Eddie up and down.

"Yeah, this is an old friend," Marlee said, not looking at Kristie for fear she would be able to read her face and sense the danger. The last thing Marlee wanted to do was put Kristie or Jasmine in any harm. "Talk to you later."

Kristie pulled her head back inside and shut the door. Marlee breathed a sigh of relief. At least she wouldn't have to worry about Kristie being injured or killed. As Marlee eased her own door open she peeked inside and saw Jasmine atop her lofted bed, under the covers. Jasmine caught her eye and was about to speak, but Marlee put her finger to her lips to hush her.

"I don't think my roommate's here, Eddie," Marlee said loudly. "We should be able to just pick up the diary and leave. You don't need to use your gun," Upon hearing the words, Jasmine flattened herself and pulled the blankets up over her head, leaving the bed looking rumpled and unmade. She was so slim that it was impossible to tell she was up there with the extra blankets and quilts.

"Hurry up!" Eddie barked, motioning to the gun inside his coat. "Let's get this show on the road."

Marlee walked toward her lofted bed and reached under the mattress, retrieving the notebook used to document the details of both Beth and Tim's death investigations. It was the closest thing to Beth's personal diary that she could produce. With any luck, Eddie would just glance at it and see enough to convince him it was indeed a diary.

With a deep breath, Marlee handed the notebook to Eddie and motioned him toward the door. "Here it is. Let's get back to your trailer and release Barry. Then we

282

can forget all about Barry and I trying to get in on this fake money thing, and you can get back to business."

Eddie grabbed the notebook and rifled through the pages without reading them, satisfied that it was indeed Beth's diary. "Let's go!"

The drive back to Eddie's trailer took what seemed like four days. Marlee again drove as slowly as possible, giving herself time to think of a great plan. The only problem was, she didn't have any plan. All she knew was that she had to keep Eddie talking so he wouldn't leaf through her notebook and see that it wasn't Beth's diary after all.

"How did you get involved in the fake money scheme?" she asked, putting along behind a senior citizen driving ten miles under the speed limit.

"I thought it up and got Blake involved since he worked at the printing place. He knew enough about printing and was able to get his hands on some ink. We made our own templates and started printing money. Easy as can be," Eddie said, lighting another smoke.

"You had quite a sophisticated operation," Marlee said, playing to his ego. "Who did you get to pass the fake money around?"

"A lot of people. Some you wouldn't expect. Blake and his roommates. Beth passed some bills at 7-11 where she worked, but when they were turned over to the cops we had to cut back on circulating them here in town. I would pass them when I was playing gigs in other areas on the weekends, and I had a few friends passing them too. Like I said, the cops were on to the fake money here in town, but didn't know who was doing it. We had to lay low for a while," Eddie said, enjoying the opportunity to brag on the counterfeiting empire he built in the small town.

"Did they need the money so bad that they were willing to get involved in an illegal operation like this?" Marlee asked.

"Not everybody has money like you rich college kids. Hell, most of the college kids I know don't have much money either. Everybody has bills to pay. Plus, it's fun sticking it to the man, you know? The law has been breathing down my neck since I was a kid. Finally, I'm coming out on top," Eddie said.

"But wouldn't it have been better to just work at a steady job and earn money honestly?" Marlee asked.

Eddie snorted. "And how do I get this steady job with good pay? And even if I do get the job, will the wages be high enough to pay all my bills, fix my car, and send me on a two-week vacation? I seriously fucking doubt it. This working hard-and-steady job thing is for suckers. I outsmarted the system, and as long as nobody rats me out, I'll be just fine."

Even though Marlee taped Barry to a kitchen chair as loosely as she could, he was unable to free himself by the time Marlee and Eddie returned to the trailer. His efforts at escape were notable since he and the chair were now tipped on their sides. Barry looked up at Marlee as they entered the kitchen and raised his eyebrows.

"I guess we'll probably just get going now that you have Beth's diary," Marlee said, struggling to turn Barry and his chair back to an upright position.

"Not so fast. Just sit your ass down. We're going to look through this diary together," Eddie growled, grabbing a beer from the fridge and flopping down in a kitchen chair.

"But you said we could go after you got the diary. We kept our part of the bargain," Marlee whined, as she worked to free Barry's right arm from the duct tape.

"I said sit down!" Eddie yelled, pulling the gun from his coat and motioning Marlee to a chair next to him. He picked up the notebook and started reading the first page. As he read, his expression turned from nervous anticipation to angry skepticism. "Who killed Beth? You expect me to believe she wrote this in her own diary? What is this?"

Now that they were busted, Marlee needed to think

284

of a story and fast. "Those are some notes I was keeping about Beth and Tim's deaths. It's sort of a project for my criminology class. You know, since there's been so much going on in town the past few weeks. Our professor gave us all an assignment to keep notes on the deaths related to the university."

"Who gives a shit about your project? Where's Beth's diary?" Eddie yelled, his face just inches from hers.

Marlee wiped Eddie's spittle from her face with the back of her hand, stalling for time waiting for a brilliant plan to spring to mind. Just then the phone rang, sparing Marlee from cooking up another far-fetched story.

"Yeah?" Eddie growled into the receiver. "That nosy student and her cop friend are here now. Come on over. And bring everybody. We're going to finish this thing once and for all."

I want everyone to know that I wasn't just some drunken bimbo that got hammered and froze to death. There's a lot more to the story.

Chapter 30

Twenty minutes later, Blake, Adam, and John burst into Eddie's trailer. "What the hell's going on, Eddie?" Blake asked. "What are these two doing here?"

Eddie relayed the story of Beth's diary and how Marlee and Barry wanted in on the phony money scheme.

"Beth kept a diary? Where is it?" Blake asked, helping himself to a beer from the fridge and settling in on a kitchen chair.

"That's what we're trying to figure out. Marlee and her cop friend tried to trick me with her notes for a college project. They're a couple of liars, and I want to find out what they're really up to. And I want that damn diary!" Eddie said.

It didn't take a genius to see that she and Barry were outnumbered. Plus, Barry was still duct-taped to a chair, and Eddie possessed a gun, which tipped the odds against them even more. Her only recourse was to stall them until she could think of something else.

"If Tim was involved in the money scheme, why kill him?" Marlee asked, holding her breath as she waited for an answer.

"That was an accident!" Eddie and Blake shouted in unison.

John, the calmest of the group, spoke first. "We just wanted to talk to Tim, and things got out of hand. Tim thought we killed Beth, and he was really upset when he found out she was pregnant. We tried to talk sense into him, but Tim overreacted, and Eddie hit him a little too hard with a baseball bat."

"So, he died right then?" Marlee asked. "How did he get to the shed on the farm?"

"Yeah, he died instantly. There was nothing doctors could've done, and we didn't want to get into trouble for what was an accident. Blake knew Tim got a key from his grandfather for the shed, so we took him out there knowing it would take some time for anybody to find his body," John reported.

"Why did Tim get the key to the shed?" Marlee asked.

"After Beth died, the cops were swarming our house, so we moved our printing stuff out to the shed. When we took Tim out there, we picked up our printing materials and moved them out to the place we've been staying since the fire," John said, his winter pallor getting even lighter. "I couldn't stand to look at him, so I pulled his hood over his head."

"Why burn down the house? And why kill Tim's dog?" Marlee was still more upset about the death of Rufus than she was the demise of Stairway to Hell.

"When Eddie and Tim were arguing, Rufus attacked Eddie, and he broke the dog's neck. That set Tim off, and he went wild. We couldn't talk any sense into him, and Eddie hit him over the head with a bat. That's what did him in," John said. "The fire was a distraction. We thought the cops would be so busy investigating it that they wouldn't find Tim for a few days. And that's exactly what happened."

"I suspect you guys were hoping Tim's disappearance and fire would all be blamed on Pam," Marlee said. "And that's why you told me Tim was graduating in May and that Pam knew it. You were pointing me in her direction all along."

"Yeah, that was part of the plan," John replied. "We gave conflicting stories to keep you off balance, but kept pointing you back to Pam."

"So, who killed Beth?" Marlee asked looking around the room. "And why?"

John, who had been the spokesperson since the group arrived looked puzzled. "We didn't kill Beth. She died because she drank too much and then fell down and froze to death. It was an accident."

"No, I don't think so," said Marlee. "Beth knew she was pregnant and planned to keep the baby. I think she talked to you guys about getting a bigger cut from the fake money scheme. Since she was pregnant, she wasn't drinking because she knew it could be harmful to the baby. Somebody spiked her drink. I know she wasn't drinking garbage pail punch or beer at the party because I saw her spill some clear liquid. I think she believed she was drinking pop, but you guys put alcohol in it without her knowledge."

John shook his head from side to side. "No way. We didn't do that. She got drunk on her own."

Adam also shook his head, while Blake and Eddie made eye contact. The knowing glance told Marlee everything she needed to know.

"So how did you do it?" Marlee directed her question to the half-brothers.

"She wanted more money. She said it was to take care of the baby, but I didn't believe she was pregnant," Blake said. "Beth was drinking 7-Up and had poured it into a red plastic cup so that no one else at the party would know she wasn't drinking alcohol. We were talking in my room upstairs and when she went to the bathroom, I poured vodka in her glass. It's colorless, and she was eating cough drops all night, so she didn't know she was drinking alcohol. I didn't mean for all of this to happen. I thought she'd get a little tipsy, and I could talk some sense into her. Instead, she got bombed and tried to walk home. She was so blitzed, she even lost her coat with the car keys in the pocket. I suppose that's why Beth tried to walk home."

Adam and John both turned to Blake, their mouths wide open. "You killed Beth?" John accused.

"It was accidental," Blake shouted.

"And you killed her baby!" John accused, his eyes wide and his mouth open.

"I didn't think she was pregnant. I thought she was just saying that to get a bigger cut of money," Blake said. "When I told her 'no' she threatened to go to the cops and tell them everything. Beth was hysterical. I thought some vodka would calm her down so we could talk reasonably."

"The next morning, you knew what happened to her, and you didn't say anything!" John shouted. "Did you know about this?" John looked at Eddie.

"Look, Beth is the one to blame here," Eddie justified. "She got pregnant, and she was going to talk to the cops if we didn't give her more money. We couldn't let that happen. She got what was coming to her. If she hadn't got greedy, none of this would've happened. And Tim would still be alive too."

Everyone in the room except for Blake looked at Eddie in disbelief. Had he really just blamed Beth for not only her own death but for Tim's too?

"Beth's blood alcohol level was at a level that could have killed her even if she hadn't fallen down and frozen. You gave her more than a little vodka to calm her down!"

Blake let Marlee's comments hang in the air without affirming or refuting them.

"How much were you guys making from printing fake money?" Marlee asked. "Was it really worth killing two people over it?"

"Two people and a baby," Barry said, now that he'd pulled the tape free from his mouth with the one hand he'd worked loose. No one noticed that Barry was freeing himself from the confines of his chair.

"We make about two or three hundred apiece each week if everything goes right," Blake said.

"Really? That much?" Marlee was incredulous. "How do you turn fake twenties into that much profit?"

"Buy things with fake money then turn around and sell what we bought. I bought a new stereo with twenties last week and sold it to some college kid for a discount. And I use the fake money to buy things out of town, like gas, booze, and food. We've all been doing it and making some good money," Eddie said, puffing out his chest.

"Who else is involved?" Marlee asked.

"Right now, a couple of my friends here in town, but I'm looking to expand," Eddie said. "Now enough with the questions. Where's Beth's diary? Or does a diary even exist?"

Marlee tried to give out a nonchalant laugh, but it sounded more like a sputter. "Of course, there's a diary. We'd have to be pretty stupid to come over here and make up a story about Beth having a diary."

"I've had enough chit-chat. This isn't social hour. Where's the fucking diary?" Eddie asked, pulling the gun out of his coat and pointing it squarely at Marlee's face.

"Wait, Eddie!" yelled John. "You can't shoot them!"

"Sure, I can. Why do you think I let you rattle on about all the things we did? It's because these two aren't going to make it out of here alive." Eddie bowed his head to light another cigarette while still holding the gun.

"No way, Eddie. Tim's death was an accident. And Beth shouldn't have died either, but we never set out to intentionally kill anyone. I never signed on for anything like this," John argued.

"John, you're an idiot if you think we can let these two go. They'll run to the cops. Hell, this one right here is a cop," Eddie reasoned motioning his head toward Barry. "Now, let's get the diary and finish things up." He still held the gun just inches from Marlee's temple. One shot, and she'd be dead.

"Why should we give you the diary if you're going to kill us anyway?" Marlee asked with a level of calm that she didn't feel.

The co-conspirators all looked at each other. Blake and Eddie might be geniuses, but they hadn't planned this far in advance. Eddie strode over to Barry and put the barrel of the gun against his knee cap. "Because if you don't tell me right now, I'm going to shoot him right in front of you. Except I'm not going to kill him. I'm going to make him suffer. It will be a long, painful death, and you'll get to watch the whole thing. I'm done screwing around! Where's the damn diary?"

Frozen with fear, Marlee couldn't think of one

thing to say. She wasn't sure if her voice would even work. But she had to think of something or else Barry would be tortured to death right there in Eddie Turner's trailer while they all watched.

Barry was not as fear-struck as Marlee and spoke out. "I have it, but it's in my locker at work. At the police station. I'll get it for you, but you have to let Marlee go."

"I don't have to do anything!" Eddie corrected. "You're not in a position to make demands. And don't think I'm stupid enough to walk into the police department with you. One word from you, and I'll be swarmed by the cops."

Blake pulled Eddie aside, and the two talked in low tones. "Here's what we're gonna do," Eddie said. "Blake and Adam will go with the cop to the station to get the diary. If you're not back here in an hour, I'll know the cops were tipped off somehow. Then I'll put a bullet in Marlee's head, and we can all get the hell out of town before the cops move in." Blake, Adam, and John all nodded as Marlee and Barry looked at each other wondering what they needed to do to stay alive.

Rats always abandon a sinking ship.
Every. Damn. Time.

Chapter 31

The minutes seemed like hours after Barry left the trailer with Blake and Adam. Marlee paced as she tried to figure out the next step to keep her and Barry alive. Once Blake and Adam saw that Barry didn't have the diary, they might kill him before coming back to the trailer. Or they might wait until they came back and then kill Barry and Marlee at the same time. If Eddie and his thugs still believed there was a diary, they would likely result to torturing the student and the police officer.

"Eddie, we can't kill Marlee and the cop. We need to just tie them up and get out of town," John reasoned.

"Where are we gonna go, John? Do you have a mountain hideaway you haven't told us about?" Eddie's upper lip curled as he spoke.

"No, but we can just grab some stuff and take off. At least it will take them awhile to get to the cops. We'll have a few hours head start and..."

"Shut up, John!" Eddie interrupted. "The only way out of this is to get the diary, kill these two, drag their bodies somewhere remote so they won't be found for a few days, and then each of us take off on our own. We can meet up again in a few months in another state and set up our printing operation there."

"I'm not getting involved in killing anyone else. Tim's death was an accident, and I didn't know about Blake spiking Beth's drink until today. But that was an accident too. Shooting Marlee and the cop is cold-blooded murder. We could get the death penalty for that," John argued.

"If you don't shut up, I'm gonna shoot you too," Eddie said with a glare that meant he wasn't messing around. "You can either do as I say or get ready to meet your maker."

John held up his hands in defeat. "Okay, okay. Take a chill pill, man!"

Marlee couldn't think of a way out of the mess, but she thought that, with some persuasion, John might defect to her side. "Killing people who won't do what you say is how you and Blake operate, isn't it, Eddie?" He glared at her, but didn't offer a response.

"Beth wanted more money or else she was going to the cops so Blake killed her. Then Tim suspected Beth's death was no accident and was going to reveal the whole scheme to the cops so you killed him. Now you're planning on killing Barry and me because you think we'll squeal. And then you threaten John because he's not falling in line. Where does it end, Eddie? Does anyone get out of this alive besides you and Blake? Or are you going to do away with him too? You have all the printing materials and know how to make the fake money yourself, so you really don't need all these other guys."

"Shut up! Beth and Tim's deaths were both accidents. I already told you that. And no, I'm not going to kill anyone else other than you and the cop."

John looked at Eddie, the pieces clicking into place. "She's right, isn't she? As soon as you get the diary, you're going to pick us off one by one, and you and Blake are leaving the area."

Eddie pulled the handgun from his coat and leveled it at John. "You leave the thinking to me, John. Now sit down and shut your mouth before I knock you in the head!"

John sank into a kitchen chair and looked at Marlee. "When did you figure out that's what he was going to do?"

"I guessed," Marlee said, not attempting to bluff anymore.

"I said shut up! Both of you!" Eddie swung the gun back and forth between Marlee and John as he grabbed yet another can of beer. His eyes were glassy, and his movements were becoming unstable.

Eddie laid the gun on the edge of the table to open his beer. John, realizing that his allegiance to Eddie wasn't

296

going to get him very far, lunged for the gun. Eddie was intoxicated, but not to the extent that he lost track of his firearm. He had his hand on the gun before John could reach it.

"Go sit on the couch," Eddie directed John in a calm tone.

"Eddie, I wasn't going to do anything. I just thought she might try to grab the gun," John stammered, trying to talk Eddie out of the inevitable.

John got up from the kitchen chair after Eddie motioned with the gun. He sat on the couch as directed and began to plead for his life. "Eddie, I'm on your side. I'll do whatever you want. I'll shoot her right now! Just don't kill me!"

"I'm not going to kill you," Eddie said as he took a yellowed pillow and placed it between John's leg and the barrel of the gun. The pillow squelched some of the sound when the gun fired. Enough of the sound was blocked so that it shouldn't be heard by the neighbors. "Remember when I talked earlier about a slow death, John? Do you remember that? That's what I'm going to do to you."

John writhed in pain, grasping his lower leg as blood oozed between his fingers. "Please, Eddie. I promise I'll do whatever you want!"

Eddie watched as his co-conspirator in the money scheme fell to his side on the couch, screaming in agony. With a laugh, he turned to Marlee who had followed them into the living room area. "Change in plans, bitch. Get over there on the couch next to him."

Marlee knew there were two options if she sat on the couch. Either Eddie would kill her dead, or he would give her the same slow death torture that John was receiving. "But the diary! Blake, Adam, and Barry should be back with it any minute!"

"After they got the diary, Blake and Adam took the cop out into the country to put a bullet in his head. After that was done, Blake did the same to Adam and left them there. By the time Blake gets back here, I'll have taken care of you and John, so all we have to do is dump you two out in the country, load up the printing stuff, and head out of town."

"But what if..." Marlee's voice trailed off as Eddie's plan became clearer.

"I said SIT DOWN!" Eddie roared. As Marlee complied, weeping as she sat, he placed the pillow over the barrel again and aimed at her heart.

At that moment, the door to the trailer was flung, open and in burst Barry and Doug followed by Jasmine and Kristie. Eddie was taken by complete surprise. Doug overtook him easily and had him on the floor and in handcuffs within seconds.

"Barry, I thought you were dead!" Marlee shrieked running up to him and pulling him into a hug. "Eddie said Blake killed you."

"I'm sure he would've if Doug hadn't been tipped off by Jasmine and her friend," Barry said, motioning toward Jasmine and Kristie. "They figured out that Eddie had you at gunpoint and that you were going back to his trailer. They called Doug, and he was waiting at the edge of the trailer park when Blake, Adam, and I drove out. He pulled up beside us and pointed his gun at Blake, who was driving. Backup arrived, and they took Blake and Adam to jail. On the way there, Adam told an officer that you were still here and that Eddie had a gun," Barry said, pulling himself away from Marlee to survey the situation.

More cops entered the house along with EMTs, who tended to John's wound as they removed him on a stretcher. Eddie was led outside by two uniformed officers as they read him his rights. Jasmine and Kristie ran up to Marlee and engulfed her in a hug.

"Dammit, I told you to stay out of trouble," Jasmine said between sobs of joy. "If you hadn't mentioned coming back here, I never would've known how to track you down."

"So, you told Kristie about Eddie and me coming to the room and then you called Doug and reported everything? How did you get here?" Marlee asked.

Kristie laughed and jangled her roommate's ring of keys. "Polly should keep these in a safe spot. Anybody could take them."

Marlee laughed at the thought of her roommate and next-door neighbor stealing Polly's car to help with the investigation. "Serves her right!"

"What's this about a stolen vehicle?" Barry asked, his tone serious and professional.

"Uh, Barry, have you met Kristie? This is the friend I told you about. She was just joking about taking her roommate's car," Marlee said as she stepped behind Kristie pushing her a little closer to Barry.

"So, Barry, why did it take so long for the cops to clue in?" Kristie asked, unimpressed with the cop and his coworkers.

Marlee glanced at Barry and saw that he was already irritated with Kristie. *These two will make a good couple,* Marlee thought as she watched them chat over the pool of blood from John's gunshot wound. Jasmine and Marlee made eye contact and walked out of the trailer to allow Barry and Kristie some time to talk, even though the trailer was swarming with police and crime scene technicians.

"I wanted you and Barry to get together," Jasmine said, looking back at the trailer.

"I always told you we were a good investigative team but that was all. Maybe Barry and Kristie will hit it off. I bet you and Doug will be an item now that he's seen what a crime fighter you are." Marlee smiled as she looked at her friend. If it weren't for Jasmine and Kristie, Marlee would be shot and left for dead by now.

"No, I don't think so," Jasmine said. "Yesterday, when I talked to Doug, he said his wife was going to rehab, and they were going to give their marriage another try. I don't want to get in the middle of that."

"Well, Jazz, I guess that makes you President of the Lonely-Hearts Club, and I'm the Vice President," Marlee said with a laugh as they walked toward a police cruiser that was going to take them to the station to get their statements. "You know what I'm going to do when we get back to the dorm?"

"Make some toast?" Jasmine asked.

"Yep, and some ramen noodles. I'll make some for you too," Marlee said with a smile. "By the way, thanks for saving my life."

AFTERWORD

Marlee closed her eyes as she remembered the deaths of Tim and Beth all those years ago. She shuddered when she thought of how close she'd come to meeting a similar fate. If Barry, Doug, and the rest of the cops hadn't come when they did, she would've been shot dead.

Even though the cases had long been solved and the perpetrators punished, Marlee still felt bad for the scrutiny Pam had been under. *Imagine being accused of killing your own brother. And your own cousin*, Marlee thought. She'd been cleared in Tim's death, but the cloud of suspicion still hung over Pam for Billy's death in the shed over twenty years ago. She was the only one who knew for sure whether Billy's death was intentional or accidental.

The more she thought about the crime wave that struck her university back in 1987, the more she wondered what became of those involved. Marlee stayed in touch with Jasmine, now a fashion designer in New York and Kristie, who traveled the world as an archaeologist. Once in a while, she touched base with Barry Stevens, but hadn't heard from him in a couple years. Barry had worked his way up to Captain of the police department after years of hard work and skillful politicking.

On a whim, Marlee called him to see how he was doing. She'd heard through the grapevine that he got a divorce last year. Barry was excited to hear from Marlee and talked over her for the first few minutes of their conversation. "I've been meaning to call you. We had a big development here a couple days ago. I would've called sooner, but the kids and I had the flu. Sometimes being a single dad isn't all it's cracked up to be."

"What's the big news you wanted to tell me?" Marlee asked, hoping Barry didn't delve into the details of his flu symptoms.

"Remember Pam DeWitt and all that business at the farm outside of town?"

"Of course, I do. Why?"

"She died earlier this week," Barry reported. "She was hospitalized off and on for a few months and finally passed away."

"Died? What happened? She was only a little bit older than me. Did she have cancer?"

"Cirrhosis of the liver. Pam drank herself to death. She'd been to rehab a few times but always went back to drinking. Doctors told her she would die if she didn't stop, but either she wouldn't or couldn't," Barry said.

"That's horrible. Her poor parents. Both of their kids gone," Marlee murmured, thinking of the heartache the DeWitts endured at the death of their only son and now the death of their only daughter.

"Yeah, but that's not the big development. Pam couldn't quit drinking and knew she was going to die. The doctors told her it was just a matter of time. After she passed away, her mother found a letter she'd written to be opened after her death and turned it over to us. In it Pam tells the story of the time she, Tim, and Billy were playing in the shed. She admitted daring Billy to climb to the top and shaking the ladder, but wrote that it was never her intention for him to die. She just wanted to scare him," Barry said.

"Wow! A deathbed confession. Well, almost. So, she was responsible for Billy's death, even though she said it was unintentional," Marlee said. "Did she write anything else?"

"She asked for forgiveness for causing Billy's death and for turning the family against Tim when he tried to tell them what Pam did. She seemed to carry a great deal of guilt for both of these things, and that's probably why she became such a chronic alcoholic," Barry said.

"Those are both huge burdens to bear. She brought about the death of her cousin and caused the whole family to believe Tim was unstable. I can see why Pam turned to drinking. Did she write anything about the death of her grandmother?" Marlee recalled Grandpa Edgar asserting that Pam caused his wife to go into diabetic shock and die. He claimed Pam locked Grandma Ethel in the bathroom while he was gone. She was unable to get her insulin shot or food and died shortly thereafter.

"No mention of the grandma. My guess is if Pam had something to do with her death she would have written about it in the letter too. The letter seemed to be her confessional, and I think she was unburdening herself from the bad things she did. If she did kill her grandma, there wouldn't have been any reason to keep it a secret. Pam knew nobody would read the letter until after her own death, so there wouldn't be any legal consequences she had to withstand," Barry said.

"What happened to Eddie, Blake, and the other guys? Are they all still in prison?" Marlee asked.

"John and Adam were both paroled years ago. Adam moved away, but John still lives here. Don't think he's been in any trouble since he got out. Eddie and Blake are still at the State Pen, and I don't think they're getting out anytime soon," Barry reported.

"Well that's good. I don't want to run into Eddie again. I still have nightmares of him holding that gun to my head. If you guys hadn't burst in the door when you did, I wouldn't be here today," Marlee said with a shudder.

"All in a day's work, ma'am," Barry said with a slow Texas drawl. "What's new with you? New boyfriend, maybe?"

"No, I'm done with boyfriends. They cause too much trouble in my life. I function better when I only have to worry about myself."

"Don't let some bad experiences with men make you bitter. There are plenty of good guys out there. You just need to give them a chance," Barry cautioned.

"Thanks for the tip, Oprah," Marlee said with a laugh. "How about you? Are you taking your own advice and playing the field again?"

"No way. Women are bad news. I'm not looking for another girlfriend or another wife," Barry said. They were both still laughing as they finished their conversation minutes later.

After a few more hours, she only had one box of papers left to sort through. Then Marlee would have everything she needed to compile her folder to submit for sabbatical. If she received sabbatical, she planned to travel to Ireland to do research on their criminal justice system and compare it to the one in America. A hot cup of tea steamed near her, while Pippa sat in a box on the table observing Marlee's every move through one barely-open eye. She glanced around the dining room and smiled, satisfied with the life she'd built for herself. Marlee was a tenured associate professor in good standing at Midwestern State University, well-respected in the community, had a group of wonderful friends, owned her own home, and had the perfect pet.

Still, something was missing. *After I'm done with this sabbatical folder, I'll look at jumping back into the dating game*, she thought. *I'm just too busy now*. Finding a new boyfriend now wouldn't be the wisest decision. When the time was right, she'd know.

A knock at the front door startled her out of her daydream. She wasn't expecting anyone, so the knock took her by surprise. As Marlee approached the door she caught a glimpse of her visitor through the small window in the door. She hesitated as she contemplated her next move. Marlee smiled as she opened the door, pretty sure she was about to make a really bad decision.

When the punishment fits the crime, we say justice has been served. But has it really? Is it fair and just that Beth and I are dead while everyone else is living their life? My only consolation is that at least I'm not spending the rest of my life in prison. That would be a fate worse than death.

I hadn't told Tim about the baby because I didn't know for sure what I was going to do. Tim would've wanted us to get married and raise the baby, and I don't know that I was ready for all of that. Until I knew for sure if I was keeping the baby, I wasn't drinking. When Blake said my death was an accident, he lied. He spiked my drinks and made sure I was really drunk. I think he did it so I would have a miscarriage. Then he hid my coat so I couldn't find my keys. But the worst thing Blake did was watch me walk away from Stairway to Hell that night. He was standing on the widow's walk and saw me fall down in the snow. Blake did nothing to help. That was no accident. It was murder.

ABOUT THE AUTHOR

Brenda Donelan is a life-long resident of South Dakota. She grew up on a cattle ranch in Stanley County, attended college in Brookings, and worked in Aberdeen as a probation officer and later as a college professor. Currently, she resides in Pierre with her two Himalayan cats, Yeti and Wolfie. She loves reading, playing with her cats, and traveling.

Fatal Footsteps is the fifth book in the University Mystery Series. Brenda is currently working on her next book.

The author can be reached by email at brendadonelanauthor@gmail.com. For more information on Brenda Donelan, books in the University Mystery Series, and tour dates, check out her website at brendadonelan.com or find her on Facebook at Brenda Donelan – Author.

ALSO BY BRENDA DONELAN

Day Of The Dead

When a college professor is found dead on campus, rumors and innuendo begin to swirl at Midwestern State University. The police department and the university are mysteriously secretive about the professor's background and the ongoing investigation. Marlee McCabe, a professor of Criminology, is unwittingly pulled into the investigation leading her to question the integrity of the police department and her university. Despite warnings, Marlee uncovers information on the professor's death, making her the next target of someone who has nothing left to lose.

Holiday Homicide

Criminology professor Marlee McCabe is thrust into a criminal investigation when a janitor is murdered at Midwestern State University. Marlee's sleuthing leads her to the Lake Traverse Indian Reservation and into the dangerous underworld of trafficking Native American artifacts and sacred cultural items. Those involved are not afraid to use threats, violence, and even murder to keep their secrets buried. What will they do to keep Marlee from exposing the truth?

Murder To Go

On the second day of a week-long class trip, a body is discovered in a motel room. Criminology Professor Marlee McCabe struggles to continue the tour of prisons and juvenile correctional facilities while uncovering the truth behind the life and death of the victim. As she protects her students from harm, Marlee begins to suspect the killer has ties to her university. What steps will the murderer take to hide the truth and prevent Marlee from revealing it?

Art of Deception

A million-dollar antique is stolen from an art show in Elmwood and Professor Marlee McCabe jumps into the investigation when her cousin, Bridget, is arrested and thrown in jail. Marlee steadfastly defends her cousin until secret details of Bridget's life call that loyalty into question. As Marlee struggles between dedication to family and the pursuit of justice, she is forced to make decisions which may destroy the rest of her life.

Made in the USA
Columbia, SC
07 September 2017